EARTH'S ECOCIDE

HOPE 2147

DAVID A. COLLIER

Earth's Ecocide: Hope 2147

Copyright © 2022

by David A. Collier

All rights reserved.

ISBN-978-1-66783-410-8 (printed)

ISBN- 978-1-66783-411-5 (eBook)

U.S. Copyrights Registration Number TXu 2-289-280

Writers Guild of America West, Inc. Registration # 2143500

www.theentity.us

Earth's Ecocide: Hope 2147 is a book of fiction. Names, characters, and events are creations of the author's imagination. Any resemblance to actual events, locales, or people, living or dead, is entirely coincidental.

No part of this book or story may be reproduced in any written form or by any electronic or mechanical means, including DVDs, movies, Internet videos, or search and retrieval systems, without the written permission of the author and the author's legal counsel.

Dedicated to those who love this tiny speck of wonder called Earth.

CONTENTS

Chapter 1:	*Let There Be Light*	1
Chapter 2:	*Discovery*	16
Chapter 3:	*First Encounter*	33
Chapter 4:	*Enlightenment*	48
Chapter 5:	*Healing*	64
Chapter 6:	*Chaos*	84
Chapter 7:	*Second Encounter*	98
Chapter 8:	*World Reaction*	114
Chapter 9:	*Security*	134
Chapter 10:	*Celsus*	145
Chapter 11:	*Third Encounter*	160
Chapter 12:	*Pyrrhic Victories*	177
Chapter 13:	*A New Life*	192
Chapter 14:	*Hunting*	203
Chapter 15:	*Stampede*	215
Chapter 16:	*Decisions*	220

Postscript 233

Author's Note on Today's Climate Change Crisis 235

About the Author 238

CHAPTER 1
Let There Be Light

"Control tower, did you see that flash of light off my right windshield?" the pilot asked just as Sterling Airlines flight number forty-five took off.

"Yeah, I saw a flash of light," responded the human air traffic controller at 2054 on October 18, 2147 at Bluegrass Spaceport in Lexington, Kentucky. With the radio interference, his words had a choppy cadence. "Autopilot, can you confirm?"

"Our instruments picked up a strong magnetic pulse of three hundred thirty-five tesla," the virtual pilot said. "The electromagnet pulse interfered with our plane's electronics for 1.27 seconds."

The virtual pilot was a quantum computer hidden below the floor of the cockpit. In this plane, the virtual pilot spoke in an emotionless female voice. In 2147, airplanes required only one human pilot, though the airplane could technically fly itself—or fly remotely—from any place in the world. The safety record of automatic piloted planes exceeded that of human pilots, though three levels of encrypted codes were necessary before a remote pilot could take over.

"Control tower, can you confirm?" the human pilot requested while rubbing the back of his neck.

"Hell, if I know. But it's gone," the baffled controller said. "We have no radar images in that area. We had one anomaly—a short, powerful electrical disturbance."

"Okay, let us know if you find out what's going on."

The plane continued its climb to a cruising altitude of eight thousand meters.

"Are all systems okay?" the pilot asked the virtual pilot.

"Yes, all systems are operating within design specifications."

"Great. I'll take a nap. Wake me if you see anything unusual."

"Yes, sir, Captain."

Down below, Tom Hickory sat on a sofa with his wife, Mattie. They owned a five-square kilometer farm in Bourbon County, twenty kilometers from Lexington, surrounded by pristine thoroughbred horse farms. Tom enjoyed being his own boss. He had never left the county because for him, he had everything he needed. An adored wife and his family and friends, and their successful farm operations made him proud.

Demand for their crops was continuing to increase. The rises in sea-levels in states like Delaware, Florida, Louisiana, and New Jersey were forcing people to higher ground, so a lot of people were migrating to Kentucky. The highest elevation in Kentucky was over 1,200 meters, and the lowest elevation was 78 meters. The mean elevation of the state was 230 meters.

Mattie had grown up on a local farm, and like Tom, Central Kentucky defined her world. When she was four months old, a family had adopted her. Now forty, she still did not know her biological parents. She adored farm life and being the mother of a wonderful young family. Though she had earned a college degree in education, she stayed home with the kids, ten-year-old Ethan, and eight-year-old Jillian. Skinny Ethan had short brown hair and brown eyes, and showed promise as a budding scientist. He was always watching science and educational channels. Jillian had short blonde hair, piercing green eyes, a couple of missing teeth, and a few freckles on her arms and face.

Other members of the Hickory family were a spoiled goat named Titan, who lived in the barn attached to a massive greenhouse, and two farm bots named Atticus and Ethel. Titan ate weeds while the bots focused on farm efficiency.

Atticus and Ethel managed the five-thousand-square-meter automated hydroponic greenhouse. The climate-controlled greenhouse used four levels of horizontal farming, and was powered by solar-powered shingles on the roof, which generated electricity. The greenhouse grew artichokes, strawberries, raspberries, basil, and parsley, and these hydroponic and bio-engineered crops went to regional markets. Sometimes the bots would help Tom plant and harvest crops in outdoor fields, but the torrid temperatures and violent storms prevented most of the outdoor farming. As a virtual farm manager, Tom managed much of the farm through this wall screen and their obedient farm bots. Their farm income was supplemented by communications-tower fees and natural-gas lease payments.

"Mattie, did you see that flash of light out the window?" Tom asked.

"No, I was reading."

Mattie looked away from where she was reading her novel on their television. Called a wall screen, it was two meters high and six meters wide, and was created through light-emitting diodes embedded in the wallpaper. Such smart wallpaper cost about twice as much as regular wallpaper, but far less than the boxy televisions of the past.

"Daddy, did you see the lightening?" Jillian shouted from the top of the stairs.

Ethan came over to help his little sister navigate the steps. She had cerebral palsy and often needed assistance. He walked in front of her and she put one hand on his shoulder and one hand on the stair railing.

Parents always screened their DNA before conception, and genetic specialists would re-engineer DNA to avoid major birth defects. However, genetic engineering was not an exact science, and unexpected errors and side effects did occur. Jillian's DNA had an unintended mutation, which caused her cerebral palsy. She had not learned to walk until she was three years old, her mouth and chin would twitch, and she walked with a slight limp, leaning to her left side.

Once in the living room, she limped over to sit on her dad's lap.

"Yes, I did, sweetie."

"Daddy, it was scary. I was putting on my pajamas next to the window, and when I looked up, the night sky had a white hole in it," Jillian said, slightly slurring every other word.

At this, Mattie turned from her novel and, with a heavy sigh, stared at Tom.

"What do you mean? Like a hole in the cloud?" he asked, eyebrows raised. He wrapped a muscular arm around his daughter's waist.

"Daddy, the flash of light made a hole in the sky." Jillian clutched his arm, her face twitching more than usual.

"Jilly, there are no storms tonight. It couldn't be lightning."

"It could be an airplane or helicopter flying low with its lights on," Ethan said, looking out the window, examining the evidence. "Dad, it's a new moon, so there shouldn't be any moonlight."

"I didn't hear any noise," Mattie said, her voice full of skepticism. She picked at a button on her blouse absent-mindedly before resuming her novel.

Tom held Jillian comfortingly, and to keep her mind off what she had seen, he started an episode of *The Mortals* from another segment of the wall screen. Years ago, he and his father would watch this old television show together, and seeing it now brought back wonderful memories—as well as some that weren't so wonderful. Like when his father developed a liver disease and he had dropped out of college to care for him. Doctors had tried to replace his father's liver by growing a new one, using his father's DNA and tissue engineering, but the body rejected the replacement liver. Tom managed the farm all the while, and when his father died, he eventually took over. This was all before he had married Mattie, fourteen years ago.

Tom's father had raised cattle, but sweltering temperatures in the summer, up to forty-nine degrees Celsius, killed them. One summer heat wave killed thirty-two. Cattle didn't sweat and relied on respiration to breathe and expel heat. Tom had been a young boy at the time, but he still had vivid memories of hauling away the dead, bloated cattle. To combat livestock losses, some farmers built facilities to provide shade, and later air-conditioned livestock pens, but the added infrastructure raised food prices and electric bills.

Tom and Mattie had left that business long ago because of shrinking markets and changing climate. The global demand for animal protein had decreased because of plant-based substitutes, which had the same nutritional value, and because forty-eight percent of the human population was now vegetarian.

They sometimes raised cotton, hemp, and soybeans in the outdoor fields, crops that were amenable to the hotter temperatures. The average global temperature was seventeen degrees Celsius, three degrees higher than it had been in the year 2000.

A precise two square kilometer grid helped Atticus, Ethel, and other automated equipment plow the fields and harvest the crops, and Tom monitored them from his living room wall screen. Automation allowed small farms and towns to thrive, for many industries were disaggregated, and no longer chained to economies of scale.

They watched *The Mortals* for a while until Tom's curiosity got the better of him. "Mattie, I'm going outside to investigate that flash of light."

"Can I go?" Jillian asked, jumping up from his lap and secure embrace.

"No, you need to stay here, young lady. Ethan, you lock the doors once I leave."

"Dad, Titan is banging around in his pen."

"I'll check Titan out too. That flash of light could have scared him. Mattie, can you get the kids ready for bed while I check this out?"

Tom pulled a programmable-matter flashlight from a drawer, buttoned his shirt, and strapped on his cooling vests before going outside.

He marched out onto his front porch, and turned on the flashlight to scan the front yard. The flashlight used catoms nanotechnology to change the amount and concentration of light beaming from it. It could generate a pinpoint laser of light or a diffused floodlight. He pressed a button and reduced the light to a concentrated beam. It lit up the greenhouse area about fifty meters away.

He searched the exterior of the greenhouse, which housed Titan and the farm bots. Everything was normal.

But he could hear Titan's whining *baa-baa-baa* and his hooves hitting the sides of his pen.

He opened the greenhouse door, walked to Titan's pen, and patted him to calm him down. Titan was a wiry black goat weighing thirty-three kilograms. Two small brown horns protruded from his head, and he had no other colors or markings. He continued to yap, so Tom pulled out a few stalks of broccoli from the small refrigerator beside his pen, and fed them to him. The animal relaxed. Broccoli was ambrosia to Titan.

Ethel and Atticus were in sleep mode in the corner of the greenhouse. Tom walked down one aisle and investigated the storage room. After searching inside, he locked the door and turned on the outside lights. He walked along the outside of the greenhouse and found nothing unusual, no source for the flash of light.

Puzzled, he walked back toward the front porch. He scanned the horizon one more time, paused, and looked down at his dad's gold pocket watch. The time was 2133. Many other e-devices could give him the time, but he wore the watch as a reminder of happy childhood times.

Before he turned to go back inside he caught sight of a dim blue light, which seemed to originate about two hundred meters away on the county road. He looked over once, and then once more. No light should have been there.

Tom walked down the gravel driveway toward Dura Road, and crossed the hot blacktopped road, feeling the day's radiant heat move upward toward his body. He made his way over to the white wood fence and with his flashlight, scanned the field where noble thoroughbred racehorses roamed. About one hundred meters farther down the road, he saw the dim blue light again, but still he could not determine its source. He slowed his movement, and when he reached the light, he had an elevated heartbeat.

He sat down in his chair, shaking his head. He tried to straighten up his messy hair by running his fingers through it. "It's a moving ball of light. It knows I was there."

"A ball of light," Mattie said, her neck muscles flexing, but did not question him further. She told the wall screen to find the police's communicator number and call it.

Tom took a minute to recover and chewed three antacid tablets. Afterward, he stood up, walked to his gun cabinet and got his stun gun.

While he held the stun gun, his communicator buzzed, showing an urgent message. It was his virtual doctor.

"Mr. Tom Hickory, your heart rate has accelerated to unsafe levels. Are you all right? Should I call an ambulance?"

"No, I'm fine. I got excited. Thanks for the call." He turned off his communicator and said to Mattie, "I'm going back out there."

"Daddy, can we go?" Jillian asked, Ethan behind her.

"No, it's too dangerous. You two stay with Mom."

He marched back down his driveway, armed with his stun gun, and looked for the blue light. It was still there. He walked up to it and aimed the gun. His hands shook, and he shuffled his feet. Facing the mysterious orb and scared of what might happen, he backed up several meters.

Back in the house, Mattie called the Bourbon County Police office.

"Yes, this is Mattie Hickory on Dura Road," she said quickly. "Come out here. My husband, Tom, found something in the field across from our farm."

"What is it?"

"Tom doesn't know."

"Is it a person or an animal?"

"No, it's a ball of light moving around in a field. Hurry up!"

"Can you say that again?" the officer asked, a hint of skepticism in his voice.

"It's a hovering light in a field—an orb—that shouldn't be there. Come see for yourself!"

"We'll be right there."

"You two stay in the house," she said to Ethan and Jillian. "Close all the windows and doors. Lock them." The kids shrugged, signaling their displeasure. "I'm going to join your father."

Mattie opened the front door and grabbed a cooling vest and umbrella. The umbrella was the only weapon she could think of, but she didn't want to go unarmed. She locked the door behind her with a verbal command and dashed down the driveway. She fell on the gravel driveway, but bounced back up and continued toward Tom and the orb. Her arms and knees were dirty and scraped.

When she arrived, Tom was standing five meters from the orb, still pointing his stun gun at it. He would step forward to watch it move backward and vice versa. The ballet allowed him to test the orb. Could the orb see him? Where were its eyes?

"Oh, my goodness," Mattie said. "I can't believe it!" After she studied the phenomenon for a moment, she whispered, "Can I pick up the flashlight?"

"Yes, yes," Tom said, straightening his posture.

Mattie walked toward the orb and picked it up. She pointed a beam of laser light at the orb. It edged backward a meter.

"Have you tried to touch it?"

"Yes, but my hand went numb."

"Let's wait for the police."

Tom continued to point the stun gun, assuming it would provide some protection, and Mattie held the flashlight. She put her free hand over her mouth, mystified.

The enigmatic orb did not move.

"Put the gun down," Mattie said. "It hasn't attacked us."

He lowered his gun to his side.

"Mattie, when I touched it the second time, I felt marvelous."

"What do you mean, marvelous?"

"Well, I've been trying to figure it out. I felt a surge of joy pass through my body."

As they waited, they stood guard. Only the faint sounds of crickets chirping and the light breeze filled the anxious night air. Later, Mattie saw the lights of a vehicle coming toward them.

"Here come the police. They won't believe it."

The self-driving police cruiser pulled up next to their driveway, its lights flashing. Tom shouted at the cruiser and Mattie waved the flashlight in the air to get their attention.

The cruiser drove the remaining hundred meters down Dura Road, and then sixty-year-old Pax Duncan lifted his short, stocky frame out of the car, pulling his gun belt over his stomach. He climbed over the wood fence, although his potbelly got hung up on the top rail for a moment. With several twists and turns, he landed on his feet and stood upright.

"Pax, don't touch that thing—it seems to know we're here," Tom said as he lumbered up.

Duncan was out of breath and his cooling vest was soaking wet. He pulled his gun from his holster and aimed it at the orb, which lurched toward him.

Surprised, Duncan fell backward, and fired his gun. The laser hit the orb and bounced off, ricocheting into the dark night.

"Pax, are you, all right? Don't shoot!" Tom shouted. He stood up from his crouched position, where he and Mattie had both ducked.

"Pax, what's wrong with you?" Mattie shouted. She used her hands to inspect her face and neck for blood. "You could have killed us."

"I didn't mean to shoot. That thing moved toward me and I got scared."

Tom and Mattie ran over to the officer and helped him up. Tom picked up the smoldering gun from the grass.

"You have a knot on your forehead, Pax," Mattie said.

"Yeah, the gun hit my head. What is that thing?"

Tom handed him his gun. With a trembling hand, Duncan placed it back in his holster and buttoned the strap.

"I told you, Pax—something protects this thing," Tom said.

"Let's get Dr. Sheppard out here—someone smarter than us," Mattie said, biting at a fingernail.

"Good idea. I'll call our office," Duncan said and spoke into his communicator. The sound of a police dispatcher could be heard, but Duncan interrupted her. "Martha, this is Pax. Get Dr. Sheppard out here now."

"But it's late."

"I don't care what time it is. Tell Dr. Sheppard to get out here on Dura Road across from Tom Hickory's farm as soon as possible. This is an emergency."

"All right, I'll call him," Martha said before hanging up.

Duncan, Tom, and Mattie stood in a huddled state of amazement. They kept blinking as they stared at the orb. Duncan's hands continued to shake. They tried to rationalize the thing hovering in the air before them and how to explain its physical capabilities and behavior, but it seemed to defy human reasoning.

"If I can't shoot it, I'll take pictures of the damn thing," an irritated Duncan said. At this, Tom relaxed, and walked with him toward the police cruiser to retrieve the camera.

They came back and began to take pictures. The intelligent ball of energy continued to emit a uniform and mesmerizing light. The light grew brighter when the orb was interacting with people, and dimmed thereafter.

After taking several pictures, Duncan stopped to review them. "The pictures are blurry," he said when he saw the first. Mattie and Tom walked over. Together they found that all the pictures were similar.

"Why would the pictures blur like that?" Tom asked.

"I have no idea. Maybe this thing doesn't want its picture taken."

Duncan snapped his camera shut. He didn't know whether to kneel and pray, run away, or shoot the damn thing again. But he knew he had to act like a brave peace officer.

The trio turned toward the glistening orb and waited. After fifteen minutes had passed, the headlights of a truck came bouncing down Dura Road. The truck pulled up behind the cruiser, and Dr. Sheppard jumped out. At seventy-four years old, the local physician had much less trouble climbing the fence than Duncan had. He was wearing a plaid shirt under his cooling vest and a Cincinnati Reds baseball cap, and carried a small blue gym bag with a University of Kentucky logo on its side.

"What is this?" he asked as he trudged toward the orb.

Duncan grabbed his arm, and said, "This thing has been here for several hours. It moves like it's alive. I shot it. It was an accident. And the laser shot bounced off."

The systematic Dr. Sheppard stepped toward the orb.

"Don't touch it," Duncan said.

Sheppard ignored the warning. He put down his doctor's bag and deliberately approached with both hands held out. When his hands were within centimeters of the orb, the light brightened. His fingers hit an invisible surface, and he inspected it, trying to decipher its composition and origin. His fingertips caressed the orb as if they were examining a newborn baby.

The orb did not move.

"It's a sphere about twenty centimeters in diameter. My hands are numb. It generates an electrical charge," he said to the group in his typical scientific manner.

"So, what's it made of—plastic?" Tom asked.

Dr. Sheppard dropped his hands to his sides and said, "Hard to know, but it doesn't feel like plastic." After a moment's reflection, he added, "It's a force field of electromagnetic energy."

"So, what do we do?" Mattie asked, still chewing at her fingernails.

"I don't know, but we need more help. We need some medical or technical experts. I'd call the governor's office. This thing doesn't seem to be biological."

"I'll call our office and get two deputy officers to guard things here," Duncan said. "They can mark off the site to keep sightseers away. I'll also call the governor's office and see if they can come out."

"I have a portable generator at my house," Tom said. "I could bring it down to power lights and a coffeemaker."

"Yeah, that would help," Duncan said, tugging at the communicator that was clipped to his shirt pocket.

"Martha, who's on duty now?"

"Marty, Tenor, and Luke."

"Send Marty and Luke out here. Tell them to bring plenty of 'No Trespassing' tape, our emergency tent, a couple folding chairs, and the folding card table in my office closet. Tell them their asses will be in this field all night. Oh, tell them to bring bug spray too."

"Yes, sir. I'll contact them now."

"And Martha, have the governor's office call me," he added.

"Done," she said.

Duncan hung up his communicator and pulled his gun belt above his belly, a decade-long habit.

"I've got to go to the hospital," Dr. Sheppard said, wiping sweat off his forehead. "I have patients who need me. Good luck figuring out what this thing is."

"Dr. Sheppard, do you have any idea what it is?" Tom said.

"My best guess is ball lightning that somehow got stuck in time and space. It's lost." With that, he climbed the fence and walked back to his truck.

"That Dr. Sheppard is a smart man," Duncan said as they watched his vehicle drive off.

"What's ball lightning?" Mattie asked.

"It's lightning generated by thunderstorms," Tom answered. "When the lightning hits the ground, it ionizes the dust particles and flings them into the air."

"But that doesn't explain the orb's intelligent behavior."

"Yes, I know. That's why we need technical experts out here."

"Yeah, and we didn't have any storms or lightning tonight," Duncan said.

The orb continued to hover above the ground, emitting its mesmerizing blue light. It watched the feeble humans stumble around its overtures, confused by its form. The orb belied human logic. Humanity needed time to evaluate its presence, and the intelligent orb knew it. Those meager human endeavors set the stage for the first encounter.

CHAPTER 2
Discovery

"Hello. This is the Kentucky Emergency Administration. How can we help you?" a calm male voice said.

"I'm the head police officer in Bourbon County, Pax Duncan. We have an odd situation here. We need help fast."

"What's the problem?"

"We have a ball of light—an orb—alone in a field, and no idea how it got there."

"What?" the emergency responder replied with a chuckle. "Why don't you put it in jail?"

"Well, sir, the orb seems to move around. We cannot bring it in."

"Are you guys drinking bourbon?"

"This is no joke. I know you think I'm crazy, but it's the truth. I tried to take a picture, but it's just a blur of light. Four people, including a medical doctor, saw this thing. Send us some damn help!"

"Has the ball of light threatened anyone?"

"No, sir," Duncan answered, "but it could."

"We'll look. Is the address the same as your communicator's coordinates?"

"Yes."

"What's your communicator number and badge number?" After Pax gave his full name and numbers, he hung up and walked back to his cruiser. Tom and Mattie had scurried back home so they could bring the farm's portable hydrogen generator to the site. They said they'd load it onto their truck.

Duncan sat alone in his cruiser with his sweaty hand close to his gun. He surveyed the darkness surrounding him, thinking something might attack him at any moment. He couldn't stop looking at the surreal orb, wanting to flee, but knowing he had to do his job.

Meanwhile, Marty and Luke left the police headquarters and headed out to Dura Road, the van fully loaded with equipment. On their way, they placed an order for hamburgers at an automated fast-food restaurant.

"We ordered two AZ Burgers," Luke said when they drove up to the AFS drive-through window.

"They are ready. Thanks for calling ahead," a female robot said. The mannequin handed them the meals. "We charged your e-account."

AFS sold entertainment, speed of service, and food with little need for human labor. At AFS, smart robots prepared food in an assembly-line fashion. They could customize orders by holding the pickle or mayonnaise. The store itself operated twenty-four hours a day, seven days a week.

AFS stores required five human employees. Each evening, two employees cleaned the equipment and facilities, emptied trash cans, and swept the parking lot. They also performed maintenance on the robots and equipment. Two other employees restocked supplies and ingredients into the automated equipment. The manager was the fifth employee.

Robots and virtual assistants augmented or automated many jobs. Bank tellers, professors, retail clerks, and pharmacists were examples.

"I see prices are going up," Marty said.

"Yes, we must pay taxes," the female robot replied.

"Do you pay taxes?"

"Sure. All virtual and physical robots pay taxes. That's how you fund universal income for humans."

"What's your name?" Marty asked the robot.

"Tatiana, sir."

"You sure are pretty. I like your orange hair. If you weren't a robot, I'd ask you out."

Tatiana smiled at both men. With a wink of her left eye, she said, "Move on, boys."

Tatiana had learned how to flirt with humans, and the humans loved it. When the robots serving customers were viewed as sexy, surveys found that AFS store sales increased 1.7 percent. Store computers operated and managed the store, and did all data analysis.

Marty and Luke laughed at Tatiana's response. With a verbal command, they directed their self-driving vehicle to leave and go to Dura Road.

Duncan saw the headlights of a vehicle coming toward him. He got out of his cruiser with a sigh of relief. He briefed Marty and Luke on what had happened. The whole time he spoke, Marty and Luke stared at the orb, which had maintained its benevolent position. They had never seen anything like it.

"Don't draw your guns," Duncan said with a stern look, seeing their hands.

"Pax, is this thing alive?" Marty, a short and stocky thirty-six-year-old man, blurted out. Tom Hickory had been the quarterback at the same high school as Marty's, though in an earlier class. As in most small towns, everyone knew one another.

"Hell yes, it's alive," Luke said, his body locked in a defensive position. As a US Army war veteran, he enjoyed being a police officer. He protected the public from harm. He helped make order out of chaos.

"Settle down, boys. It hurt no one."

Both deputies took their hands off their guns, but they kept their eyes fixed on the cagey orb.

"Men, get to work. Set up a secure area around this damn thing," Duncan said.

Marty and Luke blocked access both ways on Dura Road. They used wooden sawhorses, signs, flashing lights, and yellow tape. They set up and taped off a restricted area in a radius of thirty meters from the orb, and used sledgehammers to knock down about six meters of the roadside fence. Finally, they set up a small tent, a card table, and folding chairs.

Soon after, Tom and Mattie arrived with the generator. They started it, and plugged in a floodlight and coffee maker. The five of them sat in chairs and watched the enigmatic orb. Marty and Luke placed their guns on the card table, and no one objected.

After several minutes of reflection, Mattie said, "Tom, I should go back to the house. The kids can't be alone much longer."

"Okay, go. I'll stay here."

"Why don't you go with me? The police can handle everything now."

"No, I want to stay here."

Mattie stared at her husband for a few seconds and abruptly turned and marched to the fence and drove their truck home.

The foursome continued to gaze at the orb. It stayed in position, and the intensity of its light didn't waver. It simply waited and watched as humanity adjusted to its presence.

* * *

By 0015, two drones had arrived from the KEA. They beamed pictures back to headquarters in Frankfort, Kentucky. One drone oversaw the entire area from about fifty meters in the air. A second flew within several meters of the odd sphere of light and circled it. The face-off remained dignified and calm. Neither entity seemed to mind the scrutiny.

The moment the KEA video transmission began, government officials began to know of the orb.

Twenty minutes later, a Kentucky emergency vehicle arrived. Two armed state troopers and two communication specialists stepped out and were briefed by Duncan, then one of the state troopers walked the site using a small handheld Geiger counter, but he found no unusual radiation threat.

A state emergency vehicle set up a television camera on a tripod, which transmitted more real-time video back to the state's emergency headquarters. They illuminated the area using floodlights mounted on the vehicle's corners. The light reflected off the scattered clouds, creating an eerie blue glow.

The whole time, the orb was not disturbed by the commotion, but it knew what was going on.

Within minutes of viewing the videos at home, the commander of KEA, Chase Saladin, called the governor's office.

A minute later, he heard someone say, "Hello. This is the chief of staff for the governor's office, Bob Eagle, speaking."

"Bob, this is Chase."

"Yes, Chase. Why the call in the middle of the night?"

Standing in his bedroom at home, Saladin was wearing his Ohio State University pajamas. They had a white background and a scarlet-and-gray O logo.

"We have an odd situation in Bourbon County with an orb in a field. Can I send you and the governor the real-time video of it?"

"Ah, sure," he said, sounding uncertain.

"Once you see the video, you will wake the governor, I assure you," Saladin said.

Soon the live video was playing on the living room wall screen in Governor Jake Morris's mansion in Frankfort, Kentucky.

"Get me a cup of coffee, please," he said to an on-duty state trooper.

"Yes, sir."

"Bob, what is this damn thing?" Morris asked.

"I don't know. They tell me a local farmer got shocked trying to touch it. And the Bourbon County police officer shot at it, but the laser bounced off."

"Fine, let's stay ahead of this. We'll go to the site tonight. Get my limo ready."

At 0150 that morning, the governor's hydrogen-powered limousine began its trip to Dura Road. A state SWAT vehicle with four armed officers followed, and behind that, two armed drones made up the rear of the convoy.

Their headlights illuminated the landscape and stone fences as they drove. Gentle rolling hills and beautiful horse farms defined the central Kentucky landscape. Limestone fences surrounded many of the horse farms. Irish and Mexican immigrants had built the stone fences in the late 1800s and early 1900s, which were still intact over three centuries later. Their craftsmanship was outstanding. They'd interwoven the limestone rocks using no mortar.

* * *

At the governor's mansion, a few housekeepers and state troopers, plus the governor's wife, watched the real-time video of the orb, everyone staring at the wall screen. They tried to interpret what they were seeing with earthbound logic.

"It could be a lost spirit," one housekeeper said. With the movement of her hand, she closed her eyes and outlined the shape of a cross.

The governor's wife gave the housekeeper a befuddled look.

"No, it's an electric charge that got stuck close to the ground," a young state trooper said. "It will dissipate by sunrise."

"I hope it's not a terrorist attack," another trooper said.

"Or an alien attack," someone else suggested.

"We don't know what it is; let's not speculate," the governor's wife said.

A minute passed before someone else in the room spoke up. "I see a lot of movies, and I assure you it's nothing more than a hologram. Someone is tricking us."

A few employees stepped away from the wall screen to discuss the situation. They were told not to reveal the news of the orb's arrival to anyone, including their families. Everyone continued to stare at the video and the orb's radiant blue glow.

* * *

Governor Morris arrived at 0244. He walked to the site to see the orb, which was still hovering about ten meters away.

Two of the state troopers had their guns drawn but held them down at their sides. The four SWAT team members spread out around the orb, but at a twenty-meter distance. They aimed their guns toward the ground, but at the first sign of trouble, their job was to protect the governor.

Officer Duncan met the governor and explained the situation.

"Don't touch it," he warned.

"Understood," Governor Morris replied, a strong frown on his face. "Are you Officer Duncan who called this in?"

"Yes, sir."

"Who was first on the scene?"

"Me, sir." Tom Hickory stepped forward.

"What brought you out here?" the governor asked.

"Sir, I saw a flash of light out the window. So, I came out to investigate. I touched the orb, and it shocked me, so I ran back to the house and called the police."

"It's amazing how it floats," the governor said, staring at the orb. He looked at the small group of people that were also watching and said, "Please come over here. What type of help do we need?"

"I'd bring in medical experts," Duncan said.

"How about a physics professor?" Tom asked.

"I'd call Homeland Security in Washington, DC," a state trooper added.

The governor listened, and then called Bob Eagle, his chief of staff, patching in Chase Saladin. "Bob, Chase, I know you've been watching on television. I tell you this: it is real. It seems to defy gravity. The locals think the orb is intelligent. But it might be a hoax." The governor paused, and said, "I don't want us to be the laughingstock of the world. Who should we contact next?"

"Let's send a team from the University of Kentucky—say, a medical doctor, a physicist, and an electrical engineer. They can be there in one hour. Also, we should ask the experts what equipment we need on-site."

"Okay, get it done. By sunrise, I want this figured out, or we're calling the Department of Homeland Security and the Federal Emergency Management Agency. I'm going back home, and then to my office in the capital."

After Governor Morris and his entourage left, Tom turned toward the three officers and said, "I'm going home before my wife locks me out."

"I'm going home, too," Sheriff Duncan said. "You two stay awake and guard this thing—understood."

Marty and Luke nodded in agreement and were soon alone with the mysterious visitor.

* * *

As the State of Kentucky tried to cope with its alien guest, Bourbon County deputies Marty and Luke guarded the orb. They were sitting outside their tent in the cool night air, but by about 0530, both were asleep in their chairs. Marty's snoring woke Luke, who upon waking, immediately looked toward the inconceivable ball of light and searched for any change in its demeanor. He found none. The orb maintained its sentry position.

Luke realized he wasn't alone. Startled, he stood up, pulled his gun, and turned toward the sound. To his amazement, he saw a big thoroughbred racehorse walking toward them.

The ruckus woke Marty.

"Look at that damn horse," Luke said, his gun aimed at it.

"Yeah, I see it," Marty replied in a higher-pitched voice. "Put that damn gun in your holster. You are going to kill us."

The majestic thousand-pound thoroughbred made a deliberate advance toward the orb. Its head tilted downward, and its thick neck muscles quivered. The closer the horse got to the orb, the slower it walked. It was making whinnying sounds but these decreased to a mild whiffle as it reached within a few meters' distance. It did not seem afraid. To the contrary, the handsome horse shuffled closer to the orb. The glare of the floodlight created a monochrome glaze on the horse's velvety brown skin.

The entity remained stationery, enduring the curiosity of yet another earthbound life-form.

"Should we shoo it away?" Marty asked.

"No, let's watch."

When the horse was about one meter from the orb, it stopped. It made no more sound. It raised its head and glanced over at Marty and Luke as if to say, "You human fools, you don't understand what is before you," then continued its brave advance. Next, it touched its nose against the orb. It snorted in a muffled way and nudged the orb a second time. After a few seconds, it backed away about five meters, knelt down in the bluegrass field and lay there with its big brown eyes focused on the orb.

"What should we do?" Luke asked, an edge to his voice. They didn't know what to point their guns at: the horse, the orb, or some unknown force lurking in the night's shadows.

"How the hell should I know?"

"Let's leave it alone until Pax gets here. Our job is to guard this thing, not the horse."

Both put their guns back into their holsters and spent the rest of the night trying not to fall asleep. By 0615, several squirrels, a few field mice, and a rabbit and its three babies had surrounded the orb. Even a snake or two slithered through the bluegrass to visit the new arrival. A flock of chirping birds landed in trees about fifty meters away. Once settled, the flock also turned toward it and quit chirping.

Did the animals sense something humans could not?

When Duncan arrived at 0645, he walked up to Luke and Marty and asked, "Why is the horse here? And what's going on with those damn rabbits and squirrels?"

"They came out last night in the dark. Do you want us to shoo them away?"

"This isn't an animal farm. Yes, shoo them away."

With Duncan's order, Luke and Marty clapped their hands and tried to run off the animals, waving their hats in a shooing motion. The horse was the first to move. The majestic thoroughbred lumbered up the small hill and stood there. It clearly did not want to leave. The squirrels ran up the big nearby oak tree, while the rabbits moved farther away and nestled back down. Even at a distance, the animals were looking toward the orb.

* * *

By 0900, a team of three University of Kentucky professors arrived at the site. The team comprised a physics professor, a neurosurgeon, and an electrical engineering professor. They brought with them an optical spectrometer, a Geiger counter, and a magnetometer. They set up the equipment and began to take measurements.

"This sphere is a magnetic anomaly, with its field measuring a steady 0.5 tesla. The magnetic field does not seem to vary at all," said Dr. Jalan Breslin, the University of Kentucky's Toyota chaired professorship of physics. He had received his PhD from Ohio State University. His research focused on the thermodynamics of Earth's atmosphere and oceans.

"The spectrometer suggests a frequency of 480 nanometers," said Chao-xing Xandra, the electrical engineer. She graduated with a PhD from Tianzhu University in Taiyuan, China and specialized in optical metrology.

A spectrometer measured various technical properties of light, such as wavelength, energy, and frequency. The light spectrum included gamma and x-rays, visible light, and the far infrared.

"Can I touch it?" Breslin asked.

"Yes, but at your own risk."

He put his hands on the orb. "Yes, there is a slight tingle, an electrical current," he said as the others watched him move around the sphere. After a pause, he said, "It allowed me to touch it. Amazing."

"I used my mobile Geiger counter and found no excess radiation here," a state trooper said.

"Yes, our Geiger counter also shows nothing but normal background radiation," Breslin said. A call on Duncan's communicator interrupted their conversation.

"Professor Breslin, you have a call from the governor's office. Mr. Bob Eagle and Mr. Chase Saladin are on the line," Duncan said, handing Breslin a hand-held police communicator.

Breslin activated the communicator's speaker, so everyone could hear.

"Do you have any idea what this is?" Eagle asked.

"No, I don't," Breslin said.

"What do the rest of you think?"

"It doesn't appear to be biological, but it could be alien," said Dr. Edha Shreevallabh, the neurosurgeon. She had received her MD from Case Western Reserve University in Ohio and focused on stereotactic surgery.

"The orb is a ball of electromagnetic energy. But that doesn't explain its reported intelligence and that is what scares me," Xandra said.

"I see on our live stream that the orb is attracting animals. Any idea why?" Eagle said.

"Electrical energy can sometimes attract animals," Xandra replied.

"Is it dangerous?" Saladin asked, still at home wearing his Ohio State pajamas.

"I don't know," Breslin said. "It may dissipate. When I touched it, it felt as if there might have been two shells. The outer shell could be a protective shield."

"Is this a trick of some sort?" Saladin asked.

"I don't see how it could be a trick. I thought about the orb being a hologram projected to this remote site, but I don't see how that's possible," a perplexed Xandra replied.

"I agree," Breslin said.

"Okay, we'll call DHS and FEMA. Let's get the feds in here," Bob Eagle said, before hanging up.

* * *

"I need to speak to the director of Homeland Security, Ms. Ginger Agee," Eagle said, calling from his home.

"To whom am I speaking?" the person who'd answered the call asked.

"I am Bob Eagle, chief of staff for the governor of Kentucky."

"Is this call related to national security?"

"Yes, it could be. We have a light-generating object, an orb, hovering in a Kentucky farm field. It could be a threat to national security. It has been here twelve hours."

"A what?"

"We'll send you a live television feed," Eagle said. "What emergency channel should we use? You can see for yourself."

"Try emergency channel 602149."

Within one minute, the video was playing at the Homeland Security command center. "I see the video on our screen. I'm calling our director's private number now. I'll send her the live TV feed."

The director of Homeland Security, Ginger Agee, reviewed the video. She then asked the US chief of the armed forces to deploy military personnel to the site. Troops were to set up a restricted area around the orb.

* * *

Orders went out to the army's military base at Fort Campbell, Kentucky, directing military personnel to where they were going, but they did not explain why. So far, only four officers knew about the orb.

Military base loudspeakers also announced the deployment. The first battalion of the 303rd Army Infantry Regiment would go.

About 370 soldiers scrambled to pack their duffel bags and put on full battle gear. They locked their guns on safety and loaded into forty-four vehicles. The battalion carried rifles, handguns, mortars, grenade launchers, and laser and machine guns. It also deployed three dozen wearable robotic exoskeletons. They were armed for war, not policing their own citizens.

The battalion left Fort Campbell and traveled to Bourbon County, a drive which took four hours. Along the way, the large troop movement was noticed by the public, and news reporters from several towns, including Bowling Green, Elizabethtown, and Lexington, followed the convoy. Townspeople posted videos on UNet. The videos would soon attract worldwide media attention.

Homeland Security also deployed experts in nuclear and biological weapons and a bomb expert with a robot, while seven empty military trucks were tasked with buying steel chain-link fencing, lumber, barbed wire, posts, and ladders from a number of construction supply stores. The other customers and store employees wondered why the troops were in such a hurry. Whenever anyone asked what they were doing, the soldiers smiled and did not answer.

By 1400, the troops began arriving at Dura Road. The first thirty to arrive stood guard around the orb. Like those before them, they gawked at the nameless and, so far, purposeless orb. They erected tarpaulins to hide three sides of the area.

All the other troops set up a one-kilometer-radius security fence. They blocked all roads and fields that gave access to the orb. Row after row of soulless chain-link fence and ominous coils of barbed wire piled up at the site. The two-kilometer-diameter barrier defined the restricted area. The troops set up their air-conditioned tents and, in a nearby field, built a helicopter landing site. A fifteen-kilometer radius around the orb became restricted airspace. Fighter planes stationed at Wright-Patterson Air Force Base in Dayton, Ohio, enforced the no-fly zone.

Lt. Col. Harold Preston commanded the first battalion. Nicknamed Hawk, he was a meticulous dresser. His shoes and metals shined. Black hair cut in a short flattop haircut framed his square face. At one hundred ninety-six centimeters tall, the thirty-eight-year-old was in command, and everyone knew it. He lifted weights daily, and one could tell. He exercised and ran with his troops, and his troops loved it. Hawk was a soldier's soldier.

"Where's that farmer who first found this orb?" he asked as he strolled into the central command tent.

"Sir, he lives on that small hill," Captain Kash Kilbourne replied. He pointed toward Tom and Mattie's farmhouse.

A strong twenty-six-year-old man with black hair and brown eyes, Kilbourne had graduated from the University of Arizona. He liked the way the military got things done. Yes, they had their rules and rituals, but the military brought order to today's chaotic times. Proud of his military service and loyal to his fellow officers, he did his job with vigor and clarity.

"Get his ass down here."

"Yes, sir."

The captain ordered two soldiers to go to the Hickory house and escort Tom back to the command tent. Both soldiers carried pistols and toted Teton 2 automatic rifles. The rifles could shoot graphene-reinforced metal bullets or a concentrated laser beam. Staff Sergeant Kipp Stoner had grown up on a farm in Nebraska, while Corporal Buck Claiborne came from San Diego.

When they knocked on the door, Mattie answered.

"Ma'am, is Mr. Tom Hickory here?"

"Yes, but what do you want with him?"

"Ma'am, our commander wants to meet him."

"Why?"

"Your husband discovered the orb."

"Yeah, I wish he would have stayed home."

Tom came down the steps and walked back down the driveway with Stoner and Claiborne to Preston's air-conditioned command tent, which belied its mundane looks. Outside, the tent was a dreary camouflaged green-and-gray color, but inside, it housed the electronic brain of a military command center.

Electronic warfare and intelligence were routine parts of an officer's duties. A successful military campaign depended upon real-time updates and smart computer algorithms. Winning battles depended on superior information technology. The electronic systems included dozens of wall screens with built-in computers. Hundreds of out-in-the-field cameras fed real-time video and audio to the command center as did drones and satellites. The landscape or battlefield was modeled using 3-D scale-model holograms. Officers could simulate different battle or logistical plans in seconds using digital twins of each piece of equipment and platoon, each accompanied by a probability-of-success statistic.

The command center was protected by two automated and mobile Rapture gun turrets. The sentry guns could shoot laser beams in a wide variety of patterns. They moved on steel tractor treads and rotated 360 degrees, and were able to monitor their surroundings using infrared and visual cameras, radar, and satellite information. The robotic guns fired only after certain codes and security measures were used. Each gyroscopic stabilized gun could lock on airborne devices or ground targets. Once locked on, the fury of the powerful guns would obliterate the target.

Next to the command tent, another tent housed three dozen wearable robotic exoskeletons. These suits augmented human physical capabilities and firepower, and were powered by miniature hydrogen-powered energy cells.

"Do you think your commander is going to ask us to leave our farm?" Tom asked as they walked to the tent. He knew that other residents within the restricted area, most of whom were farmers, had been asked to leave their homes and were offered hotels at government expense.

"Sir, we don't know. Colonel Preston is an excellent officer. He'll make the best decision for your loved ones." Once they arrived outside the tent, Stoner walked through its swinging doors. The tent's plastic floors squeaked as he said, "Sir, Mr. Hickory, the farmer, is waiting to see you."

"Bring him in."

Lieutenant Colonel Preston greeted him with a firm handshake that buried Tom's wedding ring deep into his finger.

"Mr. Hickory, I understand you found the orb first."

"Yes, sir, I did," Tom replied as he moved his coveted wedding ring around his finger to alleviate the damage.

"Please sit and tell me what happened. I reviewed the orb video on my way here. Would you like a soda or water?"

Tom nodded and a soldier, who was standing by, opened a small refrigerator and handed him a bottle of water.

For the next thirty minutes, Tom and Preston talked.

"Tom, I want you close while we investigate this object. Can I post two soldiers at your house while you stay there?"

"Yes, sir. I didn't want to leave my home, anyway."

"Okay, it's done."

The colonel ordered Kilbourne to get identification documents for Mr. Hickory's family.

"Colonel," Tom said. "Your soldiers can stay in our greenhouse area at night. It has a bathroom and running water. And it's air-conditioned."

"That sounds great. And please call me Hawk."

After a second hardy handshake, Tom said, "I have a temperamental goat named Titan in the greenhouse. Please tell the soldiers that he likes broccoli."

"I hate broccoli," Preston said with a chuckle. "Mr. Hickory, you show our soldiers how to care for your animals, and we'll do it. We do things right here."

Tom walked over to the ID tent, which had been set up by the Dura Road entrance to the restricted area. There he allowed his photograph to be taken, as well as DNA samples, and fingerprint and retina scans. Military personnel was sent to the farmhouse, and the same procedures were done for Mattie, Jillian, and Ethan. Within an hour, Tom had four federal IDs in his hand, the gaudy tags representing another intrusion into the Hickory family's lives.

Governor Jake Morris, Chase Saladin, Bob Eagle, and the three University of Kentucky professors also got ID badges, as did Sheriff Pax

Duncan. Otherwise, only employees of the federal government could enter the restricted area.

Marty and Luke tore down their tent and returned to their headquarters. Sheriff Duncan told them not to tell anyone about what they had seen and he left with them.

By 1900 on Thursday, the US Army controlled the restricted area. The orb had been on Earth for twenty-three hours, and the quarantine of the orb and the Hickory family had begun.

CHAPTER 3
First Encounter

The orb glowed brighter and started to move higher off the ground. Its behavior seemed to be more definitive, more amplified. Everyone present put on the protective goggles designed to witness nuclear blasts. Soldiers guarding the orb unlocked the safeties on their guns with resounding *click-clicks*. A few troops pointed their guns toward the orb while television cameras continued to record everything. Fear and hope energized the evening.

"Get the University of Kentucky professors out of their tents now," Lieutenant Colonel Preston ordered.

Soon, all three professors were standing together, observing an unknown and puissant entity. No one knew what to expect.

"What do your instruments say?" Preston asked.

Dr. Xandra reviewed the magnetometer readings. The portable magnetometer measured the strength and direction of magnetic fields.

"The magnetic field increased to thirty-two tesla," Dr. Breslin said.

"It's moving!" Dr. Shreevallabh said, holding her hand to her head. Because of the magnetic field, one of the metal hairpins in her hair was vibrating and threatening to leap off her head.

Paper clips and metal pens flew off tables in the command tent, causing soldiers to jump up from their seats. Their electronic wall screens flickered. Military medals and service pins on soldiers' uniforms twisted and turned as if they wanted to flee.

Meanwhile, at home, the Hickory clan scanned news channels to see if there were any reports of the orb. They found none, but the local television networks did report troops going to Bourbon County, speculating that something might be going on at the US Department of Defense's Blue Grass Military Depot. The sixty-two-square-kilometer depot located close to Richmond used nine hundred munitions igloos to store weapons. According to the US Army, it had finished destroying all chemical weapons in a sustainable way in 2060. However, local people worried about a chemical or biological emergency at the depot. Calls from local and national news agencies to US military facilities went unanswered.

The Hickory family listened to the news report. They knew the truth.

"Tom, they can't keep this secret much longer," Mattie said, continuing to bite her fingernails.

"Yeah, and they don't know what this thing is, either," Tom replied. After hesitating, he said, "Mattie, I'm sorry. I should have never gone to investigate that flash of light. If I didn't go, we would be staying in a hotel and far away from this chaos—the media and military have overwhelmed our farm and our lives."

"Too late now, Tom," Mattie replied in a tart tone of voice.

"The orb's outside our house," said Ethan. "What if it explodes?"

"It won't explode," Mattie said with a sigh. "But I wish it would leave."

"Daddy, what's an orb?" Jillian asked, stumbling to pronounce the word 'what's.'

"It's a ball of light or energy."

"Why is the orb scaring everybody?" she asked, sitting on the sofa. Her head twitching more than usual.

"We have the US Army protecting us. Life around here will settle down soon," Tom said as he stood up. Ethan and Jillian nodded in agreement while Mattie lowered and shook her head.

"We need to sleep. I've got a headache," Mattie said, and gesturing toward the bedrooms upstairs. "It's been an exhausting day." She stood up and herded the kids upstairs to their bedrooms.

Mattie went to Jillian's room first. Jillian put on pajamas and slid into bed, pulling a pink blanket that matched her pajamas over her. Mattie pulled it up over her shoulders and, with a hug, said, "Try to sleep. I'll call the school tomorrow and tell them you aren't feeling well. You don't need to go in."

"Mom, I didn't get my homework done."

"I know; it's been a confusing day. I love you, young lady. Good night."

Next, she went to Ethan's room. "Did you get your schoolwork done?"

"No, Mom. I played a new virtual game. It was fun."

"Okay, I'll call the school. You'll stay home. Ethan, don't spend too much time in the digital world. It's not healthy—mentally."

Ethan sat up in bed and said, "But mom, I can't sleep. When I'm in an immersive digital world, I'm safe."

"The army will protect us. I'll leave your closet light on tonight," Mattie said as she turned on the light and shut the closet door. Good night, Ethan. I love you."

While Mattie put the kids to bed, Tom locked the doors and turned on the home security system. When he finished, he found Mattie in their bedroom getting ready for bed. He glanced out the window and saw the silhouette of the two soldiers standing outside the greenhouse. Sergeant Kipp Stoner and Corporal Buck Claiborne waved at Tom standing by the upstairs window. They were guarding the Hickory home.

"Do you think we're safe here?" Mattie asked her nervous husband.

"I have no idea," Tom replied. "But I want to stay here. I love this farm."

* * *

The farm bots, Atticus and Ethel were also asleep in the greenhouse. They looked like human mannequins, except metal tractor treads replaced where their legs should be. They used the most powerful T921 quantum computer chip, and had instant access to all human knowledge on UNet. Like most robots, they rewrote their own software as they learned.

Their telescopic and hydraulic-powered arms could lift many times their own weight, and could rotate 360 degrees, with more dexterity than the average human hand. These robotic movements and behavior annoyed Titan. While he contributed to farm productivity by eating weeds, the bots had far superior tasks to perform. Feeling perpetually hapless, Titan often butted or kicked the bots for no good reason. Jealousy was a strong motivator. In return, the bots often bumped Titan. Jillian and Ethan saw the boisterous competition between the bots and Titan, and they would respond by taking him for a walk to calm him down, or feeding him broccoli.

Stoner and Claiborne were to sleep in the greenhouse hallway, a three-meter-wide space that allowed self-driving tractors to enter and leave the building. By 2135 Thursday night, they had completed their outside security check of the greenhouse and Hickory family home. They entered the greenhouse and locked all doors behind them.

"Where's that damn goat?" Claiborne asked when they found that Titan's stall was empty. He turned on the lights and walked down the hallway while Stoner began to setup his sleeping area. Claiborne found Titan standing in front of the big greenhouse door. When the goat saw him, he made a *baa-baa-baa* sound.

"What's the matter, you stupid goat?" he asked as he looked through the double-door windows.

Titan butted his head on the door.

"Okay, okay, Titan. What's bothering you? Let's go in." He opened one of the heavy swinging doors, and he and the goat entered the cavernous hydroponic greenhouse.

The dim glow of electronic meters, gauges, and exit signs lit the facility. The four vertical levels of horizontal hydroponic crops looked daunting. Claiborne turned on the light switches along the inside wall, and the glare of the lights revealed the genius of the factory farm.

"Sergeant Stoner, come down to the greenhouse," Claiborne said into his communicator embedded in his ear.

"What's up, Buck?"

"Titan is acting weird, sir. He wanted to go into the greenhouse."

Claiborne and Titan ambled toward the farm bots in the corner of the greenhouse, both still in sleep mode. Titan followed a few meters behind him.

Stoner left his sleeping area, jogged down the hallway, and opened the greenhouse door. With a reluctant stare, he saw Titan and Claiborne.

"So, you found him," he said as he strolled up to them.

"Yes, sir. This goat senses something isn't right."

"Well, the bots are in sleep mode, so they can't be the problem," Stoner said. "You search this side, and I'll search the other."

The two men began their search. Titan stood in place, staring at the defenseless bots, before marching over to them and kicking both of them with his back hoof. The kicks made tinny sounds against the ceramic-metal composite hulls of the robots. Titan raised his head high; for an instant, he was the dominant species.

Claiborne snaked along several long rows of the greenhouse. In one aisle, he noticed a pile of vines, leaves, and eaten strawberries lying on the floor. Looking up at the four horizontal levels of hydroponic strawberries, he thought he saw something moving. Could it be an animal or human intruder? He pulled his gun from its holster and scanned the upper levels of the vertical farm. Something small was running along a steel support beam. In that moment, he realized what was going on. A group of rats had invaded the greenhouse and were eating the strawberry crop.

"Stoner, I found what's bothering Titan," he said into his communicator.

"What's that?"

"We have rats in the greenhouse eating the strawberries."

Stoner joined him and they climbed up ladders to observe the rats. They were chattering and eating strawberries. For them, an atmosphere-controlled hydroponic greenhouse growing fruit was heaven. What more could they want?

"Don't shoot them. We'll break something. Call Mr. Hickory," Stoner said. They holstered their guns.

Tom arrived and they searched for how the rats got into the greenhouse. They found a broken skylight and covered it with plywood. Then, they laid thirty rat traps on the rafters and floors.

"Okay, that's enough for tonight, "Tom said. "Thanks for calling me. You know, those rats can destroy our entire crop in a week."

"Ugh, so we did the right thing," Claiborne said.

"Yeah, I wasn't sleeping anyway."

Tom left and Stoner and Claiborne took Titan to his pen. The goat pranced out and headed back to his stall.

Claiborne locked Titan's stall, then reached into the small refrigerator nearby and pulled out more broccoli, a reward for warning them about the rat invaders.

Titan had a good day; he'd even gotten to kick the bots.

Claiborne and Stoner bedded down in the hallway with their military gear. They laid their rifles and handguns down beside their sleeping bags. As the two soldiers lay there, Claiborne said, "I think Titan is smarter than the bots."

"No, I doubt that. But the robots cannot smell a rat."

"I guess that's true," Claiborne replied. "Bots have no ability to smell."

"Get some sleep. We don't know what tomorrow will bring."

* * *

Later that night, around 2300, Jillian awoke. She threw on pink cotton sweatpants over her pajamas, and a sweatshirt with *LOVE* embroidered on the front. She worked her way down the stairs sideways, as she always did. Her carriage tilted to the left. The steps were always a challenge.

But that night, her movements were deliberate, even compulsive.

A determined Jillian bounded out the front door, knowing her destination.

Opening the door caused the home security alarm to go off, and it began to emit a loud wailing sound. Tom and Mattie jumped up from bed.

Tom rushed to Jillian's room.

"Mattie, Jilly is not in her room!"

Ethan peeked out his bedroom door, just as Stoner and Claiborne came running to the front porch.

"Tom, Mattie, are you all right?" they yelled.

"Yes, we're okay, but we can't find Jillian," he yelled from the top of the stairs.

"I'm looking in the bathroom," Mattie shouted.

Tom, dressed in dark-blue-and-green pajamas, ran down the stairs to see the front door wide open. "Start looking for Jillian. She's not in the house," Tom said to the soldiers.

Claiborne sprinted toward the greenhouse and Stoner searched around the sides of the home.

"Mattie, stay with Ethan," Tom said as he sat down in the living room and hastily put on his shoes. Then, he bolted out to the porch and began his descent down the steps. He looked toward Dura Road and breathed a sigh of relief when he noticed a dark silhouette moving by the front gate.

"Jillian's walking down the road," he yelled. "I'll get her!"

He took off running down the gravel driveway, followed by Stoner. They caught up with Jillian outside the farm gate on the side of Dura Road.

"Jilly, what are you doing?" he asked as he grabbed her tiny arm. She smiled at him but did not reply. "Why did you leave the house?"

"Daddy, I need to see the orb. It needs me."

"What?"

"Let me go, Daddy."

Jillian tried to pull her tiny hand away from his firm grip.

"Okay, we're going with you; first to the command tent."

Tom gripped his daughter's hand and glanced at Stoner. The three of them walked toward the command tent.

Stoner called Claiborne on his communicator. "Go to the house, get Mattie and Ethan, and bring them here."

"Yes, sir."

When they arrived at the main gate on Dura Road, one of the five armed military soldiers shouted, "Stop! Identify yourselves." By then, Mattie, Ethan, and Claiborne had joined them. They squinted from the glare of the flashlights and one big floodlight.

"I'm Staff Sergeant Stoner, and I'm guarding their home. Let us in."

The soldiers escorted them to the command tent, where Captain Kilbourne, who oversaw the night watch, asked, "Why are you here in the middle of the night?"

"Jillian wants to see the orb. She says it needs her," Tom said.

"What? Is this thing talking to her?"

"Sir, I don't know what's going on. But Jillian says she needs to go to the orb."

"You realize we could be in danger."

Jillian smiled at Kilbourne and said in a determined, slightly slurred voice, "Do you want to know why the orb is here?"

"All right, let's go, but you'll be surrounded by our armed troops. If anything suspicious happens, we'll pull your family out of there in a second."

Captain Kilbourne handed the Hickory family protective goggles to put on.

Claiborne, Kilbourne, Stoner, and the family walked to the orb, which was about forty meters away. The soldiers guarding the orb stepped aside but pointed their guns toward the menacing orb. With the group's arrival, the blue light the orb was emitting intensified. It eased its way toward them.

"The orb is higher in the air," Tom said.

"Yes, it's been acting weird for the last hour or so," Kilbourne said. Next, he turned to one soldier and said, "Get Colonel Preston; he left to catch some sleep."

"Do you mean wake him up, sir?"

"Yes, dammit, wake him up."

Tom held Jillian's hand tighter. Mattie held her other hand and Ethan's. They were three meters from the orb. Jillian's *LOVE* sweatshirt glistened in the orb's blue light. The three professors arrived and stood behind the family.

"Daddy, let me go. It needs me," Jillian said in a resolute voice. She tugged at her dad's strong grip.

"This thing could hurt you."

"No, it won't. It needs me."

They grappled for a while, but Tom eventually let go of Jillian's hand. A slight tug freed her from her mom's grip. Now all guns were pointed at the orb. Even Kilbourne had drawn his gun and aimed it at the orb.

The mystical orb advanced toward her until Jillian and the orb were within one meter of each other. It hovered up and down, as if it were inspecting her. Its light dimmed to a tolerable level.

Jillian reached out her hand. The orb touched her fingers, and suddenly they were one, overwhelming all who were present. A thin blue halo surrounded Jillian's body, even her arms, legs, and head. The orb had vanished into Jillian's body. The symbiotic relationship was clear for all to see. Even Preston was mesmerized.

Jillian's posture relaxed, and her head turned toward the crowd. She smiled with the complexity of a Mona Lisa smile.

"*See? The orb needs me,*" she said to her parents and to the crowd. Tom and Mattie were astounded and relieved that the orb hadn't hurt her. Stoner and Claiborne held Tom and Mattie's arms to restraint them from getting closer to their daughter.

After many seconds of quiet, Jillian said to the crowd, "*The orb loves us.*"

"Lower your guns, soldiers," Captain Kilbourne said, and then turned back to Jillian. "What does it want?"

"*The orb is here to help us. It wants me to be its voice.*"

"What?" Tom stepped forward. Mattie grabbed his hand, looking to him for answers. He could hear some people in the crowd beginning to pray. Others gawked in awe, wonder, fear, or despair.

"Jillian, we believe you," Kilbourne said, a sense of wonderment in his voice. He pushed his communicator and said, "Sir, are you coming?"

"Yes, I'm ten seconds away," Colonel Preston answered. "What's going on?"

"Sir, the orb and the farm girl, Jillian, are touching. I'm not sure who's talking, the girl or the orb. But you've got to see this."

"Don't let that girl get hurt, you idiot!"

"No, sir, I won't."

Preston arrived and stood beside them.

"Jillian, what does the orb want?" Preston asked after a moment of haunted silence.

"*To help humanity.*"

To some people in the crowd, Jillian's vibrant voice was the signature voice of an angel or even God. Others thought they might be hearing the voice of an advanced alien race or even the devil.

Jillian seemed immune to the surrounding distractions, just looked on serenely, waiting for Preston's response.

"How?" he asked.

Then, with a gentle smile, she revealed the purpose of the orb's visit: "*Your world is going to burn up. Global average temperatures and carbon dioxide levels keep increasing, while less oxygen is created in Earth's biosphere. All ice on the planet will disappear, and your oceans will rise over seventy meters. Jet streams will become chaotic. Humanity will not survive.*"

"What?" Dr. Breslin shouted, his chest heaving. "What should we do?"

"You should assemble a panel of your best scientists, philosophers, and religious leaders. Bring them here, and we will explain."

"Are you divine?" Shreevallabh asked, stepping out of the jam-packed group.

Jillian turned her head and looked deep into her eyes. *"Not as you understand it."*

"Oh, I'm so happy. We are not alone," Shreevallabh mumbled as her tears fell to the ground. She knelt down and bowed her head in prayer.

The orb remained steadfast in its position, color, and intensity. Cameras recorded each word and movement.

"Why are you in the form of a glowing orb?" an amazed Breslin asked.

"We have appeared to humankind in many forms. What form would you prefer?"

"Why not a human form?" Breslin said in a voice of exhilaration.

"We've fulfilled that request before," Jillian said, smiling.

With that, the thin blue halo around Jillian's body vanished and she and the orb separated. Her hand dropped to her side. Her eyes blinked, and then closed. The fragile girl stood in place with her shoulders slumped.

Mattie scrambled over and hugged her tightly, but Jillian's arms did not respond; they were limp and hanging straight down. The orb's light dimmed further as it moved to its original position. Mattie moved Jillian away from the orb and joined Tom and Ethan.

"Jilly, are you okay?" Tom asked when she opened her eyes again, kissing her on the forehead.

"Yes, Daddy. Was I asleep?"

"Yes, sweetie, you were," Mattie said. Both hugged her, their beloved daughter.

A dense silence engulfed the crowd. No one spoke. No one stirred. No one knew what to do. Should they pray or run? Believers versus nonbelievers, their confusion increasing. And, the US Army, including Colonel Preston, was skeptical of the orb's motives.

One could hear the mumbling of prayers in different languages. Dr. Shreevallabh knelt in prayer, as did two soldiers and one nuclear weapons expert. They believed they had witnessed a holy spirit or even God. A few confused people burst out crying and hugged one another. Others, laughed at what they had seen and thought it was a farce. And, others stood still and were silent, as if Medusa had turned them into stone.

Mattie sobbed. She felt dizzy. At that moment, she had realized that this orb would forever change their lives. Her descent down the deep trail of depression had begun.

After a minute of the crowd weeping, hugging, and praying, Colonel Preston broke the confusion by yelling, "Man your positions! This isn't a religious service or alien invasion. We have a job to do."

* * *

Afterward, the director of Homeland Security, Ginger Agee, used her communicator to contact the White House. "Please get the president on the line. I must talk to him now."

White House staff woke up the president, the Honorable Steven E. Barlow. In his bedroom, he activated his communicator and said, "Hello, Ginger. What's going on?"

"Mr. President, we have an unusual situation outside Lexington, Kentucky. I'm sending a video to your White House communications staff. We can't keep this event from the media much longer. It's been a day since we first sighted this glowing object."

"Did you say a glowing object?" Sleepily, he patted his white hair, which stood straight up on one side of his head.

"Yes, sir. It's a gaseous sphere about the size of a volleyball. It hovers above the ground with no sound or smell. It seems to be a form of higher intelligence, but it's not biological. You need to watch the video, sir. I know it sounds strange, but please watch the video."

"I will."

A White House telecommunication staffer entered the room and opened a wall panel, where a television wall screen appeared with the video already loaded.

The president sat on the edge of the bed, his wife, Elizabeth, by his side, and watched. He asked the aide to replay the video. Afterward, he called Agee back and said, "Is the young girl okay? Is the orb a danger to us? What do you need?"

"Sir, the farm girl, Jillian Hickory, is fine, but our doctors are monitoring her. We set up a restricted area two kilometers in diameter using a US Army battalion."

"Yes, the chair of the Joint Chiefs of Staff informed me of the troop deployment. He said he would find out what's going on and report to me."

"The orb asked us to assemble a panel of experts. It wants us to get scientists, philosophers, and ministers of any faith here as soon as possible. Did you hear that on the video?"

"Yes, I did. I'll get dressed, and we'll meet in the situation room." President Barlow ended the call and turned to his aide. "Get my Chief of Staff here. And tell Al Carr to meet me in the White House situation room. And get the senior military officers on-site tied in to our conversation."

The presidential aid left and Barlow stood alone reflecting on the situation and how he got in this position. A tall man with blue eyes, the president had graduated from the United States Naval Academy. To protect the USNA campus and Annapolis from rising sea levels, he had acquired funds to build a seawall. He wanted to protect the rich heritage of the USNA. Barlow thought about his twenty years in the Pacific fleet as an officer on submarines. He had become governor of Maryland after his retirement from the US Navy. And now, as President of the United States, he must handle the arrival of the orb.

* * *

As the Hickory family hugged one another, they asked Kilbourne if they could go home. The captain ordered Stoner and Claiborne to escort them. The US Army doctors examined Jillian one more time before she left and placed three electronic monitors on her body. For now, she was not hurt in any way they could detect.

Tom carried her down Dura Road, and once they were at their farm's gate, he stood her upright in the darkness.

"Why aren't you leaning to the left?" Mattie asked curiously, walking up the gravel driveway. "You're not twitching either."

"Mom, I'm tired," Jillian said in a clear, articulate voice.

"But you always lean left."

Jillian shrugged, but her parents were racking their brains, trying to make sense of the night's events.

"I still don't understand what happened. Jilly, are you okay?" Tom asked, hugging her again.

"Yes, Daddy, but I'm thirsty. I want to go to bed."

Once home, Jillian headed toward the kitchen, where she poured herself a glass of water and drank it while standing by the sink. The entire family watched her gulp by gulp. There were no twitches or sporadic movements in her body. Soon after, she walked up the stairs in one swift motion, like any healthy eight-year-old.

"Jilly, why aren't you leaning or twitching?" Mattie asked again.

Jillian gracefully turned on the steps and said, "Mom, I don't know." She continued upstairs, laid down on her bed, and fell asleep with all her clothes on.

Her feet and tennis shoes were muddy and hanging over the end of the bed. Mattie took her shoes off but decided to leave her in her clothes. She closed Jillian's bedroom door and, standing outside, began to whimper.

"Is Jillian cured of the palsy disease?" Ethan asked when his mother returned to the living room.

"Are you crazy?" Tom replied.

"Good heavens," Mattie said, still crying. "I'll take her to the doctor. The doctor will tell us."

Ethan went upstairs to his bedroom, and before Mattie turned in, she checked on both children one final time. Tom, as usual, turned on the security system and locked all the doors. He waved to Stoner and Claiborne, who were talking outside the greenhouse building and retired to the bedroom too.

There were no gentle embraces that night. Tom lay there thinking about how different their lives might have been had he not searched for the strange flash of light.

"Tom, I can't handle this; it's too much," Mattie said. She wiped tears from her face using the pillowcase.

"This thing will blow over. Then, we can resume our lives."

"I don't think so."

CHAPTER 4
Enlightenment

Conk-conk-conk went the alarm clock. It was 0700 on Friday. Tom liked the unnatural sound of bamboo striking bamboo to force him to wake up. Mattie despised it but it did the job, and she got out of bed too.

They went downstairs to prepare breakfast. Tom pulled cold eggs and sausage out of the refrigerator, while Mattie placed their worn skillet on the convection range. Tom and Mattie cherished the smell and sound of the eggs sizzling in the hot skillet.

Technology permeated every aspect of their lives, but it did not change the small-town habits of an old-time family breakfast. A 3-D food printer was the only technology allowed in the Hickory kitchen.

Preparing breakfast was a manual, team effort, with a family efficiency they were proud of. Each member of the family had specific tasks to do during breakfast. These assigned tasks gave them time to talk.

They prepared the family's traditional breakfast without saying a word. Given the previous day's incredible events, Tom and Mattie were in deep, anguished thought. They wanted the kids to sleep, so they didn't wake them. While they ate, Mattie eventually broached the subject. "What do you make of last night?"

"It's unbelievable."

"Do you think the orb is a messenger from God?"

Tom stopped eating and looked straight ahead. "Yes, I do."

Mattie refreshed their coffee but did not respond to Tom's words.

"We're Christians, Mattie, so I can come to no other conclusion."

"Yes, I agree; it's God's messenger. But why us?" She reached for his hand, and they held hands on top of the kitchen table for a moment. They continued their breakfast, but a knock at the front door interrupted them.

Tom opened the door.

"Hello, Captain Kilbourne. What's up?"

"Mr. Hickory, Colonel Preston requests that your daughter, Jillian, not go to school today. She is seemingly the voice of the orb, so she cannot leave the vicinity."

"My wife canceled school for the kids for the rest of the week. They can make up the schoolwork on UNet. Come in. Do you want a cup of coffee?"

For 80 percent of secondary schools, 100 percent of the curriculum was online using avatar teachers, but Jillian and Ethan's school used a combination of online and on-site study. The kids attended a brick-and-mortar school with human teachers for half a day, three times a week, and used UNet to complete their studies, homework, and projects. Their electronic textbooks used embedded UNet links to make the topics more relevant.

"A cup of coffee would be great."

Mattie pulled a huge cup from the kitchen cabinet and asked, "How would you like it?"

"Black is fine," Kilbourne said. "Mrs. Hickory, your kitchen smells wonderful. It reminds me of home."

"Where did you grow up?"

"Ma'am, I'm from Paris, Texas. My mom raised me. I never knew my dad."

"Well, Captain, things turned out well for you."

"Yes, ma'am, they did. I have enjoyed my career in the army."

Tom gestured that the captain sit down at the kitchen table and the three of them sat down.

"The army's request is for Jillian to be readily available as long as the orb remains here," Kilbourne said, his voice coming out strained.

"Ah. What if the orb stays here months?" Mattie asked.

"Ma'am, I don't know the answer to that question."

There was a pause as the three of them took tentative sips from their coffees.

"Do you want any breakfast?" Mattie asked, breaking the silence.

"No, ma'am, I've already eaten in the mess hall. Thank you. I enjoyed your coffee, though. Our mess hall coffee tastes like cardboard." He set the half-empty cup down on the table. "I'll tell Colonel Preston about your decision. It's a matter of national security to have Jillian available. Thank you."

"Yes, we understand," Mattie said after taking a deep breath.

Tom escorted Kilbourne to the front door.

"Is Jillian okay?" the captain asked once they reached the porch.

"Yes, but she's exhausted and still in bed."

Tom wanted to state that he was also worried about Mattie but Kilbourne had already turned to walk back down the gravel driveway.

After cleaning the kitchen, Mattie and Tom moved into the living room to watch the news. They watched two news channels concurrently on their wall screen, but turned the sound up on WKYH after an item caught their eye, and muted the other station.

"The Shuman Retirement Center is uninhabitable," the news announcer said. "At high tide, the floors are filled with seawater. Because of sea-level rise, FEMA declared it a disaster area. A wide and shallow bay has also amplified ocean levels. Sea levels around the world are increasing exponentially. The Atlantic Ocean has risen over one meter on average since 2000."

Mobile beds and black wheelchairs dominated the video. They filled the flooded sidewalks and parking lots.

"During the past week, the retirement center evacuated one hundred two senior citizens. The governor of Florida called out the National Guard to help them move to higher ground. Five assisted-living sites accepted the displaced seniors, with some rooms holding three people instead of two.

The temperature on moving day was forty-one degrees Celsius, and as a result, five seniors are being treated in local hospitals."

An elderly woman with breathing tubes in her nose was crying in her wheelchair.

The reporter asked her, "What's wrong? Are you hurt?"

"I left my deceased husband's picture in my room. A nurse went back to the room and searched but could not find it."

The announcer and video then cut away for commercials. During this time, Mattie said, "My gosh, we keep losing coastline communities."

"Yes, it's sad. Be thankful we don't live on the coast. Some big cities are sinking into the sea," Tom said.

"That's why I buy bottled water. I worry about saltwater contamination."

The announcer returned and began a second story about sea-level rise. As new video of the situation played, she said, "The Greyhound Golf Club in Dania Beach, Florida, was also declared uninhabitable. National Guard troops and local authorities helped evacuate two hundred fifty-three homes. In this coastal and gated golf course community, some homeowners would not leave. As you see in the video, police broke down the door of this home, which is standing in forty centimeters of seawater. The Coleman family has no place to go; they are homeless and have no relatives. They could not afford the high cost of flood insurance, so their home is a total loss. In Florida, only one corporation offers flood insurance."

"Local police and the US Coast Guard will patrol the Greyhound area. The state is trying to find the funds to tear down the waterlogged buildings. At high tide, a few elevated golf course greens protrude above the water. The occupants of Greyhound Golf Club and the Shuman Retirement Center have no chance of ever returning to their homes and the care center. If you would like to donate money to help them, please see our UNet WKYH website."

"This is exactly why the orb is here," Mattie said to Tom. "To help us with climate change."

"Yeah, I hear you, but will we listen."

"I doubt it," Mattie said while starting to cry. Tom went over and hugged Mattie.

After Mattie left, Tom asked Atticus for a status check of farm operations using his wall screen. Both of the farm bots had ignored the soldiers and the orb, and continued to give top priority to doing their jobs, the efficient performance of their farming tasks. Their software did not allow for distractions or intervention in non-farm activities. Based on Tom's review, the farm's performance reports were excellent.

Jillian and Ethan eventually ambled down the steps dressed. Ethan noticed that his sister didn't need help going down the steps. She walked ahead of him and straight down the steps without holding the rail.

They poured their milk and orange juice and sat down at the kitchen table. Mattie walked over to them, put her hands on their shoulders, and began a brief prayer. "Dear God, thank you for our blessings. Please keep us safe and together. Amen."

As the kids ate the fresh eggs and ham that Mattie prepared, she told them what the captain had said. "Jilly and Ethan, you are not going to school this week."

"Great," Ethan said.

"The army thinks Jillian is the voice of the orb. We must stay put."

"Mom, why did the orb pick Jilly to be its voice?" Ethan asked.

"I have no idea, but I wish it hadn't."

"What do you mean, Mom?"

"Things were good before this thing came. Now I fear our lives will never be the same."

"But Mom, Jilly doesn't have palsy anymore," Ethan replied.

"We don't know that for sure. Jilly must see the doctors," Tom said.

The kids looked perplexed as they tried to decipher the family discussion. Then, Ethan asked his father, "Can we go see the orb today?"

"Ethan, the government controls who sees it now."

Jillian and Mattie said nothing.

"Dad, did you know orbs have been observed for centuries? Even astronauts see these things flying around their spacecraft," Ethan said. He'd clearly been researching the topic on the UNet.

"Yes, son, but we still don't understand orbs."

"Are they angels?"

"Ethan, that could be. Or it could be an electromagnetic ball of energy that the earth and clouds somehow generated."

"But, Dad, it spoke to us through Jilly," Ethan said.

Tom smiled, signifying his agreement with his son's logical conclusion.

* * *

President Barlow presided over the 0800 meeting in the White House situation room. Jerry Bragg, the White House Chief of Staff, sat alongside him, and the Joint Chief of the Armed Forces and four-star general Al Carr also attended. Ms. Ginger Agee, Director of Homeland Security, and Lieutenant Colonel Preston dialed in via telepresence, their likenesses standing as 3-D holograms.

"Good morning. I've called this meeting to discuss the orb outside Lexington. My first question is to you, Colonel Preston. Is this thing a threat to US security?"

"Mr. President, I see no signs the orb is an immediate threat to our country. It is a remarkable event that is being played out. But, over time, we might discover it's a trick by a foreign power." For a second, Preston marveled at the fact he was now speaking to the president of the United States. He cherished the moment. But he quickly turned his attention back to the conversation and the job he faced.

"Ginger, what do you think?" the president asked while taking notes.

"Mr. President, I do not think it's a national security threat. In fact, it could be a gift."

"What do you mean?" he replied, tapping his finger on the table.

"Well, sir, the farm girl says the object is here to help humanity. I believe her."

"Do you think the orb is a hologram?"

"No, Mr. President, it's not a hologram. It's real, but our scientists are puzzled about its nature.

"What do you mean?"

"The orb seems to be massless, yet we see a physical form."

"I've replayed the video of the orb and little girl many times. Al, what do you think?" President Barlow asked.

"Mr. President, I see it as a security and military threat. Once word gets out about the orb to the media and government leaders, it could trigger worldwide turmoil. Coping with climate stress places an extra burden on civilized society, and now the orb. The military should prepare for the worse scenarios."

"Can we keep this secret?" the president asked.

"Not for more than a day or two," Ms. Agee said. "Local media followed the troop movements out of Fort Campbell, and reporters are still trying different ways to get inside the restricted area. All troops are under strict orders not to reveal anything they see or hear. And the Central Intelligence Agency is monitoring the hackers, who we believe are trying to steal video from our encrypted cameras. But, sir, it's only a matter of time before someone will talk."

"General, do you recommend we go to a higher level of military readiness?" the president asked, still tapping the table with his finger.

"Yes sir, I think we should. If this thing is here to help humanity, it's still unclear how it plans to do this. Will it help all nations or only a few? Sir, it could disrupt trade, trigger wars, wreck religion, and destroy social and government order."

"Al, I know. I know."

Jerry Bragg cleared his throat and said, "Sir, with the worldwide media, we could also have a Tower of Babel on our hands. How do they know if the orb video is real or faked, for example?"

"I watched the video four times. It seems genuine. Is there any way this could be a hoax or a terrorist plot?" the president asked.

"Not likely," Chief of Staff Bragg said. "We've asked scientists on-site and other world experts. In their professional opinions, the orb and its behavior are beyond our technology. It seems to be aware of what's going on. It moves with intelligence and responds to human interaction. It seems to be massless and a laser bounced off it. We know of no earth-bound technology capable of these feats."

No one spoke as the president continued to take notes on their discussion.

"Anyone here think it's an alien invasion, and we don't recognize it yet?" Barlow asked.

"Sir, it could be alien," Carr said. "Experts from our Unidentified Entity Program (UEP) are on site and evaluating the orb now."

"Okay." The president paused for a moment of thought, then said, "It's been on the ground for how long?"

"About thirty-six hours, sir. The farmer first sighted the orb around 2100 Wednesday evening."

"Let's get ahead of this. I doubt we can keep it from the media much longer. Too many people have seen it. We should show the videos to the world. Should I go on television now? Is this the right time?"

"Yes, sir, we believe this is the best move. The media will find out soon," Bragg said.

"I've heard enough. What are your final recommendations? Carr, you begin."

"Mr. President, I would recommend we go to a higher state of military readiness and call up more troops for onsite security. We need to create a second and larger restricted area—say, six kilometers in diameter. The population of Bourbon County is small. We could move all people in the two restricted areas to safer locations."

"Mr. President," Colonel Preston said, "we also need to deploy a mobile fusion generator to Bourbon County. We need the electrical power."

Military fusion power plants, which were carried on a mobile semi-truck, were often deployed in wartime to bring their own electricity-generating capability to the battlefield. To be combat ready, the US Army needed massive amounts of electricity. Laser weapons, electronic equipment, vehicles, air-conditioning, and hospitals needed power. Special permission by the president of the United States was necessary to deploy the mobile power plants in civilian situations.

After a long pause, Barlow said, "Ginger, any recommendations?"

"Mr. President, I agree, we should increase our military alert status. We can take no chances. And we should assemble the team of experts the orb requested. We can debrief them and get them to the site as soon as possible. I'd say six to nine more experts. That includes the three University of Kentucky professors already onsite. Each of the six major continents should have at least one representative. The world must see this as an international initiative."

"Mr. President, I'd announce the orb's arrival to the world no later than tonight. I recommend your speechwriters get started now. We should show the orb videos and tell people what we know to date."

"Is that it?" President Barlow asked.

"No, sir," Bragg said. "We need the cabinet to prepare whitepapers and videos about the orb. What should we say or not say? We need to provide stability to existing government, economic, religious, and social structures. We do not want human institutions to collapse."

The president took a few more notes, thought for a moment, and then said, "Okay, here's what we'll do."

"First, I do not want to increase our military alert status yet. Such a move will alarm the world and create even more chaos; other nations will also increase their military readiness status, moving us closer to war."

"Second, call up more troops and expand the restricted area around the orb. Also, get me the papers to sign to deploy the mobile power plant to the site of the orb. Fourth, set up the international panel of experts. And ask the cabinet to prepare whitepapers and videos about the orb's arrival. Finally, I'll go on television tonight and tell the world about the orb's arrival and what we know to date. The world has a right to know."

"All must be started by the time I give my speech tonight. Anything else?" No one responded, so Barlow stood up, pushed his chair back from the table, and said, "Good. We have a plan. Now, make it happen."

* * *

General Carr called Brigadier General Stephanie Tucson, commander of the 303rd Army Infantry Regiment, and patched in Lieutenant Colonel Preston.

"Steph, we don't have time for small talk. I want you to set up a six-kilometer-diameter restricted area in Bourbon County. It will surround the smaller security area. Colonel Preston will brief you and get you up to date. You two figure out how many more troops you need to do the job. I don't want anyone to get in or out of the restricted areas. Seal them tight. Do you understand?"

"Yes, sir."

"Colonel Preston, figure out where to set up the second perimeter. General Tucson will arrive soon. I want this done by 1930. The president goes on the airwaves at 2000. Questions?"

"No, sir," Tucson and Preston replied, after which, the communication ended, and the wall screen went blank.

Preston knew Tucson well. They had worked together at Fort Campbell and in two previous situations, once on a hurricane relief effort in New York City and another time in a civil war in Brazil.

After Carr hung up, the wailing alarm sounded at the Fort Campbell military base. The alarm did not stop. Neither did the notifications on their e-devices. They scurried around as their orders became clear: get ready to leave the base within one hour. They had to construct a second restricted area.

From Fort Campbell, they called up four more battalions of the 303rd Army Infantry Regiment. They loaded their gear, trucks, helicopters, weapons, tents, and communications equipment, and set off for the site of the orb. The US Army would have over two thousand troops deployed in a two-layer perimeter around the orb.

By 1300 on Friday, the vanguard of troops arrived by truck. The troops did not know what they were to be guarding, only that they would set up a restricted area.

Again, townspeople stared at the military convoys driving the highways toward Lexington. The public seldom saw such large troop movements, and local and national news stations covered the movement. This time, the military convoys were many kilometers long.

Brigadier General Stephanie Tucson arrived at the site at 1145 by helicopter. She marched up to the thirty-by-thirty-meter command tent, which was surrounded by communication vehicles, mobile robotic laser guns, other tents, and armed troops, where Lieutenant Colonel Preston came out and met her. They saluted one another.

"Hello, Colonel Preston."

"I'm glad to see you, General," he replied. They both entered the command tent.

Tucson exhibited a quick wit and a strong physical appearance. With short auburn hair, piercing green eyes, and an athletic body, the forty-eight-year-old had earned a reputation as a tough, smart, and fair commander. In Brazil, Tucson had helped mediate a civil war while commanding US and UN troops. She had also helped stop the war between Turkey and its neighbors over water shortages.

In the twenty-second century, climate change had made water more valuable than gold. Water shortages ravaged Europe and Africa, where millions of abandoned water wells occupied the landscape. Higher seas mixed with fresh water polluted the groundwater. Expensive desalination factories eased some of these freshwater shortages, but many nations couldn't afford to operate large-scale desalination. The results were devastating. Water shortages triggered war and sometimes the overthrow of governments. The water shortages also spread disease, shut down schools, and stopped economic development.

"Can I get you something to drink?" Preston asked.

"Yes, black coffee would be great," Tucson replied as she smoothed down a clump of hair that protruded from the back of her combat helmet. "Get the hologram maps up, Hawk?"

"They're over here, General," Preston said. He switched on the holograms, and they were able to see the surrounding terrain. They both stood over the hologram table, and discussed where and how to set up the second restricted area.

"Let's use these country roads as part of our restricted-area boundary. That way, we cut across only fifteen fields to secure a perimeter." Preston pointed out the roads on the hologram with a laser pointer.

"Your plan looks good, except why not use this country road as a perimeter and not the field?" she asked, using her own pointer to highlight another road.

"That's one less field to traverse," Preston replied. He then marked the second restricted-area perimeter. The plan was set.

"When the first troops arrive, use them to secure the roads and fields," Tucson said. "No one sleeps or eats until this second restricted area is done. No tents or mess halls are to be set up until all is secure. Troops sleep on the ground tonight. Understood, Colonel?"

"Yes, ma'am," Colonel Preston said. "Captain Kilbourne, get all the officers in here. Brief them on the location of the boundary of the perimeter, assign them to an area, and have the exterior built by 1900. The first battalion of the 303rd Army Infantry Regiment will continue to manage the interior restricted area. Assign new troops to the larger restricted area."

"Yes, sir."

As the extra troops arrived, they were also tasked with guarding farms and villages, and escorting people to hotels. They built entrance and exit gates and fences, and manned sentry positions. By 1400, all troops were onsite.

Tucson and Preston drove around the perimeter in an electric-powered V9H armored vehicle, discussing sites for the mess hall, living quarters, latrines, and security stations. During their drive, they encountered a group of soldiers standing in front of a farmhouse. Tucson and Preston drove up to them. The troops stood at attention while Kilbourne saluted.

"What is the situation here, Captain?"

Tucson and Preston got out of their vehicle.

"Ma'am, these people will not leave their farm," Kilbourne said, gesturing to the farmer and his wife who were standing on the porch. "I've explained to them we need to set up a restricted area for their safety."

Tucson looked up, and smiled at the farmers. "Sir, ma'am, we need to clear this area for your safety. Did the officer explain that we would station troops around your home and farm? We'll feed your animals. We'll protect your property and give you updates. All we need is your contact information. You'll stay in a hotel at government expense. We'll give you vouchers for three meals a day."

"Yes, we understand that, but we have a pregnant mare who may give birth soon," the man replied. "We need to be here."

Tucson turned to Kilbourne and said, "Hire a horse van to take the mare to a Lexington veterinarian of their choice."

"Yes, sir," he replied.

"The US Army will pay for everything. Tell your vet to call this number." Tucson handed them her business card. "Please leave the area, and if you need anything, call me."

They both thanked the officers and went back into their house to pack. Kilbourne turned and saluted Tucson as she walked back to her Jeep.

* * *

The announcement from the president started at 2000, the special presidential message interrupting other media outlets.

The Hickory family sat on their sofa to watch. Staff Sergeant Stoner and Corporal Claiborne stood behind them, having been invited in to view the president's message.

The president sat behind his Oval Office desk. He wore a dark blue suit, a stiff white shirt with no tie, and a small pin depicting the American flag.

"Good evening, ladies and gentlemen of the United States of America and of the world," he said. "Tonight, I want to inform you of a developing story that is taking place. It is happening in a farm field outside Lexington, Kentucky."

"About forty-eight hours ago, a glowing light, an orb, began hovering in a farm field in Bourbon County."

"A farm family first found the orb. To protect their privacy, we will not reveal their names. Scientists have examined this ball of light and the videos you are about to see. The orb exhibits some level of consciousness and clairvoyant intelligence. Our scientists conclude this mysterious orb is of no immediate threat to the United States or the world."

"I directed our armed forces to erect two restricted areas around the orb. One area is two kilometers in diameter. The outer security area is six kilometers in diameter. Kentucky media have reported large troop movements from Fort Campbell, Kentucky. This is true. We have over two thousand troops providing security within these restricted areas and have evacuated residents that live there."

The president paused and picked up a crystal glass of water on his desk. He took a drink, glanced at the elegant White House logo on the glass, and continued.

"I have directed the members of my cabinet to provide all the information we have about the orb to date. Immediately after this announcement, we'll show these two videos. The first video from the state of Kentucky shows the object hovering in a field. It emits a glowing blue light.

Our scientists are not sure what state of matter the orb is. Their best guess is an electromagnetic plasma with little or no mass. A drone took this first video."

"In the spirit of full disclosure, the US government provides the second video. It shows an eight-year-old girl interacting with the orb. And, we have blocked out the young girl's face to protect her identity, as well as all other faces. This video requires some prior explanation: Prior to this video, the young girl seemed compelled to see the orb. She left her bed and home at night to visit it. She said, and I quote, 'The orb needs me.' Her family and a significant number of US Army troops were watching when she touched it. After this, the girl became the voice of the orb. We don't know why she was selected for this role. It could be a random occurrence. The young girl doesn't remember the interaction. Medical doctors have examined her, and she remains in good health."

"What you will see in the second video is not a trick, hoax, or Hollywood film. It is actually what happened. We have added the conversation in unedited English in subtitles—that is, open captioning. The conversation is between the farm girl and our experts on-site."

"The US government takes no position on what the orb might do or say next. To our knowledge, it is not an alien invasion, a terrorist attack, or a plot to overthrow any government. The United States makes no statement supporting or refuting religion."

"The orb, through the voice of the girl, said, and I quote, 'Your world is going to burn up. Global average temperatures and carbon dioxide levels keep increasing while less oxygen is created in Earth's biosphere. All ice on the planet will disappear, and your oceans will rise over seventy meters. Jet streams will become chaotic. Humanity will not survive.'"

"These claims are profound, and we do not know if they are true or not. It is our responsibility to inform the world about this ongoing situation. We will now show the two videos. You can make your own judgment. This news announcement concludes when the last video ends. I will not answer questions. Thank you for listening."

The two videos played. The first lasted 1.3 minutes, and the second lasted 3.7 minutes. When the last video ended, the announcement came to an abrupt halt, and the local television stations regained control of their networks.

After he signed off, President Barlow remained sitting at his Oval Office desk and asked, "Are the cameras off?"

"Yes, sir," replied one of the producers.

"Jerry, I hope I'm doing the right thing."

"Mr. President, I think you are. We might have been able to delay the announcement another day or so, at most. It's better for the world to hear it from you first than the media."

"Yeah, I agree. Please get me the heads of state on the phone hotline—first Russia, India, and China. Make sure they don't wait on me. I'll wait on them."

"Mr. President, you should wait on no one," Jerry Bragg replied.

"Jerry, I'm trying to prevent the ultimate peril: war."

"Yes, sir, Mr. President."

CHAPTER 5
Healing

"I'll call Captain Kilbourne to see if the doctors can examine us today," Tom said to Mattie Saturday morning during breakfast.

"Good. We need help. I want the doctors to examine Jilly. And, after the president's speech, everyone will be trying to find out our identity."

"If we didn't need protection before the speech, we sure need it now. I'm glad we have the protection of the soldiers."

Ethan interrupted their conversation as he entered the kitchen, saying good morning, and opened the refrigerator. He found the biggest glass, poured himself orange juice, and drank half of it while still standing up.

"Do you want eggs?"

"No, Mom. I'll have cereal." He opened the pantry door and pulled out a box of EcoWheats. As he was pouring the cereal into a bowl, he dropped the box, and it fell, the contents spilling out onto the kitchen floor.

"Oh! Clumsy of me."

"Sweep it up," Mattie said as she and Tom looked down at the floor. "That box of cereal is expensive."

The price of a five-hundred-gram box of cereal was ð14 ecoins. Forty-two percent of wheat was grown in corporate and automated hydroponic greenhouses. Food accounted for a much higher percentage of daily living costs than in the past because of the erratic weather and heat. Automated greenhouses and logistic systems were expensive to operate. Even with the help of modern economies to supply food to less developed nations, millions of people died each year from malnutrition.

"Sorry about the spill," Ethan said as he swept up the cereal. His second attempt to pour himself a bowl was successful.

Once he was seated, Mattie asked, "Did you sleep well?"

"No. The president's speech upset me. The media will hunt us down."

No one responded to Ethan's outburst as they continued the family ritual of breakfast. Jillian arrived soon after and poured herself a glass of milk. Joining them at the kitchen table, the family held hands to say a prayer.

"Dear Lord, thank you for all that we have. We don't understand what is happening, but please protect us. In God's name, amen."

After the prayer, Tom stood up and kissed each of the kids on the head. As he left the kitchen, he hugged Mattie.

Tom turned on the living room wall screen to see a flurry of news reports on the orb and commentary on the president's speech. The very sight of these frantic news reports caused him to have a panic attack sitting in his chair. His chest hurt and his rate of breathing increased. He began to sweat and chills ran down his arms.

"Mute the wall screen," Tom said, trying to calm down.

He had done a good job of hiding these panic attacks until now. He wanted to be strong and positive for his beloved family, but inside he knew he had lost control of their lives. He blamed only himself for triggering his family's torturous pathway by searching for the flash of light last Wednesday evening.

Once he calmed himself, he found an educational show on the impact of sea-level rise on the state of Louisiana. He could escape his reality by seeing others cope with their reality. Climate stress dominated worldwide economics and lifestyles now, and the orb's arrival seemed to be fracturing society even more.

The television narrator said, "The state of Louisiana has lost ten thousand three hundred forty-nine square kilometers of marsh, mangrove, and land due to an ocean that has been rising since 2000; one and a half times the land area of Delaware. The cost to Louisiana's oil industry alone these past one hundred years is over forty-two billion ecoins. Shipyards, refineries, pipelines, and seaports were left to rot away. Only a few of these industrial assets were built anew or replaced."

"Meanwhile, the sea continues to corrode equipment and buildings, and swallow up the land. The economic impact is devastating to energy companies and the people of Louisiana, and the emotional impact is greater. Some families have had to give up their homes, hometowns, family history, and way of life."

After a moment of reflection, he turned the wall screen off.

An acidic taste bubbled up his throat and into his mouth. He reached beside his chair and took two acid reflux pills. He picked up the encrypted communicator the soldiers had given them and called Kilbourne on a direct line.

"Can your army doctors give our family medical exams?" he asked.

"Sure, Tom. No problem. We'll have you go to the mobile hospital. We have scanning equipment and a small laboratory for tests there. When do you want to go?"

"Today would be great—say, after 0900?"

"Yes, that's fine."

Tom paused for a brief moment, and then asked, "Uh, do you have a psychiatrist on duty?"

"Yes, we do. I'll make sure she's available to see your family."

Shortly after, while the kids were still eating breakfast, Mattie told them that they'd be going to the mobile hospital.

"Mom, I'm always tired," Jillian said. "And, Mom, I think my palsy is gone."

"Oh, my goodness. We need a doctor to help us with both of these issues."

The possibility that Jilly might be cured of cerebral palsy was both a joy and a worry to Mattie. The joy came from the wonderful excitement of Jillian being free of a dreadful disease. The despair came from realizing the orb most likely cured her. If the orb's healing power became public, Mattie thought, billions of people would want to touch the orb and Jillian.

Later that morning, Stoner and Claiborne knocked on the front door to escort them to the command tent, where Kilbourne would drive them over to the mobile hospital.

Three US Army doctors greeted them when they arrived. They administered blood samples, scans, and other medical tests. The family gave their medical histories. Each family member completed a physical exam, including vision and hearing tests. After lunch, they had psychiatrist appointments.

* * *

US Army Captain Brigida Hansley had earned her first medical degree from the German Medical Faculty of Heidelberg. Her PhD in clinical psychology was from the University of Chicago's Pritzker School of Medicine.

Dr. Hansley led Mattie through the stark hallways and plastic floors of the medical tents. They entered a windowless exam room furnished with a table with an ugly black plastic top and four folding chairs. Two glasses of water were waiting for them on the table. Hansley asked Mattie if she would like something to drink, but she declined.

They each took a seat.

"Mattie, tell me about yourself," Dr. Hansley asked.

Mattie spent several minutes describing her parents and high school experiences. Later, she focused on family life with Tom and the kids.

"And then, Tom went outside to see the damn orb."

"Are you angry at Tom?" the doctor asked calmly.

"Yes. If he hadn't been so nosy, we would be staying in a Lexington hotel, and the orb would not have ruined our lives."

"So, you feel Tom is to blame?"

"Yeah," a nervous Mattie answered, rubbing her hands together. "Every time I see a soldier, I get angry at Tom."

"Do you feel guilty for blaming Tom?"

"Yes. I blame everybody."

"Who is everybody?"

"I blame Tom, the orb, the media … I blame the government. Our wonderful life is gone."

"How are you sleeping?"

"Not much. It's wearing me down. And I'm taking too many pills."

"I'll review your medications after we talk. How about your eating patterns?"

"Fair. My kitchen time is one of the few things that relaxes me." Mattie took a drink of water and wiped the tears that had begun to fall from her face.

"Have you had any thoughts of suicide?"

"Oh no, Dr. Hansley. I love my family. I would never do that."

"So, you do have something to live for, right?"

"Right."

"Mattie, you have no family history of mental illness, but you're in a state of severe depression. Given what's happened to you over the last few days, this is understandable."

"I see no way out."

"There are treatment programs for depression. We could try antidepressant medications and regular counseling sessions. Try to exercise more. Once I talk to your family, we can find ways for them to be more supportive too. You have much to live for. A beautiful, loving family is worth fighting for."

"I know, but everything around us is falling apart."

"After I talk with the rest of you, we'll design a treatment plan for you with the help of our doctors. We'll get you going strong again. We'll work on a solution for the family."

Dr. Hansley stood up, and Mattie joined her, though her posture was stooped. They walked out of the exam room side by side.

Next, Tom entered the exam room. He talked to Dr. Hansley about the orb experience, the media, his high school days including football, and his family. Toward the end of their conversation, Hansley asked, "What worries you most about the experiences of the last few days?"

"I worry my family might break up," Tom said as he placed his elbows on the table. He covered his face with his hands.

"Why do you think it would break up?"

He pressed his hand against his throat as he tried to answer her question. Finally, he said, "Dr. Hansley, my family is everything to me. Mattie blames me for putting us in this situation. I can't even comprehend how famous Jillian is now. The media will never leave us alone. We are under siege."

"Tom, your family is going through a difficult time, but I seldom see such a loving family unit. Your love will keep you together."

Tom reflected on Dr. Hansley's advice, and then added, "I'm about to lose the farm too."

"Yes, you may well lose the farm; you need to learn to accept this. Explain to your family why it might be best to leave. Physical things aren't as important as your family's well-being."

Tom stared down at the tabletop.

After a moment of silence, Hansley asked, "How are your panic attacks?"

"The pills help, but the panic attacks are getting worse."

"We'll continue with the same medical treatment for your panic attacks. I'll also get another doctor to prescribe meds for your acid-reflux."

"Okay. My acid reflux is also getting worse," Tom replied, dejected, as he looked into the doctor's eyes. "On the farm, I'm the quarterback. On the football field, the quarterback is the center of control. But now I'm in control of nothing."

"I understand, Tom. Beside our medical treatments, would you be willing to meet with a psychiatrist alone, and maybe at times with Mattie, too?"

"Yes, that would be good. Thank you, Doctor."

"Now go hug your loved ones."

As they walked down the hallway to where his family was waiting, the doctor said, "Tom, it's acceptable to lose control sometimes. You can't always influence external forces. Our soldiers know that reality firsthand. War is chaos; no one has complete control. You plan, and you do the best you can."

Tom gave Mattie a hug while Dr. Hansley gestured to Ethan to follow her to be examined next. The doctor found Ethan to have a healthy young mind. He had retreated into the world of immersive reality as a ruthless warrior in a medieval war. His worries were about his mother's and sister's health and not seeing his friends, but he exhibited no major psychological or medical problems.

Ethan was mystified by the orb's appearance and the fact it didn't fit the human-based frameworks of science. Hansley told him, he was not alone. Many older and great scientists of the day were befuddled by the orb's presence and behavior. This thought seemed to placate the young scientist as he left the exam room.

When it was Jillian's turn, Dr. Hansley reached out for her and they held hands as they strolled to the exam room. Once they were inside, Hansley asked, "Jillian, how are you handling the media attention?"

"Okay," she said with a shrug of her shoulders.

"So, the experiences of the last few days do not bother you?" she asked, a perplexed look on her face.

"No. Once I get to the orb's location, I remember little. But I have some weird feelings I can't explain."

"What type of feelings?"

"Uh, I don't feel like I'm in my body. I'm outside of it."

"What else?"

"When I watch the video replays of the orb and me, it's hard for me to believe I did those things. It's scary."

"Yeah, I understand. No one knows how this stuff happens."

Jillian picked up a glass of water on the table and took a drink. Hansley also took a drink of water. Hansley paused to collect her thoughts and said, "Do you feel isolated?"

"Sure. I miss my friends. And the news reporters scare me."

Dr. Hansley said, "Jillian, you can always make new friends. Does this idea frighten you?"

"Yes, I was happy in Bourbon County."

"Do you realize, you may have to move?"

"I don't want to move."

"I know, but try to prepare yourself." The doctor dictated a few notes on her e-device. After the pause, she asked, "And how do you feel in general?"

"I'm tired all the time. I have headaches," Jillian answered.

"We can help with that. I'm going to give you medications that boost your energy and reduce your headaches."

"How is your mental health?"

"Okay, I guess. I don't remember anything from my orb encounter."

"Is there anything else that worries you, Jillian?"

"I worry about my mom and dad."

"Yes, we're all worried about them. We're going to help them."

"Good."

Jillian and Dr. Hansley left the exam room and rejoined the family. Mattie hugged her daughter. Soon after, another doctor, Dr. Florio Del Valle, a colonel in the US Army, walked up to them.

"We'll write a summary medical report on each of you," Del Valle said. "If you are available later today, I would be happy to come to your home to explain our diagnoses and go over the written reports."

"We'll be home," Tom said, hesitating slightly. "Call us. We can't go anywhere, you know?"

* * *

Brigadier General Tucson continued to monitor the outer restricted area from the command tent, watching videos of the ever-increasing crowd. The outer wire fence was in place now. Concrete barriers were arriving daily. In another part of the tent, Colonel Preston was talking with troops.

At the 1300 status-report meeting, Tucson asked, "What is the situation at the outer restricted area?"

"Ma'am, we estimate the crowd at five thousand and growing. After the president's speech, people are pouring into the county," Kilbourne said. "Our medical personnel are trying to triage the civilians. We hand them over to local and state medical caregivers as soon as we can. We'll need more state police to break up fights. We'll also need more ambulances and medical clinics for the bigger crowd."

"All right, let's get more federal help. Local and state resources are at their limits. Kilbourne, get on the phone with General Carr, and tell him our recommendations."

"Yes, ma'am."

* * *

Later that day, Dr. Del Valle entered the Hickory home carrying paper copies of the medical reports and an e-device, ready to summarize and explain the doctor's findings.

"Would you like homemade iced tea, hot tea, or coffee?" Mattie asked.

"Yes, iced tea would be wonderful."

Mattie went to the refrigerator and poured him a glass. They all sat down in the living room.

"Thank you for looking after my family's health," Tom said, commanding the wall screen to be silent.

"We have completed our analyses of your medical and mental health. We find your family to be in good general health. We found a few problems and one surprise." He turned toward Mattie and asked, "Do you want me to debrief everyone, or should you excuse the children?"

"I'm fine with Jillian and Ethan listening," Mattie said.

Tom looked at her and said, "If the doctor thinks it wise, we should hear the reports first."

"Let's have the parents hear our diagnoses and prognoses first," Dr. Del Valle said. "Then, we can chat with Jillian and Ethan."

Mattie agreed and asked the children to go to their rooms. Jillian complied and began to make her way up the steps with ease. Ethan labored his way upstairs, wanting to hear if his sister was cured of cerebral palsy.

"What's our situation?" Mattie asked the doctor.

"Mattie, let's take you first. Your health is good, but you are borderline anemic. The ordeal of the last few days may have caused your red blood cell count to go down. The cause is stress. Your heartbeat is elevated, and you may have noticed that your skin is pale. You also complained of headaches, shortness of breath, and little sleep, and we observed the nervous habit of biting your fingernails. You also show strong signs of anger and depression. We recommend the following medications, an exercise program, and seeing a psychiatrist."

The doctor showed Mattie a list on his e-device. "I'll send these prescriptions to you, your family doctor, and our pharmacy. Also, we would like you—and Tom—to meet twice a week with our psychiatrist. And, we recommend both of you exercise more—say, walk five kilometers daily. Questions?"

"No, Doctor. I know I've got to calm down and accept our fate."

The doctor then turned toward Tom. "Tom, you're in good health for a forty-six-year-old man. You do exhibit symptoms of gastroesophageal reflux and frequent panic attacks. We want to do an esophagogastroduodenoscopy on you."

Tom cocked his head. "What the hell is that?"

"We put a tube down your throat and examine your esophagus. It's called an endoscopy for short. And we recommend these drugs for you." He passed the e-device to him to show him the list. "We recommend continuing the panic-attack medicines. You should also walk with Mattie daily. And, when you and Mattie meet with the psychiatrist, we will work on your feelings of isolation and anger."

"Okay," Tom said. "What about the kids?"

"Ethan is the healthiest in the family. We found no significant physical or mental issues in our examinations. But he is escaping reality by doing immersive reality games too many hours a week."

Both parents grinned at this and knew he needed to reduce his time in digital fantasy worlds.

"What about Jilly?"

"We find no significant medical or mental issues with Jillian. She has no recollection of her encounters with the orb, which leads us to believe that the orb might be protecting her. The surprise is we found no medical signs of cerebral palsy. We think she is cured of the disease."

"It's a miracle," Mattie said, with tears meandering down her face.

"Are you sure?" Tom asked.

"Yes, ninety-nine percent sure. We had three of our doctors examine Jillian. Each reached the same conclusion. Her joints, reflexes, and gait all seem to be normal. Her posture is normal, and we observed no twitching in her face. One doctor who is religious thinks her cure is a divine intervention by God. The other two doctors see the cure as simply unexplainable. We see no reason to continue her cerebral palsy medications or physical therapy."

"Doctor, please do not tell anyone. We can't have the media find this out. It would support media hysteria and rumors that Jilly and the orb can heal people."

"Our medical analyses are confidential. We will not share them with anyone unless you authorize it." The doctor paused to take a sip of his drink, and then continued. "If our prognoses are acceptable to you, I'll have our staff assemble all the medications. We'll deliver them to your home tomorrow, and we've scheduled a joint appointment with you two and Dr. Hansley for Monday. Please ask General Tucson, Colonel Preston or Captain Kilbourne, and they will assign soldiers to escort you on your walks and jogs."

"Thank you for your help," Mattie said as they stood up and walked toward the front door. Tom shook hands with the doctor and closed the door behind him.

* * *

After Dr. Del Valle left, Mattie and Tom stood behind the closed door. Tom said, "Wow! Jilly is cured!"

"Yes, the kids are doing much better than we are."

"Yes, as long as the kids are good, we can cope with our problems with some medical help. Mattie, thank you for pushing us to get medical help," Tom said, pulling her into an embrace.

Mattie went upstairs to speak to the kids and take a nap. Tom sat down in his living room chair to reflect on the news. It had been another stressful day, but he felt his family would not have to cope with the orb alone. The US Army was helping them.

* * *

The family rested until the evening, when Mattie awoke to cook dinner. Soon, the rest of the family joined her downstairs. After dinner, Tom and Ethan sat in the living room, Tom watching weather reports and studying farm productivity reports, and Ethan watching a young scientist's tutorial on astronomy. They avoided all news channels now. Mattie and Jillian had gone upstairs to their bedrooms.

"Dad, Titan is yelping. Can you hear him?" Ethan said.

"Yes, but Sergeant Stoner will feed him."

They continued to watch television, and then Ethan said, "Dad, did you hear that?"

"No, I'm trying to decide whether to sell our strawberries to buyer A or B."

Ethan looked down the hallway toward the back door and laundry room. Before Tom or Ethan could respond, they could see a tall, gangly and shadowed man standing in their hallway, carrying something. He was dressed in military fatigues with muddy black shoes. A US Army ID dangled from his neck.

Tom jumped up from his chair and pulled out his stun gun from the end table.

"What do you want?"

"Mr. Hickory, don't shoot!" the man shouted as he renewed his grip on the child. His lips trembled. "Don't shoot! Don't shoot!"

"How did you get in here?" Tom asked. With Ethan standing behind him, he pointed the stun gun toward the man, with a slight shaking of his hand.

"We sneaked in to see Jillian, Mr. Hickory."

"What?"

"Sir, my son has a form of Down's syndrome called mosaicism. Your daughter can help him." He held the young infant out for Tom to see.

Mattie and Jillian heard the commotion and came down the stairs. At the sight of the man, Jillian screamed and jumped into her mother's arms. They stepped behind Tom holding the stun gun. How did this man get through security? Tom thought.

"Mr. Hickory, can I sit down on the floor and lay my child down? I've carried him many kilometers."

"Yes, but I need to see your hands. Move slowly or I'll shoot."

"Please don't shoot, Mr. Hickory. You might hit my son."

The man bent down and sat on the floor. He laid his son in front of him, who wailed when the infant touched the hardwood floor. The man then raised his hands in the air.

"Sir, I am no threat to your family. I am a family man too. My son is fourteen months old and needs your help."

Jillian hugged her mother's leg. Tom stood in front of his family.

"Do you have a gun?" he asked.

"No, sir. I have no weapons, only hope." After a moment of confused silence, the peculiar man continued. "Mr. Hickory, you can search me."

"How?"

The child on the floor continued to wail.

"Sir, I will stand up, turn around, and put my hands on top of my head, and you can search me."

"Do it."

A nervous Tom searched the man and found no weapons, though he did find a small communicator in his pocket. Tom stepped back and said, "Pick your son up. Can you stop the crying?"

"I'll try."

The man picked up his son and cuddled him. Soon, the child's unrelenting cries turned into whimpers.

"Sit back down on the floor. What's your password for the mobile communicator?"

"Hand it to me; I'll open it."

Tom handed the man the communicator, and he turned the device's camera toward his face to open it. Then, he handed the device back to Tom.

"So, your name is Steve Ebelson. You live at 1354 Worthington Trail, Lexington, Kentucky." Tom continued to scan the man's e-driver's license, hoping to find more information.

"Yes, sir," Ebelson said.

"What's your son's name?"

"Liam, Mr. Hickory."

"Tom, we should call Sergeant Stoner and Corporal Claiborne," Mattie said.

"Mrs. Hickory, if you would hear me out, you can call whoever you want. They can arrest me. I just need to help my son."

"What do you want?" Tom asked.

"Sir, your daughter can cure him."

"What?"

"I saw Jillian on television. She has been touched by God's hand."

The room fell silent. The Hickory family stood motionless.

"If you will let Jillian touch my son, that is all I ask. After that, you can have me arrested."

Tom was still pointing the stun gun toward the man. He looked at Mattie and said, "What do you think?"

"Oh my God!" Mattie raised her hands in the air, and then covered her reddened face. "Jillian can heal the whole world!"

Mattie's private fear that billions of people would want to touch the orb and Jillian had become a reality. Tom and Ethan were unaware of her innermost fear, and were not quite as perceptive as Mattie.

The family had backed up to the closed front door, looking for an escape route. Their heart rates accelerated, which made their communicators ring: their smart clothing had notified their virtual doctors.

After taking a moment to calm down, Tom asked Mattie, "Is it okay for Jilly to touch this man's child?"

"I suppose so, if Ebelson backs away," Mattie replied.

"Daddy, I should go to them. Lay the child on the floor," Jillian added.

With that, Tom led his daughter over to the child while Mr. Ebelson laid the infant on the floor. Tom held Jillian's hand, and continued to point the stun gun toward Ebelson. The man's smile widened and he backed away from his squawking son.

Jillian said nothing, but her graceful movements and kind expression calmed everyone down. The eight-year-old Jillian laid her hand on the infant's flattened forehead.

As her hand stayed in place on the baby, the young boy stopped whimpering. No one spoke. Then, the inside of Jillian's hand began to glow, and a shaft of blue light radiated from her palm. They could see every vein, artery, and bone in her hand. The child's forehead also glowed a faint blue. Finally, the crystal-blue light diminished, and Jillian pulled her hand back. She and Tom walked backward to join Mattie and Ethan.

"God bless you," Ebelson said and lowered his head in prayer.

They watched the infant's short neck extend before their eyes. His face and eyes reconfigured. The physical changes were subtle and slow, but unmistakable.

"Praise God! Do you see this?" Ebelson yelled out. "Praise God!"

"No, we can't see him," Tom said. "What's happening?"

The family moved toward Ebelson, and saw Liam's tongue recede from his distorted mouth. In a similar manner, the child's mouth reconfigured to a more normal appearance.

"Oh! Dear God!" Mattie yelled. "I see! I see!"

Tom lowered his gun to his side, and hugged his kids. Mattie held on to them as well in a family embrace. They were speechless.

Jillian smiled with the serenity and confidence of a true savior. Something or someone had taken over her being during that incredible moment. The family knelt down, and joined the man in prayer. They had seen a miracle. Its power and grace awed them.

"Mrs. Hickory, your daughter is a saint. She has cured Liam," Ebelson said as he stood up, holding his son. Then, with tears pouring down his bony face, he said, "I am so thankful. Thank you! God bless you! God bless you! You can arrest me now."

***

For an instant, Tom debated with himself whether to call Stoner and Claiborne. He quickly decided the security of his family was top priority, and Ebelson may be one of many who try to see Jillian. So, he used the US Army communicator to call Sergeant Stoner. In less than one minute, Stoner and Claiborne were knocking at the Hickorys' front door.

"How the hell did you get in here?" Sergeant Claiborne said as they saw the man standing there. He seized the man's arm while Stoner grabbed the child from his grasp.

Ebelson did not answer or resist. Tears continued to drip down his face as Corporal Claiborne handcuffed him.

"Are you folks hurt?" Stoner asked the Hickory family, holding the man's infant son.

"No," Tom said.

"Mr. Hickory, I apologize. We thought no one could get through our restricted areas," Stoner said, his ears turning red. "We'll take them down to the command tent and provide you with a full report." He wondered how the breach could have happened. They must have spent too much time feeding and playing with Titan.

Now they had to face their commanders.

"Tell the officers to call me. I'll tell them what happened," Tom said while handing Ebelson's communicator to Claiborne. "He came in from the back of the house."

"Yes, sir."

"And tell the officers Mr. Ebelson was not armed. He did not threaten us."

"Yes, sir. I will tell them."

Stoner and Claiborne escorted the handcuffed Ebelson out of the Hickory home. Stoner carried Liam.

When they entered the command tent, Captain Kilbourne greeted them.

"Sir, this man broke into the Hickory home."

"Say that again, Soldier," Kilbourne replied in a loud voice.

"Sir, somehow, this man got into the Hickory home. He evaded the outer restricted area."

"How in the hell did he do that? You're guarding the house."

"Yes, sir. But this man entered from the back. He got through our security."

Kilbourne turned toward the man and said, "Sit down. I want to hear your story. Is the Hickory family okay?"

"Yes, sir. They were not harmed. This man had no weapons and did not threaten them."

"Why did this man break into their house?" Kilbourne asked.

"Sir, he wanted Jillian to heal his son," Claiborne replied.

"Did she?"

"Yes, sir. It seems she did."

"Oh hell! She actually healed the infant?"

"Yes, sir," Stoner replied.

"Officer, I will tell you how I got past your security," Ebelson said.

The armed soldiers placed him in a chair and stood behind it.

"Take those cuffs off him," Kilbourne said. "He's no threat."

Claiborne took the cuffs off as Kilbourne stood facing Ebelson sitting in the chair.

"Hand the child to its father," Kilbourne ordered Stoner. "Can we get you or your son a drink or food?"

"Yeah, water would be great for both of us." After Kilbourne handed him a canteen of water, they sat down. Ebelson helped his son to drink from the canteen by pouring drops of water over the infants' mouth.

Meanwhile, Kilbourne filed through the contents of Ebelson's communicator, which also served as his e-wallet.

During the next five minutes, Steve Ebelson explained how he had gotten past the outer security area. He worked as a cameraman for a Lexington television station, so he had access to modern, high-end television cameras.

He explained to Kilbourne that he had bought US Army clothing at a local military-surplus store and forged an army telecommunications ID. He'd taken a camera from his television station and held his young son with one arm. He'd told the guards at the main gate he worked for a military television crew, and was tasked with filming the crowd. He'd explained to the troops he had found the sick child and wanted to take him to the mobile military hospital.

The US Army guards had believed him and let him enter. Ebelson then found his way to the Hickory home. He had entered the home through the unlocked back door.

"Captain Kilbourne, the orb cured my son. It's a miracle. Do you understand? Jillian cured my son!"

"Yeah, I understand," a dismayed and angry Kilbourne said.

Ebelson cuddled his whimpering son, tears rolling down his dirty and sweaty face.

Kilbourne closed his eyes for a moment and rubbed his forehead. "Mr. Ebelson, I'm not going to arrest you. But I don't want you or your son to leave the restricted area. We'll set you up in a separate tent. You can eat with the troops in the mess hall. If you need anything, including medical attention, we will get it for you. Your son should see our doctors. And you can call your family to tell them where you are. But do not—I repeat, do not—tell anyone about Jillian healing your son. Two of my soldiers will take you to the doctor first. They will also get you set up, issue you ID cards, and put an ankle security alarm on you. Two soldiers will guard you at all times. And, by the way, take a shower. You smell."

"Yes, sir," a grateful Ebelson said.

Ebelson left the command tent, escorted by two soldiers. Kilbourne's posture stiffened as he turned toward Stoner and Claiborne and shouted,

"Get your asses up to the Hickory home! From now on, one of you should be stationed in front of their house, and one should be behind. Sleep on the ground with the rats! Is that understood? I mean, twenty-four hours a day. And stop feeding that damn goat."

"Yes, sir."

Later that night, Stoner and Claiborne left the greenhouse carrying their gear. They set up two small tents, in front and behind the Hickory home.

"We have six rat traps. You take three and I'll take three," Corporal Claiborne said.

"That's not enough, but that's our penalty for screwing up. Now we sleep with rats," Staff Sergeant Stoner replied.

"Those bastard rats left the flooded coasts and came here for the strawberries."

"Yeah, I know. The bots can't smell them; only Titan," Stoner said. "You take the back of the house and I'll take the front."

CHAPTER 6
Chaos

After four hours of intermittent sleep, Captain Kilbourne left his tent Sunday morning and headed toward the command tent. Sleepless nights were a part of military deployments. He had watched the president's speech Friday and now the world knew about the disquieting orb. And, the US Army, his army, guarded it.

Guarding the Hickory family was another story. Kilbourne's commanding officers, Tucson and Preston, were furious about the security breach with Mr. Ebelson and his infant son. They added more troops to the outer security fence and several intelligence officers at the main and construction gates.

As he walked toward the command tent, his communicator buzzed. "Captain Kilbourne, we have two people at two o'clock trying to climb our security fence."

"I'll be right there."

Kilbourne hopped into his Jeep and drove to the site. The nineteen-kilometer circle of the outer restricted area was like a clock, and only the troops knew the location of the benchmark 00. Upon arrival at where 0200 fell, he could see two people on the other side of the chain-link fence arguing with the troops.

"What's the situation, soldier?" he asked.

"Sir, two demonstrators tried to climb the fence. We stopped them. They say it's their right to see the Savior."

Kilbourne's body stiffened. He turned toward the demonstrators, looking through the chain-link fence that separated order from chaos.

"Gentlemen, if you breach our perimeter, we'll arrest you. We'll put you in our makeshift jail, and then transfer you to a military jail in Fort Campbell, Kentucky. Those are our orders."

"But you have no legal right to do this, you asshole," one tall demonstrator yelled. "The Savior is here for all people, not a select few."

The man was wearing a T-shirt that said, "Doomsday, October 18, 2147." Kilbourne noticed that his eyes were gray with a hollow death-like glaze. Dirty brown eyelashes and a mustache framed the man's weather-beaten face.

"Gentlemen, take that up with the president of the United States. The US Army has a job to do, and we'll do it." He then turned toward his troops and said, "Corporal, well done. And remember, your orders are to use minimal force to stop any breaches of the restricted area. If someone shoots at you, you can fire back. But no lethal shots to kill. Understood?"

"Yes, sir."

As he walked back to his Jeep, something hit him on the chin. *Slap.* He looked down at the ground to see a small, sharp-edged bolt, which had been thrown through the fence. He stopped and held his fingers to his chin. It hurt. Blood poured onto his hand, dripping onto the trampled bluegrass.

A nearby soldier scrambled up to him and examined the wound.

"Sir, you have a three-centimeter gash. You need to see a doctor." Then, the soldier ran off to his own Jeep to get him a towel.

When he returned, Kilbourne held the small towel over the wound. He turned toward the unremarkable demonstrators, and holding his bloody chin with one hand, screamed, "Who did this?"

"I did, you bastard." The man wearing the doomsday T-shirt stepped forward to the cheers of his colleagues. The man, who had tattoos around his neck, waltzed up to the fence with his chest out and his scarred chin high. "You can't stop me."

Kilbourne turned on his body camera and walked over so that their faces were within a meter of one another, divided by the chain-link fence. He could smell the demonstrator's rancid body odor even over the smell of his own blood, which now covered his hand and the drenched towel. This deluge of blood coming from his chin embarrassed him greatly. He hated showing any sign of weakness.

"You are under arrest for harming an officer in the US Army!" he bellowed.

"You can't arrest me, you idiot," replied the demonstrator with a laugh. The wind blew his dyed blond hair to reveal about eight centimeters of dark brown roots.

"You lowlife, my body camera is on. We'll identify you and have the police bring you to our military jail. We'll see who has the last laugh."

Kilbourne stared at the man for a few seconds before walking back to his Jeep. He drove to the battalion medic to have his chin treated. His head ached, and the bare wound was throbbing.

Three shallow stitches later, he went back to his tent and tried to rest. He thought a short nap might stop his throbbing headache. He lay down on top of his sleeping bag, thinking about what he might do to the demonstrator. Later today, he would have a specialist run the man's picture on their facial recognition systems. Cameras were everywhere. The world collected over a septillion terabytes of video data per day. Once identified, he would file assault charges against the man.

Before he tried to take a nap, he laid his sparkling pistol beside him. He was glad he hadn't used it on the demonstrator.

* * *

After directing the last truck for Sunday delivery, Sergeant Rajeev Biswas, one of the enlisted men, had finished his job by 1500. They had inspected each truck for intruders at the construction entrance to the restricted areas. The truck shipments included tear gas, food, water, masks, rubber bullets and guns, medicines, and one thousand six hundred-kilogram concrete barriers.

Perspiring from the effort, he made his way outside the restricted area, ordering four of his men to come with him. The site of the orb had become a happening unto itself. People from around the world had come to see the spectacle. Some arrived in expensive motor homes and trailers.

Fifty media trucks and thousands of people surrounded the outer restricted area. Vans, school buses, and recreational vehicles converged on the site of the orb, and a hobbit encampment had been erected, with tents serving as homes and stores. Poets, ministers, scientists, and society's dropouts descended upon the site, the tall bluegrass giving way to its new masters.

The crowd had brought their belongings, including their pet dogs, goats, and even pigs. Quilts, plastic sheets, plywood, and blankets served as floors. Some arrivals had made makeshift plywood and cardboard huts and teepees, with not-so-sanitary homemade latrines and communal kitchens. Smelly trash piles dotted the landscape and were growing bigger by the hour. Merchants had even set themselves up, selling water, groceries, and souvenirs to the growing assembly of people.

Biswas and his armed soldiers walked down the row of tents, cardboard houses, and teepees. When the troops walked by, the demonstrators who were eating, drinking and standing around talking to their neighbors, stared at them.

As an American citizen and a native of India, Biswas had an inquisitive mind. When time permitted, he read religious books, trying to find answers to humanity's fate. It was this curiosity that led to his desire to watch the demonstrators. The ragtag group had paused their everyday lives to get a chance to be close to the orb. Many true believers, whatever their causes, had left their jobs—if they had one, that is.

Biswas walked through the corridor of unshaven, untidy, and foul-smelling people. The thought occurred to him that humanity might not be worth saving.

At one tent, he stopped and looked at a selection of T-shirts that a vendor had for sale. They boasted slogans, such as "Behold the Prophecies of Nostradamus," "Satan Is Coming," and "Behold the Apocalypse."

"You should be on the other side of the fence, Soldier," the scruffy merchant said as he flipped his braided hair out of his face.

"Yes, I should, but I wanted to see the demonstrators," he replied with a broad smile.

"Are you a religious man?" the merchant asked.

"Yes, I am Hindu. I think the orb may well be God's messenger."

The man reflected upon his answer and said, "So you believe global warming destroys Earth?"

"Yeah, it could."

"Don't worry, my friend. In the end, only robots will survive."

As he spoke, a brilliant red Kentucky cardinal landed nearby, and began to hop about on the merchant's T-shirts. The man shooed it away and said, "We humans may end up like this bird. Did you know birds are descendants of dinosaurs?"

"Yes, I knew that." Biswas picked up a T-shirt with a picture of the orb and the words "The End of Days Begins" imprinted above the picture.

"We all have a purpose in being here," the man said as he continued to fold and stack T-shirts.

"What's your purpose?" he asked.

"I'm a member of the Mayan Temple of Tikal. We believe the orb's arrival is the beginning of the apocalypse." The merchant gave a satisfied smile. "I sell T-shirts to support my lifestyle."

"Really?" Biswas said with a grin. "What destroys Earth?"

"It doesn't matter. I hope it's not an asteroid hitting Earth."

"Why?"

"I've got too many T-shirts to sell."

Both men laughed. Biswas bought a T-shirt that depicted a bright blue light emitting from a picture of the orb. One of his soldiers bought a T-shirt simply stating, "The Orb" and "October 18, 2147" on the front and "Roswell" and "July 8, 1947" on the back.

"Sir, too many people are following us," another said.

About thirty people surrounded them. Biswas turned to the crowd and said, "We're here to buy T-shirts. Nothing more."

He realized that they needed to return to the restricted area, fast.

"Yeah, but you won't let us see the orb," one disgruntled onlooker replied.

"Yes, that's true. But we'll never find out what the orb wants unless we protect it. We're not here to hassle you; in fact, we are providing you with medical and sanitary services," he said.

The onlookers didn't respond to this and stepped aside. They knew Biswas's words were true: whenever any of them were sick or had accidents, the troops helped them.

Biswas and his four soldiers walked back to the entrance. On the way, they passed tents that showed off stuffed orbs and alien creatures for sale. Other cult groups were passing out pamphlets, encouraging people to join their groups as paths to salvation. Biswas paused for a minute to listen to one of their announcements. The group was soliciting deposits for a seat on humanity's modern equivalent of Noah's ark—a spaceship leaving Earth for bases on the moon.

But the merchants had no authority to sell space at the United Nations planetary bases, unbeknown to their customers. The international colony of 310 people on Earth's moon lived in natural lava tubes that shielded people from intense radiation and meteorites. Earth–moon shuttles rotated people off the international moon base. The weightless environment required rotating people on their tours of duty.

"Sir, we could buy this stuff and sell it to our troops," one soldier said.

"Yes, but we would be in trouble. And say nothing about our visit outside the restricted area."

"Yes, sir."

* * *

Later that day, Tucson, Preston, and Kilbourne sat down in the air-conditioned command tent where an intelligence soldier debriefed them on security issues during the last few hours.

"General Tucson, you need to see screen eight," the soldier said.

On the video, they watched a dozen members of a cult group shake the rickety wire fence. Preston frowned, and Kilbourne shook his head, but Tucson remained stone-faced.

"General, the fence is about to fall. The protestors will rush in," the soldier said.

"Get more troops over there. Use tear gas to drive them back," a staunch Tucson said. "And get more fence and erect a second set of posts."

"Yes, ma'am."

"Let's see if we can calm these people down," Preston said.

"We'll go in my Jeep," Tucson said. "Kilbourne, you stay here."

As they stepped into the Jeep, Tucson's red hair continued to stick out of the back of her helmet, as if she was in a hurry while Preston adjusted his gun belt. They wanted to be on the front lines, not sitting in a command tent far from the action.

They went to location fourteen and saw the crowd pushing on one side of the fence. More people were converging around it. They wanted to see the orb. The troops were pushing back on the other side, trying to keep the fence upright. One truck was working its way forward through the frenzied crowd, running over a demonstrator's foot in the process, ready to position itself to push the fence over.

Tucson pulled out her pistol and shot two times in the air, before running toward the troops to try to stop the breach. Preston decided not to draw his revolver and ordered the troops to stand down.

"You people get back from the fence!" Tucson yelled, causing some of the demonstrators to pause. "If you don't stop, we'll use tear gas. If you cause real trouble, we'll shoot you in the legs if you enter the restricted area."

The indignant group stepped back from the fence.

"Who are you people?" she yelled.

A tall man with muscular arms and long white hair stepped forward and said, "We are the Order of Gaia." He held up an ornament hanging from his neck, a depiction of the god, and said, "The orb is Gaia, the mother of all life. She will save us."

"What do you mean?"

"The orb signals the end of the earth. Our prophecy is being fulfilled." He continued to hold the ornament with one hand and raised the other hand high into the sky.

"Glory to Gaia," his followers yelled.

The protestors' chants didn't amuse Tucson. "This is not Armageddon, people!" she shouted. "We are here to protect the orb, not to fight you."

The cult group kept chanting. "Glory to Gaia."

Amid the chaos, a massive military truck carrying fencing, barbed wire, and steel posts arrived. A second truck followed, which delivered more troops, gas canisters, guns, and masks. About fifty troops unloaded the items and began to reinforce the fence, arming themselves with tear-gas guns.

"Do you see the tear gas?" Tucson shouted through a bullhorn, still holding her smoldering revolver. "We'll use it. Stop pushing on the fence!"

Soldiers with gas masks and tear-gas guns began to approach, and the demonstrators backed away, giving up in their attempt to breach the fence, suddenly realizing the general's threats were real.

"Don't mess with Tucson; she's tough. I served with her in Brazil," one of the troops said.

Tucson and Preston got back in their Jeep and drove to the central command tent. Preston asked a soldier to research the Order of Gaia. Later that day, the soldier approached Tucson and Preston and said,

"Sir, the information on the cult group is ready."

"Good. What is this group about?"

They sat down to listen to the soldier's report.

"The Order of Gaia is a heretic group founded in San Diego in 2088," the soldier began. "The cult has eight major groups located around the world in cities like Beijing, Mumbai, New York, and Istanbul. Gaia is the Greek goddess of the earth. They believe that a death star called Nemesis will collide with Earth in this century. The rationale for this prophecy is that an undetectable brown dwarf star circles our sun every twenty-seven million years. When it enters our inner solar system, its gravity pulls asteroids out of orbit. Some debris hits the earth. It also makes Earth wobble more on its axis and changes our climate. And if the dwarf star itself hits Earth, all life is over."

"What about the big white-haired fellow? Who is he?" Tucson asked.

"Ma'am, he is the leader of the North American sector of the cult. His name is Cadmus Abhay, but his legal name is Devon Baldwin. He attended a trade school to become an electrician but dropped out and has since worked for a small electrical contractor outside San Diego. His criminal record includes drug-related charges and resisting arrest."

"Any other information on this man?" Preston asked, standing up from his chair, surveying the busy command center.

"Sir, he writes a blog on UNet wherein he proclaims to be the incarnation of this Greek god."

"Oh great! So now we have a deity outside our gates," Preston said.

Tucson and the troops grinned.

Preston turned toward Tucson to say something more, but was interrupted by their communicators ringing.

"Sir, we have other problems outside the restricted area," a soldier said. "The crowd made makeshift latrines, but they don't work. The smell is pungent and with the high temperatures today, things are getting worse. People are getting sick, asking for water, and some are even being hit by vehicles. They're asking our troops for medical treatment, but there's only so much we can do. And, sir, today, forty-nine of our soldiers became dehydrated and required medical help."

"Hawk, you handle this," Tucson said. "I'm going back to my tent."

Tucson walked to her tent, closed the opening, laid down on the cot, and covered her eyes with her combat hat. Her thoughts focused on how to keep things under control. She was the commanding officer on-site. It was her responsibility. In the course of these thoughts, she fell asleep with all her clothes on, including her pistol belt.

Back at the command tent, Preston turned to Kilbourne and said, "Captain, call the Red Cross and the Kentucky Emergency Administration. Ask them for help. And, call Fort Campbell to tell them we need more hospital tents, equipment, and medical staff. Tell them we need an extra truckload of fresh water bottles every day. And rent a hundred more portable restrooms from a local supplier. We also need more state police officers to patrol the crowd."

"Yes, sir."

While Kilbourne was making the calls, a sergeant walked up to him and saluted. "Sir, the demonstrator who hit you with the bolt is in our military jail. Do you want to see him?"

Kilbourne paused, and then said, "No, Sergeant. Find an excuse to keep him there for three days; then after he's done the time, release him. I won't press charges."

"Yes, sir."

In the next six hours, the Kentucky Emergency Administration (KEA) brought portable restrooms and twenty more state police officers. The Red Cross arrived with dozens of portable restrooms and set up two emergency service centers. Shortly after, a convoy of four military trucks arrived, which set up three white hospital tents. The horde of demonstrators did not block any of the convoys; they knew they needed the help.

"Colonel, KEA managers told me six demonstrators have died. Some deaths were related to the intense heat and poor sanitary conditions. And, sir, the size of the crowd is continuing to increase. It's estimated at fifteen-thousand people now," Captain Kilbourne said.

"Six deaths. Awful." Colonel Preston shook his head. "We're doing all we can. Have we lost soldiers?"

"No, sir. Our military housing is air-conditioned and our soldiers fit. Our medical services are much better than what's available to the demonstrators."

* * *

"How's it going over there?" Carr asked Tucson Sunday afternoon.

"Sir, the president's speech has triggered a huge response. We estimate fifteen-thousand people surround us now. We have cult groups, news reporters, tourists, religious groups—you name it. Our barriers and fences were not strong enough to hold them back, but we're halfway through reinforcing them. Our hospital is overwhelmed with military and civilian patients. We are adding more hospital capacity. And the Red Cross and Kentucky Emergency Administration are helping. It has been a very hectic few days."

"Yes, I've been watching the demonstrators on the news and military channels. It is disturbing. The president is aware of these things. What can we do to help you, General Tucson?"

"Sir, my concern is what to do if the number of demonstrators keeps growing."

"Yes, the joint chiefs have been discussing the crowd issue with White House staff. We need to close airports and stop all trains and vehicles into the area."

"Yes, I would agree. Can you assign someone to do this, Al?" Tucson said.

"Yes, we'll develop a regional shutdown plan, and I'll present it to the president. Steph, you are doing a superb job there. Keep it up. Call me if you need anything."

* * *

Within the hour, General Carr set up a meeting to develop a plan to shut down the region's transportation services. After a meeting in the Pentagon, a set of recommendations was ready to present to President Barlow.

"President Barlow," Carr said as he entered the Oval Office late Sunday afternoon, "thank you, sir, for seeing me on such short notice."

"Al, glad you're here. The television pictures coming out of there are alarming. My communicator is constantly ringing with heads of state asking me what's going on."

"Sir, the crowd surrounding our restricted area is fifteen-thousand people now," Carr said. "We have control of the restricted areas and are reinforcing the perimeter. Our troops are doing a magnificent job. But we need to shut down all incoming traffic to the area. Otherwise, we'll soon have more than a hundred thousand people there. I met a few hours ago with your secretary of transportation. We developed a plan to stop incoming traffic to the region, yet allow outgoing traffic."

"What do you recommend, General?" President Barlow asked.

"Sir, we recommend restricting all incoming air flights at eleven area airports. We also recommend only one or two emergency flights per city per day."

"What does Kentucky say about this?"

"Mr. President, none of us are happy with our options, but this is a matter of national security. It is a regional shutdown."

"What about vehicle traffic?"

"Sir, we will block all roads at the Bourbon County line. The county is seven hundred fifty-six kilometers square, and the population of this county is thirty-five thousand people. We'll issue all residents

ID tags, so they can enter and leave their home county," Carr said. "Mr. President, we considered stopping all vehicle sharing. But ninety-two percent of the vehicles within the region are booked. We could ask the firms to not deploy the cars, but we decided against it."

"Let them have all the vehicles they want as long as they stay out of Bourbon County. What about the trains?"

"Two freight trains pass through Bourbon County, Mr. President. We'll stop them at the county line and inspect them for hideaways. As for conventional passenger trains, they will be rerouted. The vactrain doesn't go through Bourbon County, so no problem there."

A vactrain was a magnetic, levitating high-speed train. It moved through a strong nanotechnology-designed tube. The tube was continuous and immune to outside traffic, weather, and animals. Parts of the national tube system were underground.

"Mr. President, these are the major components of our regional shutdown plan. Do you have questions?"

"No. Execute the plan as soon as possible. Jerry, please get the governor of Kentucky on the line for me."

Soon after the meeting, the president and governor discussed the situation and agreed to call up Army National Guard troops. The troops would help patrol the five Kentucky airports and check the trains.

President Barlow looked at the green leaves outside his window. Due to the heat, leaves didn't turn colorful until late December.

The White House windows used programmable-matter glass that could rearrange its molecular structure in different ways. The smart glass could stop high-power bullets, lasers, and electromagnetic pulses. The windows helped him feel safe.

As he stared outside, he rubbed at his chin, thinking about the orb's arrival. While the glass represented security and stability, the orb was a great uncertainty to an already frail human existence. It's arrival, he thought, could undermine or build human society. It was too early to tell which scenario would happen.

After a short deliberation, he realized he had to play the hand he'd been dealt. He felt good about establishing the restricted areas to safeguard the orb, and he had done his duty by informing the world of its presence. But he still worried about the ongoing media frenzy and confusion among the world leaders. Human governments and society stood on the edge of a precipice.

CHAPTER 7
Second Encounter

"Daddy, I need to see the orb."

It was 1919 on Sunday evening, four days after the orb's arrival. Tom put his fork down on his plate with a clink and stood up from the dinner table.

"Jillian, how do you know the orb wants to see you?" he asked.

"I get this strong feeling it needs me."

"We'll go after we finish eating and cleaning up the kitchen."

"No, Daddy. I must go now."

Tom looked at Mattie. She had also stopped eating and pushed her chair back from the kitchen table. A tear rolled down her face.

"We can't even eat dinner without an interruption," she said.

"I know," he said, "but dinner can wait. Let's go. I'll call Sergeant Stoner and Corporal Claiborne."

Mattie put her hands over her face. The orb and the military controlled their lives. Tom called the soldiers.

Within minutes, the soldiers were standing on the porch, waiting to escort the family to the command tent. Armed with flashlights, the family opened the front door to the darkness and uncertainty of the night.

"Jillian wants to meet the orb again," Tom said to the armed soldiers.

"Yes, sir," Sergeant Stoner said.

The six of them walked toward Dura Road. This time, there was a marked difference to how Stoner and Claiborne viewed the family. It now felt as if they were escorting royalty. Jillian and her family had become household names.

The media had figured out the identity of Jillian and her family from the videos, and news reports now ordained her as a saint. There had been forty-two billion replays of the orb videos so far. People from all cultures and backgrounds craved to hear from her. And, for some reason, most believed that if they could touch the orb or Jillian, good things would happen.

People became obsessed with every video clip, sound bite, and story on Jillian and her family. All of humanity knew their names. The media circus hounded Jillian's friends, classmates, and teachers. One news reporter disguised as an electrician had snuck into her school and photographed her classroom, desk, and belongings. Jillian's notebooks and pencils, and even her pink toothbrush, were missing. Somehow, her dental records also became public information. It was unclear whether they had copied her fingerprints and retina scans. The media even interviewed Jillian's school bus driver.

The government was now in charge. Control trumped freedom. Isolation trumped mobility. Tom had turned off all family communicators, only speaking through a US Army handheld and encrypted communicator when talking to troops and officers. He'd also asked the family, including himself, to not watch the news on the home wall screen. The family watched only comedy and educational shows.

"Mrs. Hickory, how come Jillian doesn't walk with a limp anymore?" Stoner asked.

"The doctors tell us, she is cured of the palsy."

Jillian turned her head toward the two soldiers in a normal manner as she walked with a determined, natural gait.

"The orb cured her," Ethan interjected, walking next to his mother. The two soldiers smiled but said nothing.

Colonel Preston was waiting for them when the family entered the command tent.

"We understand Jillian wants to see the orb again."

"Yes, she says it can't wait," Mattie replied, as she bit her fingernails while standing in front of Preston. At times, she was proud of her daughter being the voice of the orb but that thought quickly diminished into outrage for the orb's intrusion into their lives.

"Ugh, okay, let's go," Preston replied, reluctantly. Privately, he thought the orb could still be a devious plot to overthrow the US government by another earth-bound government or an alien species. He didn't want to go down in history as the fool who allowed the orb to dictate events and maybe even kill all of them.

Once they were at the site, the orb advanced toward them, its light becoming brighter. The Hickory family stood five meters away, with Lieutenant Colonel Preston, Captain Kilbourne, and the recently arrived Brigadier General Tucson beside them.

Mattie gripped her daughter's hand. The orb crept a couple meters closer to Jillian. She stepped forward and tugged at her mother's hand, asking her to release her grip, submitting again to the will of the orb.

Mattie watched her daughter move toward it. As with the first encounter, the crowd expected Jillian to reach out and touch it. Instead, the orb approached her, and without stopping or slowing down, it penetrated her body.

A thin blue halo outlined Jillian's body. The group of people around the orb marveled at the scene before them, and Jillian's green eyes penetrated the onlookers' gazes.

There were no ugly aliens or massive spaceship invaders, only a small, altruistic ball of energy that emitted a captivating blue light around a nonthreatening and innocent messenger.

"Jilly, are you all right?" Mattie called out as she lurched forward. Captain Kilbourne stopped her by grabbing her arms and pulling her backward. For a short time, she wriggled in his grasp, but she soon regained her composure.

Tom initially stepped backward in shock, but then also tried to move toward his daughter. Corporal Claiborne stood in front of him, blocking his attempt to help. He held out his arm across Tom's chest. "Mr. Hickory, we should stay here."

With an immaculate smile that helped negate her parents' fear, Jillian said, "Mom, I'm fine."

"Are you sure, Jilly?" Tom asked as he tightened his fists. Claiborne continued to block his way.

"Yes, Daddy."

Jillian and the orb were ineluctably bound. They defined a mutualistic partnership that wanted to help humanity survive.

* * *

Defying Preston's orders, one soldier stepped toward the orb and fired her gun at the orb. The laser shot bounced off the orb. But as she continued her march toward it, any metal objects that were attached to her— her gun, metal grapnels, a canteen and a knife—were stripped from her body and uniform. They flew through the air and formed a ball of metal held together by magnetic forces. She and her torn uniform lifted off the ground by about a meter. She kicked her feet, trying to free herself from the grip of unseen forces.

"Stand down! Do not fire your weapons!" Preston yelled, as his gun broke its hoister strap and flew away.

Standing five meters away, a metal pen in Tucson's pocket tore through her shirt and flew into the air. Her pistol was ripped from her hoister. Corporal Claiborne, standing next to Tom, noticed something pulling on his rifle and metal helmet. They vibrated for a second, and then flew away slamming into the growing ball of metal.

Metal objects were hurling through the air, and everyone, including the Hickory family, dropped to the ground to avoid being hit. Only Jillian continued to stand.

Colonel Preston, laying on the ground, yelled, "What the hell was that?"

"Sir, I think the orb disarmed us," Captain Kilbourne said.

"You got to be kidding me! This damn orb disarmed my soldiers! How the hell can that happen?" he screamed.

No one could answer Preston's query.

About thirty soldiers, including Tucson, Preston, and Kilbourne, were disarmed within the immediate vicinity of the orb. It shut down any potential for hostility, stopping anyone or anything that might try to interfere with its mission. The metal sphere had grown to over two meters in diameter. Several soldiers walked over to the mound of metal and tried to pull a gun from the pile. But they could not pull anything away.

Soldiers in the command tent, much farther away, had small metal items like paper clips, grapnels, and pens fly out the command center door to join the growing pile of metal. But the precise gravitational forces created by the orb were not strong enough to move large metal items like metal chairs and rifles in the distant command center tent. The two mobile laser guns guarding the tent did vibrate but didn't fly away.

Humanity had challenged the entity, and it had responded.

The crowd could sense the wonder and power of the orb. It was clear that it would protect itself and Jillian from any perceived threat. The soldier still hung suspended in the air; it only took a few seconds for her to drop, but it seemed like an hour. When the soldier, now unarmed, fell to the ground, two other soldiers ran to help her up and walked her back to her duty station. She was shaken, but unharmed.

Tucson hurried to confront the soldier who fired at the orb and asked, "Why did you disobey Colonel Preston's orders?"

"Ma'am, I don't care what you people think, this orb is a hoax, and I wanted to prove it to you."

"Well, you'll prove it in jail, soldier. Arrest her and take her to Fort Campbell."

Tucson rejoined Preston and Kilbourne as the shooter was escorted away from the area. Jillian had remained standing upright during the flurry of metal objects flying through the air. She turned toward the stunned crowd and said, *"The orb harms no one."*

General Tucson pulled Preston back a few steps and motioned the crowd to move away from Jillian and the orb. Everyone straightened up and dusted off their torn uniforms and clothes.

* * *

Jillian looked toward them and asked, *"Is the panel of experts here?"*

The second encounter had begun, and the orb and Jillian were directing it.

"Yes. Do you want to see them?" Tucson said.

"Yes."

Colonel Preston turned to Kilbourne and said, "Get the panel. They're working in the mess hall."

"Yes, sir."

A specially-formed committee of US cabinet members and top executives of the United Nations had chosen the twelve experts. These individuals had flown to Bourbon County as fast as they could, except for the three University of Kentucky professors who were already on site. The panel were experts in topics ranging from carbon sequestration to simulation models of Earth's hydrologic cycles, and even a Hindu priest.

The most notable expert was Dr. Madia Rabab, who had won the 2129 Nobel Prize in genetics. Her first PhD, in thermodynamics, was from the University of Moscow Technological Institute. Her second PhD, in life sciences, was from ETH Zurich, Switzerland. Dr. Rabab was a member of the faculty at Istanbul University's College of Science and Technology, Turkey.

They all arrived at the site not knowing what to expect. A couple of the experts simply stood in awe of the alluring ball of energy, while most took a scientific approach. Two experts were somewhat skeptical of the orb and the entire situation.

"Who is the spokesperson for the experts?" the orb said, through Jillian, with the thin blue hallo encompassing her body.

"I am," Breslin said, stepping forward.

"Professor Breslin, what language would you prefer?"

"What languages do you know?" Breslin asked.

"From your planet, 6,862 languages and dialects."

"Aha! I suppose English would be good," he replied, laughing at his naivety.

"Please listen."

A gentle breeze blew Jillian's blonde hair back from her face, and her green eyes surveyed the experts. She captivated the fragile crowd with her smile. Her two missing teeth reminders of her profound innocence—she was the perfect messenger. A few soldiers were tempted to kneel and pray but dared not defy Colonel Preston's orders.

In a tranquil voice, Jillian said, *"We are here to help humanity. Humanity must terraform Earth. Others have done so successfully, and you must too. To do this, you need to first understand the physics, chemistry, and thermodynamics of your planet, how biotic, hydrologic, geochemical, radiation, temperature, and physical Earth systems interact. I will send these formulas and a system of interrelated equations to one of your computers."*

"Get me a computer—any computer!" Dr. Breslin yelled.

Captain Kilbourne ran to the command tent and repeated the request. "I need a computer! Delete all files on it and get it to me."

"Sir, we have a new quantum device here," a technician said, pointing to a small box under a table.

"Open it up and get it operational."

Two soldiers tore the box open, and laid the pocket-size computer down on the table, so they could set it up. It did not take long, and a soldier was soon carrying it to Kilbourne, who placed it on the ground in front of Jillian.

Jillian glanced at the crowd with the thin blue hallo around her body, and then turned her attention to the computer by her feet as if to dissect it. She raised her palm toward the computer, and a brilliant beam of crystal-blue light emerged from her tiny hand and hit the computer.

After several moments, the beam of light vanished. Jillian lowered her arm and tilted her head to the side with a nonhuman jerk. She looked at Dr. Breslin and said, *"You now have the knowledge to terraform planet Earth. Your team of scientists must study this knowledge as soon as possible."*

Before anyone could blink, the orb emerged from the left side of Jillian's body. It returned to its original position a meter above the ground. For now, the symbiotic relationship had ended. The orb's light dimmed. It had fulfilled part of its purpose. The expert team now needed time to digest the knowledge.

Jillian collapsed into the bluegrass field. Her family ran over to her. Tom picked her up and with one knee on the ground, held her in his arms. Mattie and Ethan hovered over them.

The military officers and soldiers gave the family space. They watched to see if Jillian would survive the orb's intrusion into her body.

"Jilly!" Mattie said. "Can you hear me?"

Tom kissed Jillian's head several times and pushed her hair back from her face. Jillian's head turned, and her eyes opened.

"What happened, Daddy?"

"Ugh, you and the orb became one."

Still in her dad's embrace, Jillian tried to move her arms and legs and found that everything felt normal. Tom held his precious cargo, trying to protect her from worldwide scrutiny. Encrypted military cameras recorded the second encounter with the orb from every viewpoint.

"Jilly, how are you feeling?" Mattie asked with tears in her eyes.

"Mom, I'm not sure. Can I stand up?"

They helped her stand. Ethan held her hand. At first, Jillian wobbled a bit, but soon she stood upright.

"Would you like water, Jillian?" Kilbourne asked.

"Yes," she replied, reaching for the bottle. She took several greedy swallows. She swayed, so Ethan steadied her.

After the second encounter, the twelve experts argued about what they had seen. Neither scientific nor conventional logic explained the phenomenon. After reaching no conclusions late Sunday night, some of them retreated to the mess hall to discuss further, while others went to their temporary tents to think or sleep. They would meet Monday morning to discuss the orb and begin to review the information it had transmitted.

"Let's go to the command tent," Kilbourne said.

Inside the tent, the family sat down and the soldiers provided them with drinks. Everyone was silent. They were trying to regain their composure and reflect on what they had seen.

"Do you want anything to eat?" Preston asked them.

"No, we still have food sitting on our kitchen table," Mattie said in a strained tone of voice.

A doctor gave Jillian a thorough examination, and said, "Jillian's vital signs are normal. Her reflexes and body movements are normal. Please call me if any of you experience problems."

"Can you escort us back home?" Mattie asked the three officers.

"Yes, Mrs. Hickory. Stoner and Claiborne will be with you. If you need anything, please call us," Tucson said.

Once home, the Hickory family went upstairs to prepare for bed.

"Jilly, how do you feel?" Mattie said as she helped her put on pajamas.

"Tired but okay."

"Do you know what happened?" she asked, giving a gentle squeeze of her hand.

"I remember nothing."

"Were you aware it entered your body?"

"No, Mom, what do you mean?"

"We'll discuss it later, sweetie. Try to sleep. Good night."

Mattie walked to Ethan's bedroom and found him in bed. She sat down on the edge of the bed.

"Mom, the orb could be an angel," he said.

"Yes, it could be."

"Why did the orb pick us?"

"No idea. We are victims of something much greater than us, I'm afraid."

Ethan glanced at his mother, pulled his covers up over his shoulders, and Mattie left the room. Once she reached her bedroom's bathroom, she took two nerve pills.

"Are the kids okay?" Tom asked.

"Yes, I think so."

"Are you okay?"

"No, I'm a mess. I hope I sleep."

Tom didn't reply as they both crawled into bed. He could see no solution to their precarious situation. They rolled away from one another and tried to sleep. There was no loving embrace that night.

* * *

Jerry Bragg, Al Carr, and President Barlow watched the live video of the second encounter on Sunday night in the White House's Oval Office.

"How do we handle the information transmitted to the computer?" Barlow asked Bragg, the White House Chief of Staff.

"Sir, we recommend the expert panel study the information on-site."

"Any thoughts, Al?" the president asked, turning toward General Carr.

"Yes, let them study on-site. But when do we reveal the second encounter to the public?"

"That's a tougher decision," Bragg said, looking at the president. "We can keep the information private for a few days, but once their work is done, members of the international expert team will want the knowledge and their review disseminate worldwide."

"I agree. We must release the video's and information transmitted during the second encounter in the next few days. But first, we should talk to the expert team."

"Good idea, Mr. President," Bragg replied. "I'll set up a secure virtual meeting with the expert team at noon tomorrow. By then, they'll have some idea about the content of the orb's transmittal. Then, Mr. President, you can decide when to release the information."

"Mr. President, we should also have our intelligence officers and military scientists review the information to see if there are any military applications of this knowledge that could place the United States at a disadvantage," General Carr said.

"Yes, have all transmittal information sent to the Pentagon for review and have them watch our meeting with the expert team."

"Good, Mr. President. We have a plan," Bragg said. He and Carr stood up and walked out of the office, continuing the discussion as they made their way down the White House hallway.

"Jerry, some of this knowledge and equations might help us or our adversaries build better weapons," Carr said.

"Yes, I understand. We must consider all potential threats."

* * *

By 0800 on Monday morning, the expert team had convened to study the information the orb transmitted. Captain Kilbourne was in charge of expert team security. He monitored their communications on- and off-site and had oversight of team members' housing, food, medicines, and work tent.

With six worktables, they formed a rough circle in the military work tent. There the expert team scrutinized and discussed the technical validity of the material. No printouts nor any other materials could leave the tent. Soldiers guarded the tent and searched everyone when entering and leaving.

Kilbourne handed each team member twenty-six pages of equations from the orb's transmittal. They organized the document under major headings, such as "Radiative Gradients" and "Hydrologic Cycles." Two-thirds of the pages were definitions of variables, units of measure, and model parameters, and under the graceful heading of "Integrated Energy Flows" was a harmonious system of equations, which defined the performance relationships among Earth's energy flows.

* * *

At noon on Monday, October 23, President Barlow, Bragg, and Carr hosted a top secret virtual meeting with the expert team on-site in Bourbon County. The White House situation room used six wall screen displays to show the meeting participants, the orb's system of equations, and expert team notes to date. The expert team tent used two display screens. They used no holograms during the encrypted video meeting.

"Good day," President Barlow said. "Before the United States releases the information that the orb transmitted to us during the second encounter, we thought we should hear your thoughts to date. We realize you have not had enough time to evaluate every aspect of this knowledge, but we have a responsibility to release this information as soon as possible."

The president took a deep breath and drank from a water glass in front of him. Then his eyes scanned the experts, and he said, "Do you see any knowledge in the orb's transmittals that might create a military advantage? Weapons? Defense systems? Even using weather as a weapon?"

Dr. Jalan Breslin, the chairperson of the expert review team, sitting at a table, said, "Mr. President, my field of study is thermodynamics, and in the past, I've worked on the US Army's heat ray weapons. The knowledge transmitted by the orb may allow military's around the world to improve on the effectiveness of these heat weapons."

The heat ray weapons generate intense and invisible electromagnetic waves or radio waves, which heat the water in the bodies of any biological life form such as humans. A person feels like their skin is on fire. Crowd control is the primary use of this non-lethal weapon.

"Can this new knowledge enhance heat rays, so they can kill people?" Bragg asked the panel of experts.

"Yes. One equation provides new insights into heat transfer and could improve the design of a heat ray gun," Breslin replied. "But humanity has other weapons that are much more efficient than an enhanced heat ray weapon."

"Okay, I don't see this technology transfer issue worthy of stopping us from making this information public," General Carr said.

"I agree," President Barlow said. "What else in the orb's transmittals could be used for military purposes?"

"Someone could use the system of equations to create violent weather in certain regions of the world," Dr. Madia Rabab said. "But the result would be highly uncertain, and could even endanger the originator, say a nation or extremist group. Again, there are more certain and effective ways to wage war."

"Do any of you have reservations at this time of releasing this information worldwide?" Barlow asked, tapping his finger on the desk.

No one spoke up, so Breslin said, "Mr. President, it seems the benefits of making the information public far outweigh the technological risks."

"Alright, we'll release the orb videos and information transmittals from the second encounter tomorrow, Tuesday, at noon," Barlow said. "If any key issue comes up in the next twenty-four hours, please contact us immediately. Thank you, for your service, expertise, and counsel."

* * *

Later Monday evening, Dr. Breslin, the chairperson, stood up and said, "Let's vote on our preliminary findings by checking off the boxes on the one-page ballot. You can sign your name or leave it blank. Also, you can write a comment about what you have studied to date."

Each member of the team voted, and some wrote their comments down at the bottom of the single-page ballot.

After several minutes, Breslin announced the result. "The vote is in. Ten of you think the data from the orb is authentic and most likely valid. One person thinks the thermodynamic equation on page twenty-two is wrong. That person abstained from the vote. One expert thinks the orb copied the information from a multitude of books, so they abstained, and wrote the whole situation is a hoax."

"Jalan, can you read our comments?" Dr. Xandra asked.

"Sure," Dr. Breslin replied as he shuffled through the ballots. "Does anyone object to me reading through these? I will not reveal names."

None of the twelve experts responded, so Dr. Breslin began to read their comments.

"I have an overwhelming feeling of reverence toward this new knowledge. Humanity doesn't deserve this intervention."

"Too early to tell if this information is valid. If it is, the system of equations is amazing. I'm in awe and mystified."

"The harmony and elegance of the system of equations are beyond belief. It exceeds any Mozart symphony, Einstein theory, or Michelangelo sculpture. We need to test some of these equations. The impact of methane gas releases would be huge. If true, for centuries we have underestimated methane's impact on global warming."

"Ninety percent of these equations and formulas can be copied from published work. The other ten percent we don't understand yet. The orb provides no mathematical or empirical proof of the equations."

"Whoever sent us this system of equations knows more about the designs of nature than we ever will. I find that humbling."

"Inherent in this system of equations are the simplicity and elegance of the universe. I find myself awed. I pray I'm intelligent enough to comprehend this knowledge."

"The ephemeral orb, and Jillian's transmittal, reveals supreme intelligence exists in our universe. It sees humanity's dreadful limitations and destructive practices toward Earth. We are forcing earth to commit ecological suicide."

"A higher intelligence thinks humanity is worth saving. I'm not sure we are worth it. The earth is a living system, but we have hollowed it out."

Dr. Breslin placed the ballots in his leather briefcase. "An insightful set of comments, my esteemed colleagues. Two of the ballots were blank and two people abstained."

They agreed to reconvene the next morning, and prepared to turn in for the night.

But as they were leaving, Dr. Rabab looked around the empty tables and said, "I plan to stay up a little longer. Ninety percent of what's here we already knew. Yet, these printouts have two distinguishing features. First, some energy-transfer formulae are new knowledge. Second, complex second- and third-order interaction effects are modeled, which no one has ever done. What we have here is a single unifying system of global climate determinants customized to Earth's biosphere. We are witness to a god-like intellect."

"I understand, Madia," Dr. Breslin replied after the other team members left. "We need you alert and rested for tomorrow. Please don't work too late."

"Okay, but the set of three equations on entropy and dissipating the planet's heat is amazing. I want to develop a mathematical proof of it," she replied in a determined voice.

"Madia, I doubt these are God's equations," Breslin said as he walked out of the tent. "Notice that Jillian and the orb keep saying we, not I."

"Yes, I know," Dr. Rabab said as she opened a yellow notepad and pulled off her headband. She stared at the set of three equations.

Only a handful of people on Earth could understand these equations. Could she derive a mathematical proof for them? Did a simultaneous optimal solution exist that set terraforming performance targets for Earth?

Her sole companions were two large, glaring LED light fixtures that swung from the ceiling. Alone in a dreary tent, she stared at a blank page of her notebook. Beside her were three cheap gray military pencils. She would try to decipher the omniscient signature of an unknown and advanced intelligence—and her efforts might save the human species.

CHAPTER 8
World Reaction

Once President Barlow announced to the world on television the second encounter with the orb, human society stopped. Most countries stopped working and emptied factory, office, and government buildings. People stood in city streets and rural highways and cried, laid down, prayed, wandered around, and sang songs of hopefulness. But the announcement and video also brought out the extremist groups. The beginning or end of time was upon humanity, depending on the group's point of view.

In the first hour after the announcement, people created millions of perspectives, prophecies, and rumors about the second encounter. It was a day of awe, exhilarating excitement, desolate fear, and total confusion.

One television anchor said, "Today, humanity learns it's not alone in the universe! The voice of the orb, Jillian Hickory, proves it."

Barlow had shown a video of the second encounter at noon, Tuesday, October 24. Websites crashed as the video of the second encounter was replayed over one hundred billion times on Tuesday alone. He directed everyone to visit the US State Department's website to download the full transmittal of knowledge from the orb. After his announcement, the expert team hosted a worldwide news conference describing their findings to date and answered twenty questions from viewers. The experts became icons with one hour shows devoted to their careers.

Jillian, Tom, Mattie, and Ethan Hickory were saviors with hundreds of pictures of them posted on websites. The world knew Jillian used a pink toothbrush at her school and that Mattie always bit her fingernails. They knew Ethan's school grades, course-by-course and year-by-year. Public media knew the entire economic history of the family farm and what crops Tom and Mattie Hickory grew each year, and how much money they earned.

The family did not watch the news or any other show that focused on current events, so they were unaware of the recent frenzy surrounding their family. But the US government and US Army soldiers were well aware of all that was going on, and were doing their best to protect the Hickory family.

* * *

"Mr. President, please excuse me for interrupting your dinner—our intelligence indicates an increase in alert status of Russian military forces," White House Chief of Staff, Jerry Bragg said.

At this, the first lady, Elizabeth, dropped her teacup onto its saucer. The dinging sound resonated around the quiet room. The White House butler's face turned ashen.

"Dammit! Jerry, what's the situation?" President Barlow said as he threw his napkin down on his food.

"Sir, the Russians increased combat readiness."

"To what level?"

"Sir, the Russians' current alerts would be between our DEFCON 4 and DEFCON 3."

The United States defense readiness condition, or DEFCON, prescribed five levels of readiness. DEFCON 1 meant nuclear war was imminent. DEFCON 5 signified normal peacetime military operations and readiness.

A presidential aide entered the room, declaring, "Mr. President, General Carr is on line five."

"Thank you," Barlow replied and answered his communicator, standing up. "Yes, Al, I heard about the Russians."

Bragg remained standing on the opposite side of the table. His carriage stiffened. The first lady did not get up, and the butler stepped back from the table to regain her composure.

"Sir, our intelligence reports the Russians believe we're withholding information. All Russian submarines left their naval ports and are out to sea."

"For what purpose would we plan this?" the president mumbled, tapping his finger on the table standing up.

"Mr. President, I don't know what Premier Vsevolod is thinking, but you must call him. Also, the Chinese, and other nations, may be considering an increase in military readiness too."

"I'll call Vsevolod first, and then Guang Jiang." Turning toward Bragg, he said, "I'm going down to the Oval Office. Get me in touch with Vsevolod."

"Sir, in Moscow, it's about 0400 in the morning."

"I don't care what time it is. We have to head this off," President Barlow said as he left the dining room. Bragg followed.

"Is Vsevolod on the line yet?" the president said to his staff when they entered the Oval Office. "Make sure he doesn't wait on me. I'll wait."

"Yes, sir."

After three minutes, the premier answered the call. Voice-activated digital assistants translated to and from Russian.

"Igor, this is President Barlow. I apologize for calling you so early in the morning. I understand your military has gone to a higher level of readiness. Why?"

"Mr. President, my cabinet thought it prudent. It's based on what we see in the media about the orb and its absurd promises."

"But your unilateral action will create more uncertainty, and even fear."

"Yes, it may, but our intelligence officers believe the United States is withholding key technological knowledge. We must prepare for all scenarios."

"Igor, what can I do to convince you this is not a US plot against anyone? We released all information; all of it!"

After a pause, Vsevolod said, "One thing we need is Russians on-site with the orb. We need direct reports, not media hysteria."

"Okay, done. Get your people to Wright-Patterson Air Force Base in Dayton, Ohio, in an unmarked cargo plane. We'll get them to the orb's site. Your experts can use our communication links if you want."

"We'll send three Russian experts," the premier replied.

"Good. We'll make sure they have full access. We'll do everything possible to avoid an international crisis. And we should try to keep this visit secret. Our chairman of the Joint Chiefs of the Armed Forces, General Carr, will contact your generals. And, Mr. Vsevolod, I am not raising the US military readiness to DEFCON 4, so please lower your alert."

"Mr. President, I will but only after I receive reports from my experts at the site."

"I would encourage you to do it now. I am sure China and India are aware of your change in military status."

"Mr. President, I don't believe in God. Many Russians are atheists," the premier said in a lecturing tone. "I need my people to report to me."

"Yes, I understand," the president answered, his eyebrows pinching together. "Please call me if anything comes up. We do not want this to escalate."

"I agree. Our experts will be landing at Wright-Patterson Air Force Base within eight hours."

After they hung up their communicators, President Barlow stood up from his chair, walked over to Bragg, and said, "We need to keep the Russians' visit secret. If word gets out, we'll have to invite hundreds of other countries to the site of the orb."

"Yes, sir. We should separate the Russians from everyone else at the site. Put them in a separate mobile home, and take food to their quarters. We'll come up with a disguise for them. Tell them not to speak Russian in the presence of others."

"Good ideas, Jerry. Are there any Russians on the international team that's studying the orb's transmittals?"

"Not exactly, sir. Dr. Madia Rabab, who won the 2129 Nobel Prize in genetics, earned one of her PhDs from the University of Moscow Technological Institute. But she is Iranian."

"How in the hell did the United Nations not put a Russian on the review team?"

"I don't know, but it's too late now," Bragg said, before adding politely, "Sir, you need to call President Jiang."

"Yes, get her on the phone."

While waiting for the call to go through, he jotted down a few talking points. "President Jiang, this is President Barlow."

"Hello, Mr. President."

"Thank you for taking my call. I'm sure you and your citizens are following the story of this orb in Kentucky."

"Yes, we are. We have two Chinese scientists on the United Nations international team, but you should have informed us sooner."

"Yes, I understand. The reason I called you is because the Russians have increased their military alert level. The United States will not increase its military readiness level, and I've explained this to Premier Vsevolod, yet he will not lower it. He thinks the orb is some kind of trick planned by the US government. He also thinks we are withholding information and we are not."

"Yes, we have discussed this in our security council meetings. Many on the council think you are withholding key technological information. We are also aware of the increased level of nuclear readiness. We were waiting to see what the United States would do, but I repeat, you should have informed us earlier about the situation."

"Yes, I agree. I apologize, it's my mistake, not the citizens of the United States. And the United States will not—I repeat will not—increase its military alert status."

"We don't want to escalate the situation, either. We will not increase our military readiness for now. But if we discover any unique technological advances in your military capability that we think are derived by the orb's transmittal, the US will pay a heavy economic price."

"I understand and I assure you we released all of the information the orb transmitted, President Jiang. Together we can keep this situation under control. Thank you. The Russians will realize the orb, and its information, is not a threat to any country."

There was a short pause before Jiang asked, "Do you believe the glowing object is an alien life-form?"

"President Jiang, I wish I knew. As you know, our international expert team is evaluating the orb's information. And, I'm astounded that the United Nations left Russian experts off the international team."

"Yes, President Barlow. A big mistake."

Both leaders paused for a moment to collect their thoughts. Then, Barlow said, "I've tried to fix this with Premier Vsevolod. And I thank you again for your decision not to increase China's military readiness. Please call me if I can help you in any way."

"We'll continue to study the situation and the information provided by the orb. So far, we see no threat to our country."

They hung up their communicators, and the president sat back in his chair. He let his shoulders relax as he exhaled a chest full of air. He had defused the situation as much as he could, and bought more time for the experts and the world to study the orb's transmittals.

Bragg looked at him with a strained face and said, "Mr. President, your calls helped. You should try to sleep now. I will wake you if I need to."

During the night, the White House staff broke up into teams and watched ten wall screens with news feeds from around the world. International news feeds reported a diverse set of opinions. Some did not believe the orb story. Others were certain it was an alien or divine intervention. And some thought it was a diabolical trick by the US government to advance their power and influence over the world. The teams also fielded calls from US embassies, who were asking how to explain the situation in their host countries. Bragg would update the president at their 0600 breakfast meeting.

* * *

The next morning, President Barlow entered the White House dining room where his Chief of Staff was sitting at the side of the table, going over his notes.

"What happened overnight?" he asked as a butler poured him some coffee.

"Mr. President, my staff worked throughout the night. Here's their report." He handed the president a ten-page document.

Bragg had served as the president's campaign manager during the general elections. He was loyal, determined, and organized, and President Barlow trusted him in all respects. However, he knew Bragg could be abrupt, impatient, and demanding of his own staff.

The president put the pages beside him and said, "I'll read it later." He took a long sip of black coffee. "Summarize it for me."

"Mr. President, the report has two sections. The first focuses on the reaction to the orb by major religions. The second is the reactions from major governments and cities. I'll read parts of it."

"On the religious front, the pope and Vatican issued the following brief statement: 'Pope Salene Alvaro and the Vatican are watching the reported events about the orb. Humanity may or may not be witnessing a divine intervention. It is too early to determine the truthfulness or practicality of these events. We pray for humanity as the situation continues and for the young girl Jillian Hickory.'"

"The pope opened the Vatican, so people could pray for a peaceful acceptance of the orb, and St. Peter's Square is now packed with followers.

She did not make a public speech but instead issued the brief announcement I read to you."

Both men took a drink of coffee and Bragg and said, "The religious reactions are diverse. For example, the population of Sri Lanka is skeptical of the news reports of the orb being a divine entity. Mr. President, they practice Theravada Buddhism. To them, there is no God. The goal is human self-understanding and self-improvement."

"Yes, I understand. Jerry, I'm an agnostic." President Barlow took a bite of his breakfast, and then asked, "What about other religions?"

"Sir, most Christians think this is a divine intervention. Our virtual survey reports that only 2.8 percent of Christians think it is a hoax."

The butler refilled their coffee cups, and then took two messy dishes off the table, but it was clear she was lingering, trying to listen in to the conversation.

"Most Muslims are skeptical of the orb and its promises," Bragg said. "But like the pope, they are taking a wait-and-see attitude. Some think the orb may be a prophet, but they need more proof."

Bragg wiped his mouth with a cloth napkin embroidered with the White House seal, then continued. "Some Hindus believe that other gods exist and so believe that the orb is divine. Other Hindus think the orb is an advanced and conscious being, most likely an alien. And, all religions worry about all the information being disseminated worldwide and the possibility of economic or military conflict."

"What about government reactions?"

"Sir, our White House communicators are ringing twenty-four hours a day. Our embassy staff have explained to their host countries what we know and don't know, but there's much distrust in the world. You must call more heads of state."

"You tell me who I need to call, and I'll call them. And talk to General Carr about what else we can do to avert a military crisis."

"Yes, I will." Bragg laid his napkin down exactly halfway between his plate and notepad. He liked to make sure all things were in order in the White House. "Mr. President, some cities, such as Paris, Beijing, and Moscow, seem to be in normal operating mode. But some are not."

"Where's the trouble?"

"To name a few: Buenos Aires, London, Mexico City, and Mumbai. We have offered their governments help, but the panic is real. The orb triggered many demonstrations outside our embassies. Some are tied to political and economic unrest; others are because they think the orb is the signal for the end of days."

"Oh, the end of days," President Barlow muttered. He pushed his chair back from the table.

"Yes, sir, the end of days," Bragg said in a soft voice. Silence prevailed for a moment, and then Bragg stood up and faced the president. "Sir, human society is under siege. We are trying to cope with climate change, the collapse of governments, wars, technology, and social decay."

"Jerry, I agree with you. These things have created a moral vacuum. But I must be positive. I must lead, not sit around and whine."

Bragg nodded in agreement, and then said, "Sir, one final thing. We need to add more security to certain US embassies."

"Why?"

"Some of the demonstrations were violent."

"What happened?"

"Well, sir, in Mumbai, a cult group called Disciples of Ptolemy hung a goat upside down on the embassy's front gate. The goat's throat was slit. Cameras recorded the entire event. The video is playing worldwide on UNet."

"Anyone hurt?"

"No, not to our knowledge. The crowd stormed embassy grounds, but the US ambassador and staff went to the lockdown room in the basement. We're not sure what happened to the marines guarding the building, but they decided not to fire their weapons."

"Where in the hell were the local police?"

"Sir, they arrived almost one hour after the crowd entered the embassy. They have now cleared the grounds, and we're working with them to unlock the safe room." He took a sip of his coffee, and then continued. "We're still getting information on what happened. It seems about thirty demonstrators climbed the embassy walls, and entered through a broken window. These cult members are a scary bunch. They dye their hair orange, and live together in communes. The men wear white dhoti-type clothing and the women wear black saris of sorts."

"How did they get the name Ptolemy?"

Bragg answered by reading from the White House report again.

"'Claudius Ptolemy was a Greek-Egyptian astronomer, geographer, and astrologist. He was born in AD 100. He lived in Alexandria, Egypt. Ptolemy authored an astrological treatise called *Tetrabiblos*. This book is often credited with being the foundation of astrology. The disciples of Ptolemy believe their god sent Ptolemy to Earth. Ptolemy's purpose was to help humanity understand the universe and humanity's place in it.' The cult group formed in France in 2047, with splinter groups in many world cities. The cult claims hundreds of thousands of followers, but my staff thinks it's more like twenty thousand."

"Why did they storm our embassy?"

"Sir, we're not sure. Indian police say this group believes the orb is a messenger from Ptolemy. The animal sacrifice was to honor the prophet and the arrival of the orb."

President Barlow shook his head. "Do whatever you think best. We should give the embassies extra security."

"Yes, sir."

"How are things on the home front?" the president asked. He was beginning to feel exhausted and it wasn't even 0700 yet.

"Most cities in the United States have had some type of demonstration. The vast majority so far are peaceful. Four people have been injured. No deaths to date, Mr. President, but the crowds are getting bigger."

"Is that in the report too?"

"Yes, sir, it is."

"And is the crowd in Bourbon County under control?"

"It's estimated at thirty thousand people now. And the crowd is growing, sir. In general, our two levels of security are working. Also, we have restricted incoming airline flights at regional airports. We don't need any more troops for now, but we may have to help local and state authorities more with the crowd's medical needs."

"I'll read the entire report later this morning. Keep me posted. We need to keep things under control."

* * *

That same Wednesday morning, a Russian plane landed at Wright-Patterson Air Force Base in Dayton, Ohio. Three Russian experts—a physicist, a chemist, and a weapons expert—dressed in civilian clothes and carrying suitcases and three equipment containers, were met by an air force colonel and two armed guards. They took a commercial airport limousine to Bourbon County, where they arrived at a mobile home in the outer restricted area.

"Good morning," General Tucson said.

She extended her hand to the Russians in turn, then introduced them to Preston and Kilbourne.

"Gentlemen, we have issued you new identities and federal ID cards," she said after they had engaged in pleasantries, a cordial chat about the bumpy flight to Dayton. "From now on, you are telecommunications specialists for the United Nations' international scientific-review team. Please read your new names and the short bios of your histories. The only people who know your real identities are here. We recommend you do not talk to anyone other than the three of us."

"Our English is good," one Russian boasted.

"Yes, we understand that, but the less you say, the better. Our soldiers would pick up on your accents."

"When can we see it, General?"

"In twenty minutes," Tucson replied. She took a deep breath, then added, "But first, you must understand a few things. You have complete access to the outer restricted area. Feel free to come and go as you please. Colonel Preston, Captain Kilbourne, or I will escort you while in the inner restricted area. Use this radio and channel fourteen to call us. You can take whatever video, pictures, or measurements you want, and you can talk with your superiors in Russia on our communication network or by any other means. You can order food from a menu, and we will bring it to your mobile home. Bottled water, snacks, and juices are in the refrigerator. And finally, if you need medical services, we can escort you to our mobile hospital. Any questions?"

"Yes. Do you have any vodka?" one of the Russians asked.

"No," Tucson replied, "but we'll work on that request."

The three Russians smiled.

"Thank you. We need to report to our superiors as soon as possible."

"We'll see the orb in twenty minutes. Be ready. It's an amazing sight to see this blue orb hover above the ground. I'll come back to get you."

Once the three officers were clear of the mobile home, Tucson said, "Hawk, you didn't say a word."

"Yeah, I've never met Russians before."

"Well, be civil to them. It's better we do this than fight them."

"Yes, ma'am."

"General Tucson," Kilbourne said. "Should we post a guard outside their mobile home?"

"No, but assign two soldiers to follow them at a distance whenever they leave."

"Yes, ma'am."

The officers drove to the command tent, where they were given an update on the status of operations and security, before returning to pick up the Russians. The three Russians came out of their mobile home, carrying several pieces of equipment and their federal ID tags hanging from their necks.

A serene blue, pink, and orange sky revealed itself as Earth's star rose higher in the morning sky. The brilliant sunlight and brisk wind made the planet come alive. Birds chirped, green leaves swayed in the wind, and grass reached for the sun. The orb and Earth knew their role in the universe, but the newcomer, humanity, did not.

After a short drive in the Jeeps, the group arrived back at the command tent.

The Russians got out and approached the orb, stopping just ten meters shy of it.

Invincible and motionless, the orb glowed a brilliant blue. It hovered about two meters off the ground. The sheer beauty of the sunrise nearly overpowered the volleyball sized orb, yet its arrival gave hope that humanity would be witness to many more sunrises.

One Russian looked at the soldiers guarding the orb and the surrounding television cameras, while the other two looked on, gazing at the bluish orb. They used their equipment to take various scientific measurements and readings, dictating their observations on their pocket-sized e-devices. One pulled out a handheld instrument, and pointed it toward the orb, which stood like a frozen sentry.

"It looks exactly like the videos," the oldest, a gray-haired man, said.

"What did you expect?" Preston blurted out.

"Can I touch it?" the Russian asked.

"Sure," Tucson said, "but at your own risk."

The Russian walked toward the bright sphere. His colleague filmed the encounter.

"Aha!" he said as he touched the entity with two fingers, and then said something in Russian.

It did not respond. It had learned to tolerate human inspections.

Preston stiffened his posture, while Tucson and Whitney stared at one another.

The Russian continued his exploration of the orb. After touching it a few seconds, the man backed away with a puzzled look. He looked at his colleagues, and then in English, said, "My skin is tingling. Some sort of electrical charge ran through my body. And, I felt the emotion of happiness."

"I see no way the cameras here could project such an image," another replied. "I stood in front of the two cameras, and the orb's still there."

"There is no abnormal radiation coming from it," the other said.

The gray-haired Russian walked back to the other two, and they talked in voices so low the officers couldn't tell whether they were speaking Russian or English.

"A surge of energy passed through my body when I touched it. The last time I felt this way, I was at the Moscow Symphony to hear Tchaikovsky's music. So inspirational."

The other two looked at him with raised eyebrows. They were not accustomed to hearing him talk about emotions instead of science.

Thirty minutes later, after spending more time investigating the site of the orb, one Russian said to Tucson, "We see no way you could create such an object. The sky is clear, the cameras are only cameras, and the ground has not been tampered with. It is not of this world. We need to report our preliminary findings to our superiors."

Colonel Preston laughed and said, "What did you expect to find in the ground—a submarine?"

The Russian didn't laugh. He gave Preston a sneering glance, and then continued to examine the orb.

Tucson didn't say anything, just kicked at the Kentucky bluegrass with her boot twice. Trying to move past the awkward silence, she then said, "Gentlemen, let's go to the command tent. We can decide how you want to communicate with your superiors." Once they were inside the tent, she looked at the three Russians and said, "Now you have seen the orb. It exists; it's not an illusion or trick, and we are trying to deal with it. It has harmed no one since it arrived. We need your help to communicate this to the world."

The Russians requested access to a Russian satellite, and Tucson provided the frequency to US Army telecommunication specialists. They asked to hook up their personal computer to their Russian communication network.

At 1056, Wednesday, they transmitted an encrypted message to their superiors. Part of the message said: "We find no preliminary evidence that the orb is a hoax or created by the US government. We have touched it and walked around the object several times. Our equipment has measured its characteristics. We find it is in no way a creation of human technology. We perceive that the orb knows we are there. We have not seen it interact with the eight-year-old girl. Our next initiative will be to meet with the international expert team to find out what they think. We have not determined if the US withheld information from the orb's transmittal yet."

"When can we meet the international team?" one asked.

"They're working now," Tucson replied. "I'll set up a meeting right after lunch—say, 1300. We'll pick you up at 1245."

Kilbourne took the three Russians back to their mobile home while Tucson and Preston stood in the command tent.

"Hawk, can I talk to you? Let's go outside," Tucson asked.

"Yes, ma'am," Preston said, walking away from other people in the area.

"Hawk, you're a fine military officer. But do not make these Russians mad."

"Okay, but I find them arrogant."

"So what?" she said in a stronger voice. "Hawk, I'm relieving you of your duty with the Russians. We can't risk a war with you around. Captain Kilbourne will take your place. You brief him on the situation, and then send him to me."

"Yes, ma'am," Preston replied, and he walked out of the tent, the veins in his neck engorged.

* * *

Later that day, Kilbourne picked up the three Russians and brought them to the tent that housed the expert team.

"The team's goal is to write a report on the validity of the information the orb transmitted to us," Tucson explained. "The final report will be available on UNet for all to read." Then, she addressed the team. "Please answer the questions of our three invited guests. There are no secrets. Thank you."

Over the next hour, the team members answered the Russian experts' questions. They exchanged technical information at a fast and professional pace, though a few times, the discussion became argumentative over how the new information could or could not be used for military purposes.

"Thank you for reviewing this information. A helpful discussion," one Russian said as they were leaving. They returned to their mobile home to compile a second report to their superiors. Much of it focused on possible theories on the origin of the orb and the science of the orb itself. They also repeated the expert panel's preliminary conclusions.

Part of the report said: "We met with the expert team and exchanged scientific information. No country seems to have the technology to suspend and move an orb as shown in the videos. And the orb somehow generated a set of intelligent equations that are remarkable. The equations help us understand the second- and third-order interaction effects on Earth's climate. Some of these interaction effects are stronger than the main effects, and are absolutely new knowledge. The US did not create the orb and we see no evidence it is a hoax."

"However, a few equations, and the insights they provide, may have military applications that we were unaware of in past weapon designs. We've concluded that the orb itself is not a threat to Russian sovereignty, but the United States could be withholding information. We recommend continuing our current level of military readiness until more evidence of the information's completeness is acquired."

* * *

Meanwhile, the Hickory family tried to hide and recover from the second encounter. Over the last two days, the orb remained placid and steadfast. The media focus shifted to the international expert team, which allowed the Hickorys time to rest and collect their thoughts. What knowledge had the orb sent? Was it valid? Could it save Earth?

Mattie had struggled from day one. Her cozy and compact world had been invaded by the orb, media, and governments. She had gone from thoughts of 'it will get better' to anger to depression and now to defeat. Their good life had unraveled. Only Jillian had a positive outlook on things, and of course, was cured of cerebral palsy.

The rest of the family were showing signs of more stress too. Tom stared into space. Ethan hid from reality by playing immersion games. They were being scrutinized by billions of people. They felt claustrophobic. They saw no way out of the media dungeon.

To escape the scrutiny, Wednesday evening, the family watched an educational documentary on worldwide food shortages.

"The last residents of La Manga del Mar Menor in Murcia, Spain, have left their homes," the documentary host stated. "Here, next to the Mediterranean ocean, sea-level rise has made this part of Spain a wasteland. The heat is causing the southern region to lose its ability to grow crops. Once one of Europe's historical havens for growing vegetables and fruit, this area is fast becoming barren, no longer able to grow crops like tomatoes, oranges, lettuce, broccoli, peppers, and cabbage."

As the reporter spoke, a video showed lines of trucks moving toward higher ground, people migrating inland. The trucks were loaded with furniture, salvageable equipment, and personal belongings. Seawater lapped at the truck tires. A second video showed a farmer holding sandy soil as it filtered through his fingers. The sixth-generation farmer told his story of selling the farm he'd built, an enclosed hydroponic farm on higher ground in Albacete, Spain, at an economic loss.

"Southern Spain is becoming a desert like the Sahara," he said.

"Dad, our lives could be worse," Ethan said.

"Yes, son. One hundred years ago, there were fewer tangible examples. Then, it was icebergs melting, coral reefs dying, a few hot days, and fish moving toward the North and South Poles. Those things didn't have a direct impact on people's lives, but now they do. We're seeing these massive movements of people to higher ground. People have lost their homes and livelihoods. And worldwide food production is struggling."

"But, Dad, hydroponic greenhouses and genetic engineering of crops are helping."

"Yes, son, but many people can't afford those expensive options. There are great imbalances of wealth and technology in our world, and climate change is making those imbalances worse."

"Not everything can be solved by technology, Ethan," Mattie added. "The farmers in Spain are destitute. They must move at their own expense."

The next segment of the documentary focused on the effects in Brazil.

"Deep in the jungle on the Amazon River is a city called Manaus. The city has been called the Heart of the Amazon. It is fourteen hundred kilometers from the Atlantic Ocean. The city sits next to the Rio Negro River, which combines with the Solimões River to form the Amazon River. Its rich history includes the production of goods like lumber and rosewood oil, and the harvesting of nuts, fruit, and rubber. Today robots do much of this work."

"During the last two hundred years, the average temperature has soared in the Manaus area by five degrees. As a result, several hundred thousand people have moved out of low-lying areas around Manaus. Coupled with sea-level rises of over one meter, the sea has widened and deepened the Amazon River. Much of Manaus's food is now shipped up the river. The feasibility and cost of a dam and lock system on the Amazon River are being studied."

"Last year, in 2146, heat-related deaths in the Manaus area totaled thirty thousand six hundred fourteen. In a city of three million people, the poorest people are the primary victims of these deaths. People can't afford cooling vests. Air-conditioning is now subsidized by the national government because people can't afford their electric bills."

A video showed people in a poor area of the city, swimming in fountains and rivers to try to keep cool, but there were so many people and so little room, they were squeezed together in the water like thirsty animals. One child sat beside a street storm drain, splashing filthy water onto herself to keep cool.

The video ended with an interview with a paleoclimatologist.

"The causes of the extraordinary temperatures in this area are complex. Deforestation explains about thirty percent of our temperature increases, based on regression analyses. Even though we plant millions of trees and shrubs ever year, the Amazon is losing massive amounts of moisture. It is drying up. We used to average over two thousand three hundred forty millimeters of rain per year. Now we get only one thousand five hundred fifty millimeters. Our tropical rainforest is degrading into a treeless savanna."

"Daddy, it's a good thing the orb came," Jillian said. "It can stop this bad stuff."

"Yeah, what the orb knows could save us all," Ethan said.

"Yes, it could."

After a few seconds to reflect on the family discussion, Mattie said as her face reddened, "The orb may save humanity, but not us!" After blurting this out, a crying Mattie hurried upstairs to her bedroom. Tom followed her up to their bedroom to find the door locked.

On Thursday morning, at about 0330, Mattie couldn't sleep and so went downstairs in her pajamas to fix herself a hot tea. Even her pills didn't guarantee sleep. She tried to read a novel on the wall screen, but often found herself staring at nothing but coldhearted pixels. She subconsciously picked at her fingernails, unaware of a bleeding index finger.

About an hour later, Tom joined her. He sat in his chair, flicking through farm performance reports on a second open wall screen. These reports were his way to recapture a sense of normality. But dark circles surrounded his blue eyes. After minutes of these superficial activities, he paused and looked at his wife.

"Mattie, we're in trouble, you know?"

"Yes, I know."

CHAPTER 9
Security

"What happens to the Hickory family now? Do we add more security? Move them?" Captain Kilbourne asked Lieutenant Colonel Preston, sitting in the command tent. It was Thursday morning, October 26, eight days after the orb's arrival.

"I don't know. I'll call Tucson," Preston said as soldiers scurried around the bustling command tent. Tucson was in her officer's quarters resting.

"General, given the worldwide frenzy about the Hickory family, what should we do? Beef up their protection? Hide them in the restricted area?" Preston asked Tucson over their communicators.

"No, don't take them away from their home. But let's beef up security; send two platoons of soldiers to surround the home and farm. Keep everyone out; I mean everyone. Hawk, you stand by, I'll call Al Carr on these questions. I'll patch you in to my conversation with Carr."

"Yes, ma'am."

Within ten minutes, Al Carr, the Joint Chief of the Armed Forces and four-star general, was talking with Tucson and Preston, each in a different location.

"General Carr," she said, "We have patched in Lt. Colonel Preston to this conversation. He's the commander of the first battalion of my 303rd Army Infantry Regiment. He oversees the inner restricted area and security around the Hickory home."

"First, the president and I wanted to thank you for your performance in handling the orb situation. We thank you, and so do the American people," Carr said. "Second, I want to tell you, Brigadier General Tucson will be promoted to Major General, Lieutenant Colonel Preston to Colonel, and Captain Kilbourne to Lieutenant Colonel."

"Thank you. We appreciate the confidence you have in our leadership," Tucson replied.

"Yes, thank you General Carr. It is an honor to serve you and our country," Preston said.

"We will notify you in the next week," Carr said. "Now, what's on your mind?"

"Sir, what should we do with the Hickory family, given the media attention? Should we move them out of their home?" Tucson asked.

"The White House has been discussing their situation. They are most secure in their home, so they should stay in place."

"I added two platoons to surround their farm and home to provide more security."

"Good, and cut off their access to websites and communications connections. We don't want hackers watching them on their own home cameras or stealing their electronic information. Use only our encrypted handheld devices to communicate with them."

"Sir, their health is deteriorating," Tucson said.

"Yes, we see the doctor's daily reports. But they must stay put. The orb remains after its second encounter, so it may need Jillian to be its voice again. We don't know what's going to happen."

"Anything new on the Russian alert status?"

"No, and President Barlow is steadfast in not raising our alert status, against my advice," Carr replied. "Steph, we also have a request from the United Nations for you to lead the peacekeeping troops on the Bangladesh-India border."

"What's happening?"

"Sixty-seven soldiers have been killed along the border in nine small skirmishes. Sea-level rise had forced millions of people in Bangladesh to be displaced. Bangladesh's government is close to collapse, India closed its borders, and millions of people are crossing the border into India. People are dying from starvation, disease, and neglect."

"But, I've got a job here."

"Yes, I agree, but you are famous worldwide; everyone knows your name, Steph. You guard the orb and the Hickory family." Many in the US media wanted Tucson to run for President of the United States.

All communicators were silent as Preston listened to the conversation between two competent US military generals.

"Steph, the president will make this decision, not me. But I thought you should know what's going on."

"Sir, I'd like to complete my mission here first."

"I know, but the directorates' of the UN and the leaders in India and Bangladesh think your presence would help stop the hostilities. Without hostilities, humanitarian groups could help the migrants," Carr said, coughing several times.

Tucson pondered the possible new deployment and knew she would do whatever the president decided. Service to her beloved USA trumped all other criteria.

"Steph, one last thing. Eventually, we'll have to move the Hickory family and place them in our Federal Witness Protection Program. Both the Federal Bureau of Investigation and the National Security Council support this plan. I'll send a FWPP agent to brief them on what this program entails. But you must tell the Hickory family this is the only way to protect them. The orb encounters have made the Hickory family a national treasure and we must protect them."

"Yes, sir. They won't like leaving their beloved farm, but I'll tell them."

"Good bye, Steph and Colonel Preston."

Tucson turned off her communicator and stretched her arms high in the air. A confident glow permeated her face as she thought about her promotion to a two-star general. As a career officer, she dreamed of being the Joint Chief of the US Armed Forces, and that dream was coming closer to being fulfilled.

She sat on the edge of the bed in her stark tent in Bourbon County. There were no pictures of family or friends, except for one of her deceased parents. Tucson celebrated her victories and disappointments only one way: alone. She had avoided marriage and decided not to have children. Career goals trumped personal goals. She stood up, ready for the next challenge.

* * *

Major General Tucson returned to the command tent and greeted Preston and Kilbourne.

"Captain Kilbourne, you have been promoted to Lieutenant Colonel. Congratulations," Tucson said with a broad smile. "They also promoted Hawk and me."

All three shook hands, and Kilbourne thanked Tucson and Preston. Afterward, Tucson said, "Okay, let's get to work. I need your advice. I must tell the Hickory family today that eventually they will have to leave their farm and home. And that an agent from the Federal Witness Protection Program will explain the details of such a move. Any advice on how to do this?"

"I can't think of anything, except be honest," Kilbourne replied. "You need to explain why they have to leave."

"What do you mean?"

"Well, tell them they are a national treasure. Jillian is a saint to most people. If they stay in Bourbon County, the media, governments, and even extremist groups will hound them. Say that President Barlow, in counsel with many experts, has authorized this move. Say that moving is an absolute necessity; it ensures their family's safety and they stay together."

"All right, thanks. I'll go to the Hickory home shortly."

***

"Hello," Tucson said as she, the medic, and Colonel Preston stood on the front porch of the Hickory home at 1000 Thursday morning. The two officers entered, but the medic stayed outside on the porch. In the foyer, Jillian and Ethan greeted the two officers.

"Mattie, Tom, can we talk to you alone?" Tucson asked, awkwardly flexing her fist beside her hip.

"Kids, can you go upstairs while we talk to the General?" Mattie asked. Neither child wanted to go upstairs, but they obeyed their parents. Once the kids left, Mattie said, "Would you like a drink?"

"No, thank you, Mrs. Hickory. We are fine."

"Would you like to sit down?" Mattie asked as they worked their way into the living room. Mattie and Tom had disconnected all wall screens and the US Army had cut off access to all electronic media, including their communicators embedded in their ears and shoulders.

"What brings you here?" Tom asked in a hesitant voice. Mattie sat on the sofa with both hands in her lap, picking at her fingernails. She'd been so stressed; the military hospital couldn't fix her battered cuticles. The doctors considered bandaging her fingers to prevent her from chewing them.

"The US government worries about your safety. The media and public will harass your family, especially Jillian, for the rest of your lives. You are a national treasure now; the world knows everything about you," Tucson said.

"Oh, really?" an indignant Mattie replied.

"President Barlow and General Al Carr consulted with several federal agencies. They think it best we move your family to a new location. Your family would enter the Federal Witness Protection Program and learn new identities. You could start a new life."

"Did you say move?" Mattie asked. She scooted forward on the sofa, her hands clasped tighter together. Her head was pounding like a drum.

"Yes, Mrs. Hickory."

"Are you saying we have to give up the farm?" Tom said, standing up from his chair as if to defend his domain.

"Mr. Hickory, the US Army will maintain your farm while you're gone. I don't know if moving means you must give it up though. It might; I'm not sure."

"Do you realize what you're asking?" Tom asked. On the sofa, Mattie cried.

The general rubbed her forehead with one hand as she tried to reconcile what she should say or do next. How had a general, a warrior, gotten into this daunting position? She knew the Hickory family had no choice, but the family didn't.

"Yes, Mr. Hickory, we do," Colonel Preston said, stepping in. "But this protects your family."

Tom walked over to the sofa and sat down beside Mattie. He placed a comforting arm around his crying wife, when he heard someone else crying. He realized that Jillian and Ethan were sitting at the top of the steps and had heard the entire conversation.

"Kids, come down here," he said. "Have you been listening?"

"Yes, Dad," Ethan replied, holding Jillian's hand. He led her to the sofa.

As Tom tried to comfort his distraught family, Tucson and Preston had time to contemplate their next point.

"Tom, the media and the public won't let you continue your old life. Extremist groups will hunt you down," Tucson said.

"If—and I say if—we do this," Tom said, "what do we do now?"

"Nothing now. But you must learn more about the witness protection program. An agent is coming to meet you, explain things, and answer your questions."

Tom looked dismayed. Jillian and Mattie cried and hugged one another, and Ethan became more upset.

"Mattie, do you think we should do it?"

"I told you it would come to this—long ago. Do you see what you've done?"

"No, Mom," Ethan shouted. "What about our school and friends?"

Mattie looked up and wiped her teary eyes. She asked the officers, "What happens to these kids and school?"

"Mrs. Hickory, we will homeschool your kids at the government's expense, but the agent can answer those questions," Tucson replied.

Tom stood up, wiped the tears from his face, and looked at his sequestered family. He raised his head and said, "I guess we have no choice; we'll have to leave."

Mattie hugged both kids. She had foretold this moment when the orb first arrived.

Tucson stepped toward her and reached for her hand. "Mrs. Hickory, I know these are tough times, but you're doing what's best for your family."

With the news shared, Tucson and Preston opened the front door to leave. Tucson turned toward the family and said, "We'll help you any way we can. We have a medic outside, and he'll stay here for the next hour in case you need anything."

The two officers walked back to the restricted area.

"Well, we did it," Tucson said to Preston as they neared the command tent.

"Yeah, you did it; not me. We should fight wars; not this charitable stuff," Preston said.

"Times have changed, Hawk. You need to adjust. Human society is fracturing. The world needs the structure and organization of the US Army more than ever."

* * *

"Mr. and Mrs. Hickory, I'm agent Janice Sutherland with the Federal Witness Protection Program," a thin, tall lady said, standing on the porch, late Thursday afternoon. Agent Sutherland wore a light tan trench coat.

"Yes, we were expecting you," Tom said, opening the door and directing Agent Sutherland to the living room sofa. The children joined them in the living room.

Mattie came out of the kitchen, wearing a Bourbon County Fair apron, depicting a faded picture of the famous racehorse Secretariat. The Triple Crown winner had lived out his life in Bourbon County, but the Hickory family would not.

"Before I describe our witness protection program, I'd like to say it is an honor meeting you. Your family is my most famous client. Thank you for seeing me," Sutherland said while opening her briefcase. She handed Mattie a package of papers, a small video player, and a communicator that encrypts all information.

"The Federal Witness Protection Program will create new identities for your family. We'll sell your Kentucky farm and buy you a new one, placing your family in a new location with new identities. The government pays for everything. You'll go through extensive training off-site to learn your new backgrounds, how to answer questions, and so on. You'll practice saying your names thousands and thousands of times until it's automatic."

A slight chill and silence permeated the room. The slim and stoic Sutherland wasted no time explaining the FWPP proposal.

"So, we have to sell the farm?" a shaking and nervous Tom asked.

"Yes, too many people are searching for your family. We'll sell the farm and you will receive the entire sales price in hidden payments over five years."

"Oh!" Mattie cried out in anguish. Tom grabbed her hand and squeezed.

Agent Sutherland looked down at the floor, breaking eye contact for a moment. In time, she looked at the beleaguered couple and said, "I know it's difficult to lose your old life, but you are the most famous family in American history. This way, we can protect you."

Mattie laid her head on Tom's chest and wept.

"Ma'am, my family and I loved our life on this farm," Tom said as he held her. "And you tell us to give it up."

"Yes, sir. Our team considered all the options for your family. We considered moving you to another continent. We even considered splitting you up."

"What!" Tom yelled as Mattie whimpered in his arms.

"Mr. Hickory, it's easier for the media, governments, and other groups to search for a family of four. One alternative was to put one parent and one child together each and move you to two different locations. But we can avoid that disruptive option. We can change some of your physical characteristics. We have the best plastic surgeons in the world."

"Do the kids require plastic surgery?" Tom asked.

"No, they will grow and change as they age. They don't need surgery."

"What about their schooling?" Mattie asked.

"We'll home-school your kids for two years. We use the best teachers."

"Do we have any choice?" Tom asked.

"Not really, Mr. Hickory. But please think about our proposal. Call me on this encrypted communicator with questions. Our virtual assistant will always ask for the code written in this folder; otherwise they will hang up."

Although Sutherland looked ordinary and wiry, she had a big heart. She devoted her career to helping people get out of dangerous situations. As a top agent for the FWPP, she had a great amount of empathy for families with kids.

Agent Sutherland had helped hide lots of people, including judges, spies, national presidents and governors, undercover police, and renowned scientists. People were always being hunted, whether it was by governments, extremist groups, organized crime syndicates, or the media, and with trillions of cameras and electronic devices tracking and recording human practices and behavior, it was easy to find people using biometric and artificial intelligent algorithms. Only with the expertise and help of the US Federal Witness Protection Program could people truly disappear.

Sutherland stood up and walked over to the door, saying, "You'll stay here until the orb situation is resolved, but you are welcome to call me anytime. Meanwhile, destroy all items that could be traced back to you or Kentucky. For example, you must destroy the Bourbon County Fair apron you're wearing."

The Hickory family had to confront their destiny head-on—no old friends, no memories, and no choice.

* * *

"Steph, pack your bags, you're going to India," General Carr said in a call to Tucson Thursday evening. "President Barlow thinks your visibility in India and Bangladesh will enhance the United States' reputation and its worldwide perception of trust."

"Yes, sir. Can I take my officers with me?"

"We would like to have at least one of your officers stay in Bourbon County to provide continuity in protecting the orb and the Hickory family."

"Okay, Colonel Preston will stay put and manage the two restricted areas. I'll take Lieutenant Colonel Kash Kilbourne to India."

"You decide, general. Those officers report to you. A plane will pick you up later tonight and bring you to the Pentagon."

"I'll be ready."

Tucson packed a small duffel bag and went directly to the command tent. She entered and walked up to Preston and Kilbourne.

"Gentleman, I'm going to India and Bangladesh, along with Kilbourne. President Barlow made this deployment decision. Hawk, you are the commanding officer of restricted areas surrounding the orb. Protect it and the Hickory family. And be cordial to our three Russian visitors. The Pentagon and General Carr are watching everything that happens here, so be alert and professional."

"When do you leave?" Colonel Preston asked.

"Tonight."

A surprised Kilbourne said, "Do you mean tonight?"

"Yes, Colonel, I mean tonight. Get your bags packed and I'll meet you in the command tent in one hour."

CHAPTER 10
Celsus

"We need your help. We cannot cope with the millions of refugees trying to enter India," Ms. Indira Neelesh, the Prime Minister of India, said to start the United Nations meeting. "Much of Bangladesh is barely above sea level. The rise in sea-levels is taking away their homes and land, and the heat is killing them. We are using two thousand two hundred robotic Celsus warriors, one thousand one hundred drones, and twenty thousand Indian troops to block off our West Bengal border. But this is not enough; we need help."

"Long term, we need to build the refugees new cities and camps on higher ground," a general in the Bangladesh army added. "But in the short term, we need to stop the migrations and deaths. We estimate that six thousand four hundred refugees died last week. We cannot handle this crisis alone."

They held the United Nations meeting at noon on Friday, October 27. United Nations officials and military leaders attended virtually, using flat wall screens and others using holograms. Nineteen countries, including Australia, Bangladesh, China, and India, were present.

The situation at the India-Bangladesh border was a human atrocity. Every day counted—Bangladeshi refugees were dying. With no homes and little food or medicine, the refugees lived wretched lives.

"How can we help?" General Carr asked from his Pentagon office in Washington, DC.

"Sir, we need the UN peacekeepers to separate the refugees from the India border. Then, they can build a barrier with a buffer zone," the

Bangladeshi general said. "We need the Indian military to pull back from the border to avoid more military conflicts."

"Okay," Carr said. "What if the UN peacekeepers land in both Bangladesh and India and move toward the border? This will prompt the Indian and Bangladeshi militaries to retreat. Our UN troops will fill the void and begin creating the buffer zone. We'll build temporary housing and provide food and medical services for the refugees."

"Yes, we agree to this plan with two additions," the Bangladeshi general said. "First, we made a request to the UN earlier that US Army General Stephanie Tucson lead the UN troops. Given the orb events, she is a leader that everyone recognizes and respects. People on both sides will do what she says. Second, we want India to remove all Celsus warriors from the border as soon as possible. They are ruthless killers."

A Celsus warrior was a robotic soldier run by a quantum computer in its chest. It weighed two hundred thirty-five kilograms when armed. The warrior mimicked the human body in shape and stood at three meters tall. Its head used six cameras and four microphones to observe and communicate with people and its environment. There was no need for human-like ears, nose, or a mouth in its long cylindrical head. Each robot was made of a ceramic and stainless-steel composite with a tough, nanotechnology-based skin, and powered by a miniature nuclear reactor. Its hands could hold and fire several weapons and two guns were mounted in its back and rotated to the top of its shoulders.

The weapon's manufacturer named the robot warrior after Celsus, a third-century Roman anti-Christian philosopher. He hadn't understood why Christians would not take up arms or defend themselves. To Celsus, war seemed to be a logical way to resolve human disagreements.

The Bangladeshi general's requests resulted in prolonged silence.

General Tucson brought hope to the border crisis, while the Celsus warriors brought a callous fear. The autonomous robots had a long history of killing humans. Refugees knew the history of the Celsus warriors, and this was why they dared not cross the border.

"President Barlow granted you the first request," General Carr said at the UN meeting. "General Tucson is here with me in the Pentagon and will soon lead UN troops. Your second request is a decision that only the Indian leadership can make. It would be helpful if the Celsus warriors moved away from the border," General Carr said.

"I will agree to a two-phase retreat of our Celsus warriors," Prime Minister Neelesh said. "But only after our military generals approve each phase of the retreat. We must ensure they don't breach our borders."

"One last question," Carr said. "How many UN human troops, automated monitors, and drones do we need?"

"We've analyzed the situation," a Pentagon official said. "We recommend forty thousand UN troops, ten thousand ground-based electronic monitoring devices, and five thousand drones. An electronic fence will be built along the border using ground-based monitors and drones. The West Bengal portion of the India and Bangladesh border is two thousand two hundred kilometers long. Most migrations happen in the southern third."

"Does anyone object to the plan? If so, what are your recommendations? If not, I'll ask the UN to approve our plan and mission goals. The United States Army will commit eight thousand of our troops to this mission," General Carr said. He picked lint off his uniform as he waited for a response, but no one offered an objection to the planned deployment.

"Major General Stephanie Tucson will lead the UN troops," he said and turned to where she sat at the Pentagon table. "General Tucson, do you have anything to say?"

Tucson tilted her head back and collected her thoughts. She said, "I have worked with many of you before in Brazil and Turkey. You know how I work. We work together and avoid missteps and injuries. We'll get it done. Tomorrow, Lieutenant Colonel Kilbourne will lead the US contingent to Khulna, Bangladesh. I will go to Kolkata, India. We'll set up command centers at both locations. That's all I know for now."

Carr dropped his head and smiled. He knew he had picked the right officer to lead the initiative. World leaders would follow her.

The UN meeting ended; everyone said their goodbyes.

* * *

Tucson arrived in Kolkata, India, on Sunday morning, October 29. Three US Army LE-304 military cargo planes landed with them: one carried a mobile command center tent and equipment; a second carried human soldiers, nineteen US-made Tallis13 robot warriors, and two automatic Rapture laser guns; the third plane unloaded more troops and fifty Thanos B-2 robotic exoskeletons, which soldiers wore to augment their physical capabilities and firepower.

The Tallis13 warrior was similar in size to the older Celsus warrior. Tallis13 had a spherical head with a human-like nose and mouth, but no ears. Tallis13 had smarter software and learning algorithms, more powerful laser guns, and connections to orbital satellites and weapons.

A similar arsenal of equipment arrived in Khulna, Bangladesh. Lieutenant Colonel Kilbourne set up the command center, and by Monday morning, the two command centers were communicating with one another.

UN troops began arriving by plane, rail, and truck, but it would take a month to achieve the goal of forty thousand troops.

"Can we get these Celsus warriors moved away from the border?" Tucson asked a general from India. It was Monday afternoon, October 30, four days after Carr had called about her new deployment.

Driven by heat and sea-level rise, this mass migration had become one of five ongoing global migration tragedies. Bangladesh, like forty-six other countries, had nuclear weapons, so Tucson's number-one priority was to prevent a war, and then help the migrants.

Tucson arrived at the border by helicopter, accompanied by military officers from Germany, Japan, and India. No fences or barricades existed yet, only a weed-laden field with a few e-monitors and Celsus warriors. Kilbourne would arrive, accompanied by military officers from Argentina, China, and Bangladesh, by a United Nations truck convoy and meet them in that field.

With Tucson leading the way, the contingent of military officers walked toward the border, past a Celsus warrior. The robot turned toward where they stood, its steely eyes surveying companions, using facial-recognition software and UNet to identify each one of them.

Tucson stared at the robot. She knew little about Celsus warrior 4273, but it learned everything about her. UNet provided the warrior with not only her personal and career information, but also her behavioral profile. Warrior 4273 knew, for example, that on September 26, 2147 at 1209, she'd ordered a vegan hamburger with lettuce, tomato, and mayonnaise, but no onion. She'd e-paid for her favorite meal at the AFS store at 13541 Tarpon Avenue in Fort Campbell, Kentucky. To date, she had ordered the meal twenty-two times in 2147.

"General, it's a great honor to meet you. Thank you for coming," a skinny Indian officer said, breaking her stare-down with the robot. "The only reason the refugees don't storm our border is because they know the Celsus will kill them. These prodigious warriors have no souls. Our human soldiers understand the plight of the refugees and won't shoot, but the Celsus obeys only its creators and the State, not God."

"General Tucson, how are things?" came the voice of Lieutenant Colonel Kilbourne, talking on his communicator. "We're walking up to the border now."

"Good to hear your voice, Kilbourne."

Sixty UN armed soldiers and three US Tallis13 robot warriors cleared the crowd as they approached, and the two groups met at the border in an unnamed field.

The scars of human activity were everywhere on the land—trash, trampled and dead grass, human waste, and pitiful human souls searching for homes. After a while on the border, the rancid air smelled normal, but on first approach, it contained the awful smell of decay and death.

"We need to move the refugees back from the border," Tucson said to Kilbourne, standing side-by-side. "And we need to move these damn Celsus warriors back."

"Yes, general. I see the problem," Kilbourne replied as he looked at two menacing Celsus warriors, which were separated by one-half of a kilometer. Not much intimidated the young colonel, but he kept one eye on the warriors.

"We have enough troops to move these noncombatants back a kilometer. We should work in teams in both north and south directions," he said.

"Yes, I agree."

"Do we have enough fence and electronic monitors?" Kilbourne asked an officer from India.

"Yes, we have confiscated almost all the fence, wire, flags, and monitors in the state of West Bengal. We'll get more from other states too," the Indian military officer said.

"Okay, we'll build the buffer zone as we go," Tucson said. "In the meantime, try to provide food, water, and medical service to the refugees."

"They are a pitiful lot," Kilbourne said, looking back toward the refugees who were sweltering in forty-eight-degree-Celsius heat. Standing in front of the crowd was a malnourished boy of about ten years old and a younger girl. The boy weighed only twenty-five kilograms. He was wearing only a torn pair of dark cotton pants with no shirt. A filthy bandage covered his elbow. The little girl held his hand, her only source of security. The dance of death surrounded them.

The girl and boy were fighting with a larger group of children. Kilbourne ordered a soldier to break up the fight and bring the girl and boy to him.

"Why are you fighting?" Kilbourne asked the boy.

"We want to sleep under the bushes; they do too. We fight for shade."

"What are your names?"

"I'm Yash, and this is Rishita," the boy replied in broken English.

"Where are your parents?"

"We don't know our parents."

Upon hearing this, the captain took their hands and said, "If you go with us, we'll get you a shower, clean clothes, and food."

Tucson smiled as she watched Kilbourne walk away with the children. She had seen the plight of destitute people before, but the young and kindhearted Kilbourne had not.

Tucson walked back toward their helicopter, which was parked on India's side of the border. Kilbourne went to their UN trucks with the two children on the Bangladeshi side. "What happens to these people once we build the buffer zones and security fences? Once we feed them? Once we leave?" Kilbourne asked a Bangladesh officer.

"That's not for us to say. Your question is a political and economic question, not a military one."

As they drove off, Kilbourne shook his head, pondering the officer's answer.

* * *

Tuesday, two thousand more UN troops arrived in Kolkata, and one thousand five hundred in Khulna. Kilbourne worked in the command tent planning the deployment of the new troops. Their mandate was to focus on the southern part of the border.

"Lieutenant Colonel Kilbourne, we have a problem," a soldier said.

"What's the problem?"

"Sir, it seems a Celsus warrior approached the refugees, twenty steps or more, crossing into the Bangladeshi territory, scaring everyone. Our electronic fence data confirms this. The warrior turned its head around twice."

"That's odd," Kilbourne said. "It could be a shoddy computer module or programming error."

The warrior didn't need to turn its head because of the six cameras embedded in its cylindrical head. And its sensors could scan far beyond the ten meters to the border. The warrior held one twenty-caliber machine gun using metal bullets and one laser gun on its shoulders.

Turning to the soldier, putting on his combat helmet, Colonel Kilbourne asked, "Where did this happen?"

"Sir, ten kilometers south of here."

"Okay, let's check it out. Send a drone too."

The colonel assembled two UN trucks with soldiers armed with Teton 2 rifles and handguns, and two Tallis13 warriors.

They arrived at the Bangladeshi side of the site to find over two thousand refugees. It had rained earlier, so the migrants were searching for dry places to bed down for the evening, choosing spots on the ground, beside rocks or under bushes.

A bewildered Kilbourne made his way through the herd of refugees, each one begging for food and water. The troops moved among the malnourished bodies and weathered faces.

Once they arrived at the border, he saw a Celsus warrior standing guard on the Indian side. Behind the machine stood a dozen Indian soldiers. They jumped up as Kilbourne and his troops approached, but they dared not step in front of the Celsus warrior.

"We understand one of your Celsus warriors crossed the border," Kilbourne yelled from twenty meters away.

"Yes, this warrior may have crossed the border," an India officer replied. "We don't know why."

"Can you shut it down?"

"Sir, we cannot. Their software accepts orders only from our central command."

Kilbourne scanned the area, seeing families bedding down and kids playing soccer. He looked over at the Celsus warrior to find it watching him. To him, the warrior was only tolerating his presence.

At the same time, a drone from the command center arrived. It hovered fifty meters in the air, transmitting pictures back, as well as recording the surrounding sounds—refugees talking, sick or hurt adults moaning in pain, and children chattering and playing.

"Will you report the border breach and odd Celsus behavior to your commander?" Kilbourne asked.

"Yes, sir. We have."

"Good," he said, pausing for a moment to watch two dozen kids playing soccer. The kids were a ragtag bunch. One child's eye was infected. He had wrapped his head and upper face in a torn red T-shirt. Another child was wearing an old taqiya cap far too big for his head. One girl, barefoot and wearing her hair in a single braid, was wearing a tattered, muddy yellow dress that looked out of place in this Machiavellian world. They were close to the border, kicking a frayed soccer ball, the object itself being the only source of happiness in their lives.

"Let's go home."

Kilbourne and his soldiers began loading into their trucks.

Seconds later, a boy kicked the frayed ball over the invisible border. The kids followed it.

In an instant, Celsus warrior 4273 took a step forward. The humans had violated the border-protection rules. With no record of the migrants on UNet, the killer robot could not identify the intruders. In a loud, artificial male voice, it said, "Stop! You are in sovereign Indian territory. Go back across the border now!"

A few kids heard the warning, and in their native language, yelled, "Run, run, run!" Other kids kept playing soccer.

The kids ran in different directions, some going deeper into sovereign Indian territory. At this, the robot's head moved forward a few centimeters, viewing the intruders in visible and infrared light. It decided the kids had violated the sacred Indian border.

With methodical grace, the Celsus warrior raised its two shoulder guns. Without hesitation, it fired its weapons, the powerful bullets and laser shots hitting the children and nearby adults with cataclysmic force. The shots made shrill zipping sounds. When the shots hit human bodies, the drone's microphone picked up the sickly thud sounds.

Heads and bodies exploded. The kids continued to run for a moment, unaware of their fate. After five seconds of fury, the guns stopped. The damage was catastrophic.

Carnage replaced suffering. Survival replaced civility. Death replaced hope.

Hundreds of migrants ran away from the bloodshed as fast as they could. With mind-numbing fear, the Indian troops backed away from the Celsus warrior. They worried the horrific machine might turn its fury on them. Their hands and lips trembled. Beads of sweat flowed down their horrified faces. One soldier vomited onto his gun.

The Celsus warrior retracted the two shoulder-mounted guns, stepped backward and regained its sentry position, scanning the carnage for signs of life. It had fulfilled its mission without the curse of human emotion. It had protected the Indian border from intruders.

The drone's microphone picked up the screams of refugees and a few muted sounds of the victims moaning in pain. A few refugees were still alive, but no one helped them. The terrorized refugees had scrambled away from the border, and no one dared venture back into the killing field. The smoke from the gunfire swept over burnt bodies and the dismal battlefield.

Kilbourne and his troops heard the shots and ran back to the site of the massacre. Kilbourne ran to aid the wounded, dropping his rifle. One little girl was moaning in pain on the India side of the border. The shots had blown her foot off. Blood was pouring from her frail leg. She would die soon.

Oblivious to the surrounding danger, Kilbourne knelt down and took his belt off to use as a tourniquet.

His face and the front of his uniform were hidden from the Celsus warrior. He was now an unidentified soldier who had breached India's border. The Celsus warrior saw him as a threat.

"Stop! Stop!" a brave Indian officer yelled at Celsus warrior 4273. "These people do not threaten us!"

The warrior did not respond to the pleading. It raised its two shoulder-mounted guns and fired.

In less than a second, the shots obliterated Kilbourne's arm and shoulder. He looked up at his merciless assassin for an instant, but his youthful eyes soon became hollow. He fell to the ground on top of the girl. They died together.

The Celsus warrior again retreated to its sentry position. Kilbourne's troops took cover but didn't fire their weapons. The soldiers on the Indian side cowered behind military equipment and vehicles.

* * *

Suddenly, a blue orb appeared above Kilbourne's mangled body. It moved through the young officer's body, as if the orb wanted to capture Kilbourne's spirit. The orb exited his body and stopped beside it for a second. Next, the orb moved at a persistent pace toward Celsus warrior 4273.

At first, the warrior didn't recognize the volleyball sized orb as a threat; it was not in its databases. But soon it realized the orb was identical to the blue orb in the news and video reports in Kentucky. By then, the orb hovered three meters from the warrior and about two meters above the ground. The orb and Celsus warrior were facing one another.

Warrior 4273 raised its arms and deployed its two shoulder mounted guns, making a ratcheting sound. The orb stood in place as troops on both sides of the border hid behind vehicles or dove to the ground. The drone transmitted the video back to both command tents on each side of the border.

But Celsus warrior 4273 shoulder guns stopped before they reached the top of its shoulders. The robot's head, arms, and legs squeaked and thrashed as cameras and speakers were pulled back inside its head. Soon, all cameras and speakers had disappeared inside its head. Within a few seconds, its head twisted and growled as it became distorted and smaller, and collapsed into the trunk of the robot's body.

The robot's fingers and hands collapsed into its arms and its arms collapsed into its remaining body. Hydraulic cylinders and hoses broke and disappeared. Fluids leaked from the twisted metal frame as parts melted and burned. An invisible force sucked the heat and smoke into a growing ball of hot metal.

Soon the disfigured warrior became a black chunk of hot metal no bigger than a basketball as it continued to get smaller and smaller. The overhead drone used the zoom feature on its camera to follow the suspended and smoldering sphere of metal as it shrunk to the size of a marble, and then to a black grain of sand as it dropped to the ground.

Everyone who witnessed the collapse of the warrior into a black grain of sand couldn't believe their eyes. After the pandemonium subsided, the blue orb also vanished at an accelerated speed human eyes could not follow.

With the orb and warrior gone, the stunned troops creeped out of their hiding places and moved toward the massacre. They pointed their guns at disparate places and worked their way to the dead and dying victims. They dragged Kilbourne's body to safety and loaded it into a truck. A US soldier and medic in the truck checked for Kilbourne's pulse and said, "Kilbourne is dead."

"Get a shovel and dig up the ground where the Celsus warrior was standing," a German officer ordered. The soldiers found the one shovel of sand too heavy to lift. Using the shovel, two soldiers could not lift the soil into the container. The German officer tried to lift the shovel and soil, and to his surprise, couldn't lift the shovel. The officer turned toward the enlisted soldiers and said, "That grain of sand must weight hundreds of kilograms." He ordered a Tallis13 warrior to grab the shovel and lift the soil and gain of sand into a container, and then the container into a UN truck. The bewildered German officer and troops drove away in the truck.

* * *

On the India side, they called General Tucson to come to the command tent. She had been in another tent talking with United Nations officials about supplies they needed for their mission.

"What's going on?" Tucson asked as she entered the command tent.

"General, a Celsus warrior killed Lieutenant Colonel Kilbourne," a soldier said.

"Oh, no, no!"

She watched the drone video, and slammed her clenched fist into a table. Tucson put her hands over her face to hide her tears. Other soldiers were shaking their heads in disgust and some walking away to hide their grief. She replayed the video and sat down next to a computer for several minutes. No one approached her.

General Tucson had felt the anguish of fallen troops before, but she had brought the young officer here; it was her request. Maybe if Preston had come instead of Kilbourne, the older and wiser Preston would have avoided such a fate.

After a deep sigh and wiping tears from her face, Tucson began dictating an e-message to all UN troops and their commanders. It read:

"Today a Celsus warrior, a machine of our own making, assassinated at least sixteen people. Most of the dead were kids. Included in the death count is US Army Lieutenant Colonel Kash Kilbourne, who died trying to save a wounded girl. I plead with Prime Minister Indira Neelesh to withdraw all Celsus warriors from the border. I am sending a drone video of the massacre."

* * *

"I'm so sorry about Colonel Kilbourne," General Carr said Tuesday evening over a secure communication channel.

"Thank you, sir. I can't believe Kilbourne is dead," Tucson replied. "He was a wonderful young officer. Can you get me in touch with his parents?"

"Yes, Steph. I'll get the contact information to you." After a long pause, Carr continued, "It's good news they shut down the Celsus warriors. I have sent a thank-you message to Prime Minister Neelesh."

"Yes, the Celsus warriors are ruthless. It is a misapplication to use them to patrol borders or to monitor humanitarian initiatives. They are not programmed for those purposes," Tucson replied.

"I agree. But we must deal with the media. They like to focus on our missteps. But it's not your job to answer such questions. You had nothing to do with it. The Indian government and military used these lethal robots. Tell the media to ask them why they deployed such weapons to the border," Carr said. "Again, I am sorry Kilbourne died. I'm sure he was top notch."

"Yes, sir. He was a fine officer."

"Our scientist here in the Pentagon have studied the video and slowed it down. The blue orb entered and exited our reality using an Einstein-Rosen wormhole that opened and closed in 0.091 seconds. This is the first time in human history we have recorded an actual wormhole."

"Do they know how the Celsus warrior vanished?"

"Our scientist's preliminary theory is the orb created a tiny black hole inside the warrior that ate the warrior's body. They weighed each grain of sand in the soil sample and found one that weighed two hundred thirty-three kilograms."

"How can a single grain of sand weigh that much?"

"I know, Steph. I don't understand it either, but that's what their preliminary report says. They say the grain was almost infinitely dense."

In part of her final Celsus-massacre report, Tucson wrote to the United Nations, Pentagon and General Carr.

"The Celsus warrior is a magnificent weapon for war, but this advanced weapon is not appropriate to use in our quest to achieve humanitarian goals. Our factories produce a robotic soldier every few minutes. Every modern nation buys these autonomous machines. The machine is indifferent to moral and humanitarian considerations. There is not enough guidance from the creators and users regarding their use. They must develop better programming and learning algorithms. The Celsus massacre documents these failures in robot design and tactical decision-making."

"I applaud Prime Minister Indira Neelesh's decision to move the Celsus warriors away from the border. The UN peacekeepers will do everything they can to secure the border, prevent further hostilities, and provide care for the refugees."

With the Celsus warriors gone, occasional groups of Bangladeshi migrants entered India. The numbers were small compared to the millions seeking refuge, and India returned most migrants to Bangladesh. UN troops focused their energy on building the buffer zone, building latrines and camps, and caring for the refugees. The demand for humanitarian services far exceeded the troops' resources.

Even wealthy nations were reluctant to help solve the Bangladeshi refugee problem. Canada's prime minister said it best at a United Nations committee hearing: "Wealthy nations have too many financial obligations. The extra cost to mitigate climate change far exceeds our resources. The world's population exceeds ten billion people, and Bangladesh's population is two hundred fifty million. Sea-level rise has destroyed eleven thousand one hundred seventy square kilometers of Bangladeshi land, which—to put in comparable terms—is about the size of Delaware plus Rhode Island. The Bangladeshi government has collapsed. The refugee problem and the risk of war remain at the India-Bangladesh border."

Tucson continued to lead the UN mission in India and Bangladesh. She lay awake every night mourning Kilbourne's death. While eating dinner with officers from Germany, Japan, and India in the command tent, Tucson asked her fellow officers, "What could we have done to prevent Kilbourne's death?"

"General, Kilbourne ran into hostile fire to help the wounded child. He underestimated the Celsus Warrior. He was young and naïve. If we had been there, we would have tackled him," the India officer replied.

"Yeah, I agree."

CHAPTER 11
Third Encounter

"Mattie, things will work out," Tom said.

For Mattie, the gaiety of life was gone. The orb uprooted their lives upon its arrival, thirteen days ago.

Ethan sat beside his mother on the sofa, holding her hand. Jillian was curled up in a ball at the other end. The medical doctors treated the family and provided hope, but the intruder and Jillian's healing powers had brought back the fear that had plagued them.

"Mom, we'll be okay," Ethan said, trying to cheer up his mother.

"No, we won't."

Seeing Mattie like this upset everyone. Tom put his arms around her. Meanwhile, Jillian watched her family's confusion and pain, not quite understanding it herself. She had no memory of the orb encounters and only through videos and the soldiers' presence did she realize the magnitude of events. She curled up into a tighter ball.

"We can't escape," Mattie mumbled as she buried her face in Tom's chest.

"Mom, if Jillian can heal people, isn't that good?"

"Ethan, it's wonderful. But the entire world wants to see her now."

Ethan did not reply, contemplating his mother's wise answer.

"We can't solve this tonight," Tom said, "so let's eat. I'll get the army to send us some food."

"No, I'll cook," Mattie said.

"Not tonight. We'll eat, and watch a movie or educational show."

Within forty minutes, two soldiers were knocking on the front door, holding four meals. They ate in silence at the kitchen table, with the occasional whimpers from Mattie. There were no debates, laughter, or prayer. The only conversation focused on what leftovers to keep.

"Does anyone want to watch a movie?" Tom asked after finishing his meal.

"I'm going to take a couple sedatives and go to bed," Mattie said.

"Dad, I'm off to bed too," Jillian said. Ethan nodded in concurrence.

Within minutes, Tom found himself alone, sitting in his living room chair. He sat still for several minutes, contemplating his family's plight. He had studied the information Agent Sutherland had given them, so he better understood the witness protection program.

Sutherland's literature noted the government would search for small farms somewhere in the Montana to Kansas region, give them two or three location options, and buy the farm they wanted. He wondered what life would be like on a new farm out west. Their wall screens, websites, and communicators were inactive now, so he could only imagine what types of landscape and crops were grown in this region of the country. Without the aid of immersion reality technology, he thought about the mountains of Montana and the grasslands of Kansas. Once he had exhausted his memory of these areas, he headed upstairs, took sedatives and acid-reflux medicine, and went to sleep, tossing and turning throughout the night.

* * *

Colonel Preston, meanwhile, performed his duties in the command tent. He relished his command of all restricted areas in Bourbon County now that he was in charge. Earlier, he had a conversation with General Tucson and was informed of Kilbourne's death. He told Tucson he wished he had been at the India-Bangladesh border to help Kilbourne and acknowledged that Lieutenant Colonel Kilbourne was a good and promising officer.

At 2118, Tuesday evening, a real-time video streamed across his display screens, which showed two long ladders resting up against the outer restricted area's fence. Just after, a call came in from the field.

"Colonel Preston here."

"Sir," an excited soldier said. "A group of people are climbing over our fence. What should we do?"

"Fire shots in the air, and shoot tear gas at them," Preston said, running toward the tent exit. "I'll be there in three minutes."

He jumped into his Jeep and drove to the site. The Jeep's tires dug deep into the black dirt and the bluegrass gave way to the vehicle's superior force. By the time he arrived, demonstrators were at the top of the fence.

The air smelled of tear gas. A group of twenty soldiers were wearing gas masks. The glare of vehicle headlights illuminated the night sky.

Preston grabbed a gas mask and put it on as he ran the twenty meters toward the fence. Once at the scene, he pulled his revolver out of its holster.

Several soldiers ran up to him. "Colonel, what should we do?"

"Fire more gas canisters! And get me a megaphone!"

The troops fired more gas canisters into the crowd. Waves of hazy tear gas made it difficult to see. A toxic white fog engulfed the area. Eyes overflowed with noxious tears as people screamed and moaned in pain.

Without warning, a demonstrator jumped from the top of the fence. He landed on the sacred ground of the restricted area, the three-meter fall stunning him. He lay on the ground for a minute and then stood upright, as three armed soldiers had surrounded him.

The sturdy colonel walked out of the fog like a triumphant warrior with his gun drawn and holding it down to his side. He walked up to the demonstrator and yelled into his face, "What do you think you're doing, asshole?"

The demonstrator, still with his army-surplus gas mask on, tried to run away, but the soldiers grabbed both of his arms. Preston moved closer to the man and first pulled off the man's gas mask, and then his own. Both men were sweating and breathing hard.

Preston's face was red, and tears gushed down his face. He held his gun to his side, and put his nose close to the demonstrator's filthy nose. "Tell your people to stop breaching the fence and get off the ladders."

The lone demonstrator, who Preston could now see was wearing a "Behold the Orb's Rapture" T-shirt, gasped for air. Then, he spit in Preston's face. The ball of mucus landed on Preston's nose and slowly dripped on the ground.

In a surge of anger, the colonel pulled the trigger of his gun. *Bang!* The shot pierced the demonstrator's foot and dug itself into the ground. Heads turned toward the sound. Soldiers raised their guns.

The demonstrator fell to the ground, moaning. He held his bloody foot and shoe with both hands.

"Oh, I'm sorry. My gun went off. It was an accident," Preston said in a sarcastic tone. He turned toward his troops and said, "Get a medic."

Soon after, another demonstrator jumped down from the fence. Again, several armed soldiers grabbed him and put handcuffs around his wrists. They searched him for weapons, and dragged him to where the first demonstrator lay, who was still moaning in pain and holding his bloody foot.

Preston pointed his still-hot, smoking gun under the chin of the second demonstrator. With his nostrils flared, he said, "You have one second to get your people off the ladders, or my gun might go off again."

The man jumped up, ran the five meters to the fence, and yelled, "Stop! Stop! They shot Jabin!"

At this, the demonstrators stopped in their tracks and climbed off the two ladders. The tear gas continued to disperse, and a lot of the group coughed; a few even vomited.

"Take these two to our hospital for treatment. Then, arrest them and put them in our jail." Tears were flowing down Preston's face from the gas, but he was too mad to notice.

"Yes, sir," a soldier said.

The gas cleared enough for Preston to see the throng of demonstrators. He put his gas mask back on and walked up to the fence. Dusting off his uniform, still holding his smoldering gun, he said, "The guy you called Jabin got shot in the foot. We'll take him to our hospital. He'll be fine. He and the other guy who entered the restricted area are under military arrest. We'll get in touch with you later. Questions?"

None of the demonstrators said anything in response, but he could hear the crowd mumbling. Preston strolled back to his Jeep and drove off alone.

It was a painful sight as civilian doctors and ambulances began arriving to attend to people.

One staff sergeant standing among the troops lifted his gas mask. He said to his fellow soldiers, "Remember, it was an accident. Do you get that, soldiers?"

"Yes, sir," the troops replied.

Colonel Preston returned to the command tent, where he splashed water onto his face and washed his hands. He wet a towel and, sitting down on a steel folding chair, he cleaned the demonstrator's blood off his shoes. He clenched his fist several times in an attempt to relax his right hand, which had pulled the trigger, realizing he was the first military person to shoot an unarmed civilian here.

After taking a deep breath, he pulled his gun from its holster and unloaded it. The bullets dropped to the floor one by one. He heard each singular sound when each bullet hit the floor.

The one empty shell casing fell to the ground, still warm. He stared at it, feeling sweat drip off his face. He picked up the empty casing and reflected on what he had done. They trained US Army officers to fight in wars to protect the United States of America and its people, not to fight or shoot their own countrymen. He thought about the difficulty of policing public gatherings. Officers should not overstep military orders and mandates. He knew he had violated his orders. He had shot an unarmed civilian.

He speculated on what might happen to him and his sterling military record. His punishment could range from a mild reprimand to a reduction in rank. He realized the situation in India-Bangladesh was the same. Both were protection and peacekeeping deployments, not war.

At that moment, a soldier came up to him and said, "Sir, you did a good job of handling the breach situation. You can't see from our video exactly how your gun fired." She smiled at him.

"Thanks, Sergeant."

"Yes, sir. I thought you would want to know." She saluted him, turned, and walked back to her duty station.

* * *

In the early morning of Wednesday, November 1, the orb began acting strangely. Its light pulsed, and it moved up and down.

Colonel Preston was on duty in the command tent, watching the orb's odd behavior on a display screen. He had napped in a command tent chair, but never got much sleep.

"We better get the experts here," Preston said. "I'm going to the orb."

"Yes, sir," a master sergeant soldier replied, stepping away so he could relay the orders through his encrypted communicator.

Within ten minutes, scientists' Breslin, Rabab, Shreevallabh, and Xandra arrived, and they walked out to the site. They had studied the orb's system of equations now for two weeks and understood how they might terraform Earth's biosphere.

Overhead, two US Army automated drones circled the immutable orb. Without warning, one drone fired a burst of laser shots at it. The laser beams bounced off its surface, causing soldiers nearby, who were guarding the orb, to run for cover.

The drone continued to fire.

"Oh, no! Our stupid drone fired at the orb! Stop it! Stop!" Preston yelled, lying on the ground.

A soldier, who was lying next to Preston, used his communicator to order the command tent to stop the drone from firing. But before they could execute the order, the orb's blue light intensified and began to spin. Most of the soldiers ran farther away and took cover behind military equipment. But three soldiers and Colonel Preston remained on the ground within three meters of the spinning orb.

Twenty meters away, expert team members, the three Russians, and soldiers and telecommunications specialists hid behind military vehicles, equipment, and cargo boxes.

Suddenly, a powerful, unseen force pulled the drone downward, slamming it to the ground. It hit with a loud SMACK and THUD, and then burst into flames. Everyone ducked to avoid the hot debris.

But the orb continued to rotate faster and faster. The puissant gravitational forces warped spacetime around it. A thin, blue boundary had formed around and above the orb. Objects inside this twenty-meter diameter dome became twisted and distorted. Preston stared at his slightly warped hands and equipment inside the dome. The swirling magnetic energy field created a swirl of colorful lights.

"It's building a dome to protect itself," Dr. Breslin said, hiding behind a vehicle thirty meters away. The other scientists stood nearby. The thin, blue, and transparent dome had trapped Preston and three soldiers inside the dome.

"You got to be kidding me! This orb disarmed my army and now a dome. How the hell can that happen?" Colonel Preston yelled from where he lay on the ground, pulling grass from his mouth.

"I don't know, sir," a soldier lying next to him said.

In the command tent, outside the dome, the electronic gear began to flicker and military compasses were going haywire. As the electromagnetic field intensified, the devices in the command tent gyrated and moved beyond their measurement scales.

Watching the chaos from outside the dome, Dr. Breslin asked, "What is happening inside there?"

"The gravity inside the dome is becoming greater; some type of relativistic effect," Dr. Xandra said.

"Yes, don't challenge the orb; it's defending itself," Dr. Rabab added.

"If the gravity is strong enough, there may be a time dilation effect inside the dome," Dr. Shreevallabh said.

Two soldiers, standing outside the dome, flipped the safeties off their rifles and handguns, and probed the thin, blue wall that defined the protective dome. They used their rifles to hit the dome. BANG! BANG! But they could not penetrate the boundary with either their bodies or rifles.

"We can't get inside," a soldier yelled to the scientists.

"My instruments measure the dome at twenty meters in diameter," Dr. Shreevallabh said.

Soon, the orb stopped spinning, but the thin, blue boundary remained. Preston and the three soldiers tried to exit but could not. Preston hit his handgun on the dome's inside surface, making a heavy banging sound inside the dome. But outside the dome, they heard nothing.

"We're trapped," Preston said, turning toward the dismayed soldiers inside the dome.

"What did Colonel Preston yell? Breslin asked.

"We can't hear them. They'll run out of air soon. What can we do?" Xandra said. Expert team members huddled together discussing what to do as the Russians recorded everything.

* * *

Jillian woke up and walked to her parents' bedroom. She approached the bed and reached an arm out for her mom. Mattie woke up and turned toward her.

"Mom, the orb needs me."

"What? Uh, now?" Mattie asked as she rolled over to check the time. The clock showed 0140. Tom sat up and looked at Jillian.

"What's the problem?" he asked.

"Daddy, I must see the orb."

They got dressed and called Stoner and Claiborne, who escorted the family past the main gate. Jillian's request was not challenged as no one wanted to block an opportunity for humanity to learn from the orb.

When they entered the command tent, they found it in disarray. A Sergeant Major hurried up to them and said, "One of our drones fired at the orb, its laser shots bouncing off it. We mistakenly set the drone's software on autonomous decision making instead of "approval mode," so the drone would seek officer approval before firing. It perceived the orb as a threat. It's our error. Now Colonel Preston and three soldiers are trapped inside a dome. It's not safe out there."

"But the orb needs me," Jillian said. "It won't hurt us."

"We should go out there," Tom said. "Maybe that's what the orb wants. Jillian can rescue them."

"Okay, let's go," the sergeant major said. "Put on your protective goggles."

Jillian approached the dome's barrier, where, within, the orb slowly rose in the air and moved toward her. Jillian stepped into the barrier courageously, and it allowed her to pass through into the dome. This time, no one tried to stop her. The four people inside the dome and those outside all watched as the dome's thin blue boundary, making a zapping sound, vanished. A slight blast of air rushed pass the bystanders due to the pressure differential inside versus outside the dome.

Jillian paused and looked back at her parents. She stepped next to the orb. It nudged itself toward her, and without hesitation, it entered her body as it had done before. The crowd watched in awe as a thin blue halo surrounded her youthful body.

Jillian turned toward the expert scientists, and in an innocent voice, said, "*You must terraform your planet, or you will not survive. We transmitted the knowledge you need to do this during our last encounter. Now you must build megamachines to implement this knowledge.*"

After a moment of quiet, Jillian added, "*We need to send you the plans to build the megamachines. Do you have a computer to accept the transmittal?*"

"Yes, we do," Dr. Breslin answered. He laid the quantum computer on the ground in front of Jillian shrouded in a thin, blue hallo. She looked down at it and lifted her arm, her palm facing it. A bolt of blue light emerged from her hand, and it hit the computer, sending blueprints and equipment specifications embedded in the beams of light.

After a few seconds, the beam stopped. Jillian dropped her hand and said, "*You now have the blueprints and specifications to build the megamachines. You must place them at all major latitude and longitude intersection points, below sixty degrees latitude north and above sixty degrees latitude south. You must build at least two hundred sixteen megamachines. Given that your oceans cover 70.8 percent of Earth, you need one hundred fifty-three ocean-based machines and sixty-three land-based machines. These will take heat and greenhouse gases out of the ocean and atmosphere.*"

"Why Earth-based machines? Why not huge reflectors orbiting Earth that block sunlight?" Dr. Shreevallabh asked.

Jillian turned her head toward the nervous expert and said, "*Humanity does not yet have the anti-gravity capability or energy to execute large spaced-based solutions to Earth's profound climate change. For instance, how antigravity works still mystifies humanity and controlling the shields is difficult. And your planet's governments must agree on a fair and equitable reflector shield plan. Who receives sunlight, how much, and when?*"

"Can you give us the technical knowledge?" Shreevallabh asked.

"*In time, you will master anti-gravity and harness your star's energy, but first you must survive and master Earth's biosphere.*"

Antigravity generators and propulsion systems were an attractive idea but still only resided in research laboratories. The physics of gravity had a fundamental glitch in humanity's formulation. It would take humans centuries to discover the flaw and correct it.

Designing and implementing a Dyson sphere, for example, was far beyond current human capability. The Dyson sphere was a megastructure that surrounded all or part of a star and captured its energy. The struggling human species had not mastered such technologies, and the orb knew it. As such, the orb tailored the megamachine technology to human's current capabilities.

Dr. Breslin approached and asked, "How long to complete the megamachines?"

"No more than fifty Earth years. Others have done it faster."

"What if humanity cannot do these tasks?" Dr. Xandra asked, stepping out of the crowd, her hands clasped together over her chest.

"Your species will not survive unless you act now. The paradise of Earth is becoming barren and hot. Earth's biosphere will regenerate itself over millions of years, but not before your species becomes extinct."

"How do you know?" Breslin asked.

Jillian turned toward Breslin serenely and stared into his eyes. "We see this in ways you can't understand. Time is an illusion unique to each space-time arena. One day you may understand time as we do. But first you must survive."

"Who is 'we'?" Breslin asked.

Jillian and the orb, the ultimate symbiotic relationship, saw humanity's frustration in his question. She looked at Breslin as if she were considering whether to answer his question or not. Silence prevailed.

"What are you?" he asked instead.

"Before there was nothing, we prevailed. We created what you humans see, know, and don't see. We live as a form of pure energy."

After speaking those words, the orb retreated from Jillian's body. The thin blue halo vanished, and Jillian slowly fell to the ground, where she remained lying on her side, unconscious.

Everyone expected the surreal orb to retreat to its original position, as it had in the past, but this time it moved away, hovered above the crowd for a few seconds, and then, with no warning, it vanished. In an instant, in a brilliant white flash of light, the orb disappeared. At the same time, a pulse of energy resonated outward from the flash of light.

The humans turned away from the pulse as a slight vibration surged through the air. The departure happened in the blink of an eye. Their meager human senses needed time to process and recognize what had happened. Had it left? Where was it now?

"The genius of the orb is gone," Dr. Shreevallabh said, dropping her arms to her sides.

"Yes, it's gone," Dr. Breslin said, "and with it, hope."

He and others searched the heavens for any sign of the object. They saw only scattered low-lying clouds passing by and a few untouchable stars and galaxies light-years away.

Sadness overwhelmed them. Humanity was alone again.

"It's over, Madia," Breslin said after a moment of deliberation. "Now we must do our best to interpret what it gave us."

"Yeah, I agree," she replied, taking a deep breath.

With the protective dome gone, Tom and Mattie rushed over to where Jillian had collapsed, lying on the ground. Tom picked her up and held her, kneeling. Within a minute of his embrace, she opened her eyes. With no hesitation, she murmured, "What happened, Daddy?"

As with previous encounters, she showed no signs of having any memory of the event or any sickness. Sergeant Stoner handed Mattie a bottle of water, who gave it to Jillian to drink.

After a brief medical exam, Stoner and Claiborne escorted the Hickory family back to their home.

* * *

"Soldiers, go back to your units; get some sleep. We'll get new orders soon," Preston said, after the Hickory family had left.

Preston began his last meaningful trip back to the command tent, while the three Russians walked to the site of the orb. They used their handheld instruments to test the air and soil, but no one cared now about what they were doing.

People began to leave the sacred site. Television crew members packed their cameras and equipment. Others remained standing, looking upward in the hope the orb would return. But the night sky offered no remedy; it hid the orb in dimensions that humans could not see.

"I assume the video streamed live around the world?" Preston asked a soldier in the command tent.

"Yes, Colonel. There is a two-minute delay in transmission in case something threatens national security. Otherwise, the world is seeing real-time video."

"Good."

Preston turned toward his soldiers in the command tent and said, "Soldiers, thank you for your work. We did our job. Tell the troops we stay put until new orders arrive. Understood?"

"Yes, sir," the soldiers said in unison.

* * *

Colonel Preston received orders from General Carr by sunrise Wednesday, November 1 to disband the outer restricted area first and move the troops and equipment back to Fort Campbell, Kentucky. Once done, the inner restricted area would be dismantled except for the two platoons from the first battalion who were protecting the Hickory farm and home.

President Barlow showed third encounter videos to the world and announced the orb had left. Within hours, the blueprints and specifications for the ocean- and land-based megamachines were disseminated to a global audience.

Outer security fences and gates were taken down and the trucks loaded. The concrete traffic barriers and a few latrines were the sole remnants of the orb's visit. Four battalions of the 303rd Army Infantry

Regiment also dismantled the mobile hospital and many tents used for housing, equipment maintenance, and storage.

At the site, the public began to hear rumors that the orb had left and watched the soldiers dismantling the security fences and gates. Most didn't believe the rumors, at first. If true, many of the crowd's prophecies and hopes were dashed. Had the orb left them? What had happened to Armageddon? Was humanity alone again?

Early Thursday morning, Sergeant Rajeev Biswas was once again talking with the untidy T-shirt merchant. The merchant had been trying to sell his bloated inventory of T-shirts at discount prices, mostly to soldiers; they were his biggest customers now.

Troops had walked outside the outer restricted area and dodged trash, mudholes, and abandoned shelters. Biswas saw that two soldiers were buying T-shirts and coffee mugs. One T-shirt had "Nemesis Is Coming" printed on the front. The coffee mug's print read, "Armageddon Begins October 18, 2147."

"Did the orb really leave?" the merchant asked.

"Yes, it left," Biswas said with a smile as he searched through the piles of T-shirts. He was looking for gifts for his grandchildren. "Do you still believe the apocalypse is coming?"

"Yes, it's coming, but not as soon as we thought."

"What do you mean?"

"Well, the orb is the first sign; there will be others."

"Is your group ever wrong?" Biswas asked with a chuckle.

"Not in my lifetime. But I've still got to sell T-shirts, my friend," he replied with a hearty laugh.

"Do you think the orb is divine?"

The merchant didn't answer for a moment, folding and boxing up several T-shirts and then finally, with a sneer, he replied. "I'm an atheist. There is no God, only our pitiful daily struggle. That's why I sell T-shirts."

Biswas nodded. He stuck out his hand and said, "Good luck, my friend."

A hardy handshake ensued. Afterward, the sergeant turned and headed back to the structured life of the US Army. He returned to his family with hope, honor, and a sense of purpose to life. The T-shirt merchant returned to the unorganized life of a gypsy merchant. The merchant had no faith, no place to go, and a truck full of T-shirts. Either way, human life was frail, and both the merchant and Biswas knew it.

Thursday, the military armada drove back on the same highways by which they had come. Groups of people waved American flags as they passed, cheering them on. This time, the public knew their purpose, and the troops were proud of their duty to both their country and humanity. They had allowed the orb to deliver and disseminate its message.

"Thank you for a superb performance," General Tucson said to her regiment in an electronic message from India.

The demonstrators and public crowds packed up and left their campgrounds, leaving local, state, and federal branches of government to manage the trampled grounds. Trash trucks, bulldozers, and portable latrine vendors rumbled across the rolling bluegrass fields trying to clean up the area.

* * *

The world was trying to understand what had happened regarding the orb's exit. Television cameras had captured the sequence of events and videos of the orb's departure circled the globe.

At 1400 on Thursday, the US Army and a few international experts held their last media event. A vacant military tent in the inner restricted area served as the forum, and the expert panel sat at portable tables. Dr. Breslin, Dr. Xandra, Dr. Shreevallabh, and Dr. Rabab were now famous for their roles on the international review team. About twenty reporters attended, their cameras recording.

Dr. Breslin began the news conference by passing out a one-page press release.

"Our team has analyzed the video of the orb leaving. We studied the video frame by frame. Before we open up for media questions, a few of our observations are summarized in the press release."

The orb exited our reality through a one-meter wide wormhole that opened and closed in 0.112 seconds.

The wormhole disturbed Earth's magnetic field for almost two seconds.

Those trapped inside the dome, Colonel Preston and three soldiers, are 1.42 nanoseconds younger than the people outside the dome due to the immense gravitational forces.

It remains unknown how much energy is needed to create such a wormhole.

"What questions do you have for us?" Breslin asked.

"What is a wormhole?" one reporter asked.

"In the simplest of terms, a wormhole uses an immense amount of energy to alter the fabric of space-time. It creates a link, sort of like a tunnel, between two points in space, regardless of how far apart they might be. They can be nanometers away from one another or between galaxies—or, theoretically, between different universes or space-time arenas of consciousness," Breslin replied.

"Dr. Breslin, do you believe the orb is divine?" another reporter asked, standing up.

"Like most of humanity, the review team had a wide disparity of hypotheses on the origin of the orb. I am a religious man. My opinion is God sent the orb as a savior and not in human form this time."

"Could it originate from an alien race?" another reporter asked.

"Yes, it is possible," Dr. Rabab replied, and Dr. Shreevallabh nodded in agreement. "One could make a compelling argument that an advanced civilization has visited Earth in the past. It monitors Earth and our species and now foresees our extinction. Aliens may evaluate Earth's climate better than we can. And they might be capable of creating their own wormhole using the energy of their host star to travel through space-time and connect our two worlds."

"Was the orb a biological being?" the same reporter asked.

"The orb was not biological," Dr. Xandra said, trying to answer the question. "Our spectral analysis showed no living cells, not in the terms of how we define life. The wavelength of the blue light was 480 nanometers. Our analyses using other equipment were inconclusive. The orb appears to be pure energy, with no measurable mass. Whatever it was, it can travel through time and space without complications. The orb was like a spirit—godlike."

"Would our instruments recognize a different life-form or God anyway?" the reporter asked.

"No, I suspect not," Xandra replied.

"Why should we care where the orb and its transmittals came from?" another reporter, sitting in the front row, asked. "Isn't the goal to save the earth from overheating?"

"Yes, you are correct. We don't know the origin of the orb. I doubt we will ever know," Breslin answered, thumbing his ear in thought. Then, he cleared his throat and announced, "Ladies and gentlemen, this media event is now over. We do not have many answers so far, but we'll study the knowledge the orb transmitted. If valid, and if our governments support it, we will build the recommended two hundred sixteen megamachines. Please be patient with the scientific community. It will take time to sort out. We have much work to do. Good day."

CHAPTER 12
Pyrrhic Victories

Agent Sutherland called the Hickory family on Thursday; they agreed to the government's witness protection proposal. The process to change identities would begin at once. She told them to pack eight suitcases and they would first go to Fort Knox Military Reservation in Kentucky, the headquarters of the US Army's Seventh Cavalry and Armored Division. The US government would maintain the farm for them while they learned their new identities and way of life.

The next day, on Friday, November 3, the Hickory family were to have their last dinner in their beloved farmhouse, the military-prepared meals brought by Stoner and Claiborne.

"Mrs. Hickory, we have your meals," Stoner said when Mattie opened the front door.

"Please set them down on the kitchen table."

Tom got up from his living room chair and shook the troops' hands, while Mattie gave the soldiers a hug. "Sergeant Stoner and Corporal Claiborne, thank you for all you've done for us. Our family is forever grateful."

Meanwhile, Ethan walked over to the two soldiers and said, "Thank you for taking care of us," and held his hand out to them to shake, which they did.

Claiborne walked over to Jillian, stooped down, and said, "Young lady, it's been an honor to serve and protect you. I'll never forget what you did here."

Stoner crouched down beside his colleague and held the girl's hand. "Jillian, thank you for being so strong."

The two soldiers walked to the front door, giving the family friendly salutes before they left the house. Everyone knew the family's old life had slipped away.

Mattie didn't give the family time to contemplate their departure, instead announcing, "Kids, let's eat."

Tom opened up the containers of food and inspected the contents. "We should warm up the gravy and mashed potatoes," he said.

Mattie put the containers in the convection oven, saying, "Sit down. I'll bring the potatoes to the table."

The family held hands in prayer.

"Tom, can you do the honors? I can't do it," Mattie said.

Tom began the prayer. "Dear God, bless this land we stand on for the last time. My father and grandfather farmed this land. We loved our life here. We hope we can regain the joy we found here, somewhere else. Protect us and keep us safe. In God's name, amen."

Mattie toyed with her food for a while and then stood up, and said, "I can't eat. I'm going to lie down upstairs."

She made it to the top of the stairs before she began crying.

The family heard her. Standing up, Tom said, "Kids, I'm going to help your mother. I'll eat my food later. Don't throw it away."

Before he entered their bedroom to console his wife, he stood for a moment in the hallway. He was sweating. He felt powerless. It wasn't the first panic attack he'd had this week but he hoped it would be the last. After a few minutes, his heart rate slowed down, and the tension subsided. He finally entered the bedroom and hugged Mattie, who was sitting on the bed.

By the end of the day, they had stacked eight suitcases in the foyer and living room. As well as clothes and essentials, they had filled the cases with important keepsakes such as quilts and Christmas ornaments Mattie and Ethan had made, making sure that none of them had their names on them or any other identifiable markings.

* * *

Mattie took on the painful task of deciding what items to keep or destroy. The kids wanted to take every item, picture, and toy they'd ever owned. Earlier, she would destroy any items with logos, pictures, or names on that might trace their origins back to Bourbon County or Kentucky.

Tom and Mattie gave those items to Stoner and Claiborne. The two soldiers would burn them in a trench at night behind the greenhouse. The family's past went up in smoke. They even destroyed Tom's trusted living room chair because it had been on television during news reports.

What a dreadful job, Stoner and Claiborne thought.

"Mom, I want to take my first-grade picture," Jillian said, standing in her bedroom Friday morning, gripping the photo frame against her chest.

"Why, Jilly?"

"I want to remember my friends."

Mattie hugged her.

After the hug, Jillian asked, "Mom, will I ever see my classmates again?"

As soon as Jillian asked the horrific question, Mattie knew the disgusting answer. The truthful answer gave Mattie a woeful heart and a throbbing headache.

With a heavy sigh, Mattie replied, "Not for a while. The government wants to hide us. But if you want to take the class picture, I'll ask the government if we can keep it."

Mattie didn't have the heart to throw away the picture in front of Jillian. So, she walked into her master bedroom and the privacy of her bathroom and locked the door. She pulled the treasured picture out of its frame, tore it to shreds, and flushed it down the toilet. She sat down on the bathroom floor, holding the empty picture frame in her lap, and wept, both hands covering her face.

That evening, Ethan said, "Mom, is the government going to take Titan?"

"Yes, I'm sure Titan will go with us."

By 2100, all family members were trying to sleep, exhausted from the stress of the day. With Jillian becoming the voice of the orb, the family had paid an unbearably cruel price.

* * *

At 0120 on Saturday, Stoner knocked on the front door.

"Mr. Hickory, the helicopter is here. Please wake up your family." He looked at the suitcases in the hallway. "Sir, is this the luggage you want to take?"

"Yes, these suitcases, and don't forget Titan."

Titan would travel with the family. Tom thought the goat would enjoy escaping the perceived oversight of Atticus and Ethel, remembering how jealous he was of the farm bots. He wondered whether Atticus and Ethel would miss them, but he knew the answer. Once the family left the farm, the government would reprogram the bots. Then, their artificial friends would have no memory of them. And Tom knew, sooner or later, Agent Sutherland would want to separate Titan from the family to help protect their identity.

Four soldiers carried the luggage out the front door to where the black helicopter stood in the open field next to the greenhouse. Titan wore a loose leather muzzle on his nose and mouth and a leash tied to his collar. Beside him was a bag of feed pellets and some raw broccoli, a gift from Stoner and Claiborne.

The Hickory family came to the field and waited to board. Preston shook hands and hugged them, and then escorted them onto the helicopter. That small group of humanity would forever be bonded together.

Once loaded, the machine started its electric engines. There were no loud, choppy sounds. An engine-noise suppression system and the electric motors made the helicopter hum.

The big helicopter rose into the air against the darkness of night. Only its small red, green, and white beacon lights gave any hint that it existed. Within a minute, the dark shadow had rose from the ground, carrying the Hickory family and their possessions. The helicopter vanished into the darkness, as did the lives of the Hickory family.

The orb and the helicopter's departures were much alike: fast, silent, and mysterious.

"They are free now," Preston said, standing with a group of soldiers.

* * *

By 0900 Saturday, the troops had pulled the last stake of the command tent out of the ground. The soldiers rolled up the tent and loaded it onto a military semi-truck.

Communication dishes mounted on trucks and other equipment were already on the road home to Fort Campbell. By late afternoon, the inner restricted area had been dismantled.

Almost three hundred troops of the first battalion would leave Bourbon County with Colonel Preston. Sixty-two soldiers in two platoons remained on the Hickory farm to protect it and the empty home. The troops spaced out their tents and slept on the ground.

After the troops left, dozens of civilian vehicles drove down Dura Road, and people began to walk on the field the orb had occupied. It became hallowed ground.

The only signs of humanity's visit to the site of the orb were hundreds of concrete barriers that scattered the rolling hills, deep tire tracks in the ground, and oil and tire stains that crumbled Dura Road. The lush, peaceful bluegrass fields had given way to stampedes of hopeful people and their heartless vehicles. However, nature would replenish the trampled bluegrass on its own time scale.

The majestic oak tree had survived the orb's arrival. The wise and adaptive tree had seen the comings and goings of other life-forms and human beings before. Recently, the American Indians had shared the oak tree's place in the universe and now a motley crew of humans. The oak tree, a carbon-based life-form, was a survivalist. It had seen the folly of the human species and its disregard for planet Earth and its life-forms.

The wise oak tree was more adaptable than those disrespectful humans, and in some mysterious way, the tree knew it. It could feel the beauty and wonder of planet Earth, and knew the Earth itself was conscious in its own way, and that all things are connected. Humanity doesn't always see this, but the astute and judicious tree did.

Marty and Luke, Bourbon County's deputy police officers, were some of those that stationed their vehicle in the field. They didn't stop the onlookers and news media vehicles from examining the site. The intelligent life-form had left no evidence of its visit. In fact, the orb had technically never touched Mother Earth.

Several organizations and their leaders including the State of Kentucky, the White House, the United States Historical Association, and the United Nations discussed how they might preserve the Bourbon County site. They realized the orb's visit and this site marked a turning point in human history. Now humanity knew without a doubt that somewhere in the universe intelligence existed that far surpassed their own. The supreme intelligence was conscious, benevolent, and wanted humanity to survive. But this same intelligence challenged humanity, and its governments and organizations, to work together to terraform Earth.

* * *

Meanwhile, the UN established four international review teams to evaluate the technical merits of the orb's transmittals. They formed two independent teams called Alpha and Beta. Many of the original members of the on-site scientific team were part of the teams, including Doctor's Jalan Breslin, Madia Rabab, Edha Shreevallabh, and Chao-xing Xandra.

The Alpha and Beta teams wrote independent reports, their focus being on the validity of the chemical, physical, and thermodynamic systems of the equations. Then, the two teams combined to debate their independent conclusions and to write a summary report for worldwide distribution.

Two additional teams, Omega and Delta, studied the megamachine designs and specifications. Team Omega focused on building the one hundred fifty-three ocean-based megamachines, which would take greenhouse gases and heat out of the oceans, while Team Delta critiqued the design and specifications of the sixty-three land-based megamachines. These teams also wrote independent reports, before joining to create a summary report.

On December 4, the combined teams submitted their first report in a meeting at the UN headquarters. The thirty-two members nominated Dr. Breslin to present their findings.

"For the past month, we have studied the information the orb provided. The 249-page report documents much more information than I cite here, so please read the full thing. A link to it is available on the front page of the United Nations' website."

"Before we summarize what our expert teams concluded, I'd like to show the audience a graph that is in our report. The graph is based on ice cores drilled several kilometers deep between the years 1980 to 2040. Scientists have analyzed the air bubbles in these samples, and documented the carbon dioxide concentration and temperature back one million years. This graph documents global temperature changes. Notice the impact of human activity in the last few hundred years with a temperature increase of over three degrees Celsius. This great a temperature change has happened so fast."

"The correlation is high between carbon dioxide levels per million and temperature change. Carbon dioxide concentrations now average five hundred four per million. We know from these graphs that humanity finds itself in a death spiral of its own making. The orb and its knowledge are our last chance to avoid extinction. We need to terraform our planet using these megamachines."

"We find the orb's transmittals to be beyond human knowledge of physical phenomena. The orb's transmittals differ in two important ways. First, they provide an intricate system of equations. They tie all aspects of planetary heat generation and dissipation together. Second, the equations include second- and third-order interaction effects, something we didn't understand."

"We marvel at the mathematical elegance and wisdom of this knowledge. It is clear, harmonious, and profound—and we conclude it is valid. Also, to optimize certain variables, we can solve the orb's system of equations backwards. We can set target levels for global carbon dioxide and methane, for example, or set target heat levels for our planet. We can begin to design and engineer Earth's climate. With the orb's help, we can terraform our home and protect it. Thanks to the orb, we can be masters of our own fate."

"After this meeting concludes, you can meet the Alpha and Beta teams in the media room for one hour. We'll try to answer your questions."

The audience gave Dr. Breslin a standing ovation. The other team members onstage also stood, clapped, and shook hands.

Teams Omega and Delta would present their summary report after lunch.

When the meeting reconvened, Dr. Hwei-ru Zhuang, one of the foremost experts in thermodynamics and radiant energy, spoke.

"We studied the blueprints and specifications for the ocean- and land-based megamachines. Both machines have the capability to take heat and greenhouse gases out of our oceans and atmosphere. They generate electricity and beam heat out into space as radiant energy, and use solidified capsules to sequester greenhouse gases. Our general conclusion is that these machines can reduce greenhouse gases and take heat off our planet. With these, we can terraform our planet's biosphere."

"Before I continue with our findings, I must tell you that our teams also examined another alternative—that is, the feasibility of using an orbiting reflector shield around the earth or sun. The cost is more than the cost of building two hundred sixteen megamachines as the surface area of the reflector shield required to cool the earth is immense. We would not have the technical capability to deploy and adjust an orbiting shield such as this. As the orb suggested, we do not yet understand antigravity. We need to build antigravity or antimatter propulsion systems. Such propulsion systems would allow us to place a vast amount of shields and equipment in space. Our conclusion is that a solar shield option in 2147 is not workable."

"Let's examine an earthbound solution. Please direct your attention to the rotating holograms to my left. These holograms are models of the land- and sea-based megamachines. You will also find these holograms, blueprints, and specifications on the United Nations' website."

"Each ocean-based machine is two hundred meters square and one hundred meters high. The ocean-based machines float. They would take heat out of the ocean, convert this heat to electricity and radiant energy, and then this will be sent out into space by a powerful and constant beam of radiant energy. Mid-infrared-range energy in the eight- to thirteen-micrometer wavelengths would be used. These wavelengths have an unusual property that allows them to escape Earth's atmosphere. This window into space is one way to deposit Earth's heat, though it would require that earthbound airplanes, rockets, and ships must avoid this airspace."

"The machine would also collect greenhouse gases from the ocean and atmosphere. It would sequester the gas into a fiber cobweb within the capsule. One capsule can absorb four hundred twenty-eight times its own weight in greenhouse gases, and these have a final designed density of nine grams per cubic centimeter. They are as heavy as gold."

"A designed catalyst molecule would solidify the greenhouse gases in the fibers. We'd eject the solidified capsule into the ocean at minimal transportation cost. The process is not reversible. Capsules remain intact for at least one million years."

"The catalyst and this system are a brilliant design. We thank the orb for its supreme intellect."

"The land-based machine is two hundred meters square and two hundred meters high, and would take heat from the atmosphere. It would also convert heat to electricity and radiant energy. We'd beam radiant energy into space. The land-based machines would use a process like that of the ocean-based machines to take greenhouse gases out of the atmosphere. It would sequester the gases into smaller solidified capsules, and we could stack and store the capsules above or underground. The solidified material is not a molecule found in nature, so it would not degrade for at least a million years. It's impervious to natural forces."

Dr. Zhuang cleared her throat. The audience was stone quiet, listening to every word she said.

"The issue is not the technical feasibility of these megamachines. If built, these machines will work. The orb provided us with the knowledge and blueprints to terraform our planet."

"The problem is the cost to build two hundred sixteen megamachines. Our preliminary estimate is that one ocean-based machine will cost ð665 billion ecoins. A land-based machine will cost ð782 billion. So, with one hundred fifty-three ocean-based machines and sixty-three land-based machines, this adds up to ð151.1 trillion ecoins. In addition, we estimate service and operating costs would be four trillion ecoins per year."

"A second problem is the enormous amount of heat and carbon dioxide already locked up in our oceans and atmosphere. It will take a century to reduce this. This is the grim gift previous generations gave us, but it is one humanity must eradicate else we will become extinct. In the short term, the effects are irreversible. Even if we build these machines and they work, we still face troubling times. The orb knows this, and that is why it came to Earth. It knows we must act now to save our species."

"To do this monumental task, each nation must stop all heavy infrastructure construction. We must reassign our resources. The cost is high but not unattainable. It is a Pyrrhic victory for humanity. We now have the knowledge to terraform our own planet. The cost is enormous, but it's better than extinction. Our teams ask humanity, 'Do we have the political will to make this happen?' The adversary is not the technology but ourselves."

Dr. Zhuang smiled at the audience, which gave her a standing ovation. She bowed her head to acknowledge the approval, then walked away from the podium.

* * *

The Hickory family lived a stark existence at Fort Knox. A five-room military concrete-slab house with sixty-nine square meters of living space greeted them. Ugly, weathered linoleum covered the floor, and rays of daylight struggled to pass through the single-pane windows. The military delivered all food, ran their errands, and doctors visited them at their house. The fenced in backyard of the house was their only chance to be outside. The government did provide them with new wardrobes and connections to all entertainment channels. A personal trainer paced the family through morning exercises.

After weeks at Fort Knox, the Hickory family moved to new quarters, a modest home in a middle-class suburb in Peoria, Illinois, and learned how to live a lie. They were now the Giffords, hailing from Waynesboro, Virginia. The new identities for the family members included fake birth certificates, school records, and voter registrations. The government also built a new electronic identity for each family member. They rehearsed their fake backgrounds twice a day with nameless government coaches. They redefined their existence.

The family struggled with their new identities. Tom, who now went by the name of Chris, grew a beard and dyed his hair black. Mattie, now Arianna, changed her hair from blonde to auburn, and learned to wear a different style of women's clothing, a more formal Virginia country-lady style. Plastic surgery altered some of their facial features.

At government expense, teachers homeschooled Jillian and Ethan, using their new first names only, Briana and Dex.

Mattie learned to dye Jillian's natural blonde hair a dark brown, while Ethan retained his original brown hair, and was able to jump ahead one grade level, thanks to the government's homeschooling. The family changed from Methodists to Catholics, with instructors on hand to teach them the history and rituals of their new religion.

Meanwhile, the global media launched a vicious search for the Hickory family. The media were still searching for a young girl with cerebral palsy, but Jillian was cured of the disease. They also searched for a black goat, but the FWPP kept Titan at Fort Knox. A sad Jillian and Ethan accepted the fate of their prized goat, while moving to Peoria. With the help of Sutherland and the FWPP, they did meet with Titan virtually on encrypted channels. The family laughed as Titan banged his hooves at the wooden barn wall. They thought their beloved goat would be well taken care of at Fort Knox.

The US government sold the family farm in Bourbon County in December, and the FWPP began to shop for a farm for the family in several western states. The family were presented with two choices: one in Wyoming and another in Kansas. The government would also buy them new cars and teach them how to plant and harvest new crops.

They watched the Wyoming hologram first, which was projected on the floor of their Peoria home from six small cameras positioned in the room.

The family didn't like that the Wyoming farm was a long distance from the closest town, which was only eleven thousand people. They would feel isolated, but they recognized the higher risk of being discovered in a bigger town. They did like the idea of being close to the national parks, though.

Next, they watched the hologram of the Kansas farm, while discussing the information provided by Agent Sutherland, such as the number of churches and the cost of living.

"Daddy, I like the creek. Do you see the small dams?" Ethan said, leaning forward toward the wall screen.

"Yeah, we could fish there."

"Let's look up the town on UNet. It's called Salina," Mattie said. "It's forty kilometers away."

Tom queried the wall screen for further facts and figures. The results displayed on the first screen: population 66,921; elevation 373 meters; main crop of wheat; several light manufacturing firms; and a half dozen or more universities and technical schools.

"Well, we won't have to worry about sea-level rise," Ethan said.

"Chris," Mattie said, having rehearsed herself to call her husband his new name, even when they were alone. "Let's go for the bigger city. There's more shopping, education, and opportunities."

"I agree. What about Salina, kids?" Tom asked, trying to keep his voice upbeat.

"Dad, I like the creek. We didn't have a pond or creek on our Bourbon County farm."

"Dex, you could take advanced math and science courses in Salina," Mattie added. "They have excellent schools and colleges."

Jillian remained silent. She missed her old friends. Her school and church were becoming distant memories. The wait on their unknown fate over the past months had demoralized her. But discussing their future with actual locations was lifting her spirits.

"Jilly—oops, I mean Briana," Mattie said. "Do you like Salina?"

"Yes, Mom, it seems okay, but it's not as big as Lexington." One million people lived in the Lexington area, whereas fewer than one hundred thousand lived around Salina.

"Yes, but the farm in Wyoming is far from the town."

After another few minutes of discussion, Tom said, "So who votes for Wyoming?"

No one responded.

"Who votes for Kansas?"

"Yep!" Mattie yelled, and both kids replied with strong yeses while jumping up and down.

"Kansas, here we come!" Tom said as everyone hugged everyone. After many weeks of grueling training and isolation, they could see their new life. Later that day, Chris called agent Sutherland on an encrypted communicator line and told her their decision.

"Wonderful. We'll buy the Kansas farm," she acknowledged.

"What do we do in the meantime?"

"Just wait. I'm afraid it may take months to buy the farm, cars, and necessary farming equipment."

"Please try to speed things up. My family is in limbo."

"I'll do the best I can. I'll call you to give you updates," she said before they hung up.

* * *

The family continued their solitary lives in the Peoria home, waiting for news. They seldom went out except for medical emergencies. FWPP doctors visited them, and their groceries were ordered online and delivered to their home.

One rainy day in early December, the communicator beeped, and Mattie answered it.

"Hi, Mrs. Gifford. I have good news for you and your family," Agent Sutherland said.

"What?" Mattie said, stopping in her tracks, midway through putting their groceries on the shelves in the kitchen.

"Everything is complete for your move to Kansas."

"Wonderful! When do we move?"

"We'll have the movers visit you soon. They will take an inventory of your household goods. I'll be in touch."

"Super. Thank you."

Mattie scrambled into the living room to tell her family. "We're moving to Kansas! The government bought the farm for us outside Salina."

Tom stood up and hugged her, while the kids bounced around the floor, chanting, "Kansas! Kansas! Kansas!"

Mattie flashed a stiff smile at Tom, indicating their family's Pyrrhic victory.

Their new life would soon begin.

CHAPTER 13
A New Life

The Hickory family arrived at their Kansas ranch on December 12, two months after the orb's arrival. They drove up the gravel roadway to the ranch in their new Chinese-made hydrogen-electric van and kicked up a cloud of dust.

The rough-and-tumble West met the family face-to-face.

Two stone columns framed the ranch entrance, and two rough wood posts, half meters in diameter and mounted in stone foundations, stood straight up at four meters high. No arch connected the vertical bulwarks, and the massive posts went upward to nowhere. On top of one of the stone columns, sat a weathered and bent steel mailbox.

There was no sign of other buildings in any direction. A scan of the horizon revealed three electric poles and the top of a telecommunications tower. Nearby, a light frost lay upon clumps of grassland and shrubs; it was four degrees Celsius with a strong wind.

The Central Kentucky terrain was similar to that in Kansas. Both exhibited rolling hills and elevation changes of thirty meters, though rough and barbed-wire fences defined the Kansas fields, unlike the stone and wood fences of the Bourbon County farm. Deer and farm animals watched over the fields, while thoroughbred racehorses dominated the bluegrass fields.

The Kansas farm was 3.85 square kilometers, smaller than the one they'd had in Bourbon County. Forty kilometers away was the local town, Salina.

A pristine framed two-story house stood in the middle of the ranch. Built in 2139, the three hundred eighty-six-square-meter home was newer than the Kentucky house. A large porch with a railing encircled the front door. They could see the solar shingles on the roof that helped to power the home. The windows were programmable-matter technology, which helped reduce energy costs, and an on-site hydrogen-electric generator awaited them for use during the next power outage.

The family stepped out of their van in front of their new home. The chilly wind blew in their faces. They made the quick trip into the house to find the joy of heat and air-conditioning. US building codes required homes to have at least two air conditioners and heat pumps—if one stopped working, the other one served as a safety net. Extreme heat, not cold weather, killed over four-hundred thousand people in the United States in 2145, and around the world millions died because of heat-related illnesses.

"Well," Mattie said, "no one will find us here."

Tom chuckled. "Yes, you're right. But it's better than Fort Knox."

Synthetic wood beams, doors, and window casings defined the inside of the house, and they used ceramic hardwood on all floors. The living room had vaulted ceilings, and they later discovered that two of the upstairs bedrooms did too. The kitchen was next to the living room, its countertops made of ceramic-composite, and the open plan set-up created a large family living area.

"Mom, what room is mine?" Ethan yelled from the second-floor hallway.

"We'll decide that now."

They walked up the L-shaped staircase.

"Mom, I like this bedroom," Jillian stated. "You can look out and see who's coming to visit."

"Dex, the back bedroom is bigger," Tom said to his son. "You'll have room for a workbench for your projects."

"I'll take the back bedroom. I can see the barn from there."

Two hours later, a small rental truck arrived, and two men unloaded the family's meager belongings. As they were opening boxes, Agent Janice Sutherland arrived in a separate vehicle.

"I hope the farm and home are what you expected," she said after she'd entered.

"Yes, it's what we expected from the video tours. Thank you," Tom replied.

"You'll like Salina. It's a family town. Your homeschool instructors will take you on a tour tomorrow. Is that okay? They'll also get your groceries and run errands to minimize you time in public places."

Mattie smiled at Sutherland's comments. It was the first smile on her face Tom had seen in a long time.

"Chris, Arianna, can you sign these bank signature cards for me? We've set up local banking accounts for your family and deposited ð20,000 ecoins in your checking account. We will move the net proceeds from the sale of your farm through several financial accounts, and you will receive these funds over the next two years—we want to ensure the media cannot track you via any electronic funds." She smiled and said, "I'll leave now and give you some space."

As she turned toward the door, she stopped for a moment, her expression turning serious.

"Oh, I have bad news. I'm sure you remember Captain Kash Kilbourne." She paused. "He was killed in Bangladesh."

"Oh, no!"

"Killer robots shot him. That's all I know."

"A good young man; so sad," Mattie said.

"He protected us; he was part of our family. I guess we cannot contact his family?" Tom said.

"I'm sorry, but that's not possible. You have disappeared, and we must do everything possible to protect your new identity," Agent Sutherland said. "Please remember, we didn't split up your family."

The family spent the rest of the day setting up their new home, with Tom and Mattie helping the kids unpack their boxes and suitcases.

Jillian's room looked like it belonged to any other young girl, except there were no trophies or awards, and only one family photo. After they'd finished forming their new identities, a Fort Knox military photographer had taken the family picture.

"Mom, where's my first-grade picture from Kentucky?"

"Ah, uh, I didn't see it."

"Did I have it in Fort Knox or Peoria?"

"Briana, I don't remember seeing the picture," Tom said, giving Mattie a dreadful look. Ethan caught his expression and understood the situation, looking out the window at the frosty landscape. He knew the answer to his sister's query, but would not tell.

"Mom, that picture was my only memory of my friends. I miss them."

"Yes, we miss our old farm and friends too," Mattie replied, walking over to hug her daughter.

"I miss our hydroponic greenhouse and Atticus and Ethel," Tom mumbled.

"Why couldn't we bring them here?" Jillian asked.

"Well, someone could track the bots, Jilly. So, they were reprogrammed and sold. Now they'll have no memory of us."

"Yeah, I bet Titan is happy he doesn't have to deal with those bots," Ethan said.

The next morning, the family toured Salina, accompanied by Sutherland and two homeschool teachers called Morgan and Dean. They drove to nearby supermarkets, churches, schools, universities and the airport. They ended their day by visiting a small zoo outside of town, which the kids loved.

"I'll check on you once a week," Sutherland said once they were back home. She stepped into her car and said to Tom, "Remember to ask me for my badge number before we talk on our encrypted communicators.

I'll also get updates from the homeschool teachers. If anything comes up, please call me."

She closed her car window to avoid the cool air and drove off.

* * *

"Why do we have to miss school this year?" Ethan asked at the dinner table that evening.

"The government wants you and Briana to grow up more. You might go next year, though. At your ages, your appearances will change soon enough, and the media and the public won't recognize you anymore." Mattie answered.

"Mom, that isn't fair."

"Yes, I know, but we have no choice. Ms. Sutherland said you two can enroll in a regular school in a year or two. Briana, you'll be in the fourth or fifth grade, depending on how far you phase ahead."

"Daddy, none of this is right."

"I know. But one advantage of homeschooling is you only study four hours a day. You can organize your day any way you want. You can help your mom, study, or fish with us."

The kids grumbled at these explanations.

"Mom, can I have a chocolate layer cake?" Jillian asked.

"Sure, I'll make your favorite. It can be a celebration of our new home." She went over to the kitchen counter and opened the three-dimensional food printer. Jillian helped her mother load the four premixed ingredients into it, following the computer recipe. Mattie pushed the button to print the cake. Afterward, Ethan came over to watch the printer produce the artwork for the top of the cake: a beautiful, curved flower made of shaved dark chocolate.

After finishing the first cake, they made a second one for Ethan, but this one had basketball artwork on top instead. Jillian and Ethan sat down and ate their customized cakes.

Later Wednesday evening, the world news reminded them of the many honors the Hickory family had received the last few months. They had watched a painful replay of President Steven E. Barlow presenting them an award in absentia—the Presidential Medal of Freedom with Distinction.

Following that, they watched yet another new honor given to them. The news announcer said, "The United Nations in Beijing had awarded the Hickory family the Champions of Humanity Award. Jillian, Ethan, Mattie, and Tom Hickory are champions of the humanoid species or champiods. Through their beliefs and actions, champiods support all forms of life on earth and its extraordinary biosphere. The Hickory family's actions transcend any political, legal, economic, national or moral criteria to support human cooperation, harmony, and survival."

The accolades reminded them of their ordeal, but they knew their metamorphosis from the Hickory to the Gifford family was their best option.

The family was also aware that the State of Kentucky had introduced legislation so they could buy the land where the orb had visited. They wanted to build a shrine, honoring the orb and the Hickory family.

The next week, Tom and Mattie asked Agent Sutherland if they could join a local church. The answer was no. No school or church for at least one year. She told the Gifford family to find happiness in basketball, farming, fishing, and working the farm.

* * *

The family loved basketball and the University of Kentucky Wildcats. So, Tom added a basketball goal in their paved driveway. Mattie and Ethan formed one team, while Tom and Jillian formed the other. Tom researched simple plays and practice drills. The teams practiced almost every day, even in crisp weather, wearing heavy coats and hats. They held tournaments and kept score. The family even held virtual practices inside their home using hologram-generated players and courts.

"We need to learn two plays," Tom said in the living room. "The first is the pick-and-roll play, and the second is the center-crossover. Computer, project one-half a basketball court on the floor and scale it please. Computer, please assign a virtual defensive player to each offensive player."

He positioned Mattie and Ethan with virtual defensive players as they practiced their plays. Each team did ten repetitions of each play, and ended their virtual indoor practice.

"Good work, everyone," Tom said, slapping their hands together.

The first game outside pitted Mattie and Ethan's Titan Goats against Tom and Jillian's Kansas Sizzlers. Ethan whispered a play to Mattie, and they ran it. Mattie missed the shot, and Tom got the rebound. On the next possession, Tom and Jillian ran a pick and roll play, and Tom yelled to his daughter, "Shoot! Shoot!" The ball went in. She ran over to her dad for a hug, jumping up and down. Tom recorded the score on his makeshift scoreboard made of a hanging school notebook. The first team to twenty points and winning by over two points, wins the game. The final score was 26–22, with the Kansas Sizzlers winning over the Titan Goats.

The family put up an artificial holiday tree and decorated it with lights, balls, and icicles. When it snowed, the family used trash can tops to slide down gentle slopes in the privacy of their farm. They built a snowman and decorated it with potatoes, carrots, and sticks. Mattie and Jillian made a hat out of an old fruit basket. They were isolated, but happy.

One holiday morning, Ethan and Jillian awoke to the sounds and smells of a fresh country breakfast. They came down the stairs to find their parents making a holiday feast. Ethan and Jillian knew their tasks and pitched in to help. During breakfast, Mattie said, "A year ago, we were so happy, so at peace with our world. Now, everyone knows our names, faces, and even our favorite toothpaste."

"We'll rebound," Tom replied in a reflective tone of voice.

"Yes, I hope so. I want to see my friends one day," Jillian said.

"Jilly, we'll have to make new friends," a wise Ethan said, looking at his famous sister.

"We have much to be thankful for," Tom said. "We are together; they couldn't break up our family."

No one spoke for a moment. Mattie smiled and said, "Let's clean up the kitchen and watch a holiday movie. Anyone want popcorn or a pecan pie for desert?"

Tom met farmers at the Salina Farmers Association meetings during December, which he enjoyed. But he tried to limit his time with them because of his panic attacks. Whenever his new acquaintances asked questions about his past, he would excuse himself, go to the bathroom, and wait until he calmed down. He also slowed his speech, trying to remember to use Arianna, Briana, Dex, and Chris Gifford in conversations with other farmers.

One December evening, a news report caught their eye. After several court delays, a US Army judicial panel had reached a conclusion in the case of Colonel Harold "Hawk" Preston, who had allegedly shot an unarmed civilian. The court did not recommend a court-martial or reduction in rank. A press release said the fog from tear gas canisters and an odd camera angle made the video of the incident inconclusive, and soldier and demonstrator testimony, which was conflicting and confusing, provided no further insights.

"Grand news for Colonel Preston," Mattie said.

"Yes, those officers made our lives bearable during that troubling time."

* * *

On December 17, Sunday afternoon, Tom and the kids were planning to go fishing.

"Daddy, there's no hook on my pole," Jillian said as they selected fishing rods and reels in the barn.

"I'll teach you how to put a hook on the fishing line." Tom opened his tackle box and found a package of fishing leaders with hooks. "Take one of these. They call the line with the hook a leader." He showed her how to loop and tie one to the line. "Now you do it."

Jillian followed her dad's directions, securing the leader and hook to the fishing line.

"Now put the cork on the line about one meter from the hook. Dex, is your pole set up?"

"Yes, Dad. I'm ready to go."

Carrying their fishing poles and a tackle box, they walked to the partially frozen creek. A gorge four meters deep defined its banks. The creek itself measured one to three meters deep and averaged four meters wide. Bare but determined oak and maple trees covered its banks. Three deer stood on the hillside and watched as the trio fished in the openings in the slush and ice.

Ethan helped Jillian cast her line into the water. The cork bobbed as a slight current moved it downstream until it hit the edge of the ice.

"Cast your line into the creek and hold the cork over open water," Ethan told his sister.

She recast her line and waited.

Fishing taught one to try again if they failed, cast after cast. In an instant, the cork bobbed. Tom and Ethan watched.

"Jerk the line if you get a bite to set the hook," Tom said.

Whack. The cork disappeared. The line became taut. Jillian pulled on the fishing pole, but the line unreeled. The line cut through two meters of water like a surgeon's scalpel. *Zip. Zip.*

"Crank the reel with one hand. Use the other hand to hold the pole."

"I can't do it," she shouted. The voice of the orb couldn't do two things at once. Ethan stepped over to help her reel in the fish.

"Pull. Pull," he said as he worked the reel. Together, they flung the fish onto the creek bank, where it landed with a smacking sound.

A proud Tom watched his kids pull in the fish, a one-pound bass. He grabbed the line and held the fish up in the air.

The three stood on the creek bank, hugging and celebrating Jillian's catch. Her joyful smile documented a first-time moment. As the family rejoiced, the life surrounding them celebrated too. In the sky, birds chirped, and butterflies twirled. Below, fish and other critters splashed about in their kingdom. The fishing line connected Jillian to nature and her family. It was a fun and memorable family moment.

"What a great fish, Briana."

"Yeah, at least it wasn't an ugly catfish," Ethan said.

"That's a big fish, Daddy, but it smells."

Tom took a picture of the fish with his communicator to show Mattie later. They took the fish off the hook and released it back into the creek. The fish flapped and splashed in the cold water as it reclaimed its freedom.

"Daddy, why can't we take the fish home to show Mom?"

"Jilly, this fish has a right to live life the way it wants."

"But Daddy, we're not living life the way we wanted."

"You're too smart for us, young lady," Tom said as he walked over and kissed his daughter on the head.

* * *

Sunday evening at dinner, the family watched a news report. The new commentator said, "Trade squabbles between Japan and Korea may threaten their commitments to build the megamachines, and the Mideast Union's quarrel over water shortages may change their commitments."

"Scientists built a simulation model to forecast the impact of building fewer than two hundred sixteen megamachines. The successful terraforming of Earth's atmosphere is a nonlinear probability function. If we build and operate two-thirds of the megamachines or one hundred forty-four, the probability of reaching our target performance levels for Earth's heat content and gases is 0.39. If we build and operate the two hundred sixteen megamachines, the probability increases to 0.89. Scientists continue to improve the simulation model."

"Dad, with these many countries arguing, I don't think we'll ever build all the megamachines," Ethan said.

"I doubt it too."

CHAPTER 14
Hunting

In January, the first major winter storm arrived. The boisterous wind howled, and twenty-one centimeters of snow fell to the ground, making the countryside look a pristine white. Tree branches were bare, their leaves gone. Only a few tenacious leaves still clung to their branches.

Tom and Ethan had been clearing the snow off the driveway and porch. As they entered their home they heard a *crack-crack* sound that echoed through the heavy winter air.

"Dad, what was that?"

"It sounded like gunshots to me."

"Someone must be hunting."

"Yeah. It's easy to see the deer in the snow."

They stepped back outside and stood on the porch like frozen sentries. They searched the horizon for the source of the gunshots, but found nothing unusual.

They retreated to the warmth of their home, where Jillian was finishing her virtual homework on the wall screen, and Mattie was setting dinnerware on the kitchen table. The fireplace burned in the living room. Ethan was the official family fire builder. His dad had taught him how to build and manage a fire. The process had taught him responsibility.

They had adjusted to their new life. Things were going well.

As Mattie served dinner, they heard a clattery truck pull into their driveway. It slammed on the brakes and skidded several meters on the frozen drive.

Tom and Ethan stood up and looked out the window to see two men wearing hunting jackets getting out of a green truck. One man was dragging the other toward the front door.

Tom ran to a chest and pulled out his stun gun.

Soon, two loud, pounding knocks came at the front door, startling Mattie and Jillian. They abandoned their dinner and stood up, their eyes focused on the front door.

"Who could that be?" Mattie asked.

Tom held his gun down at his side, expecting the worst, and did not answer her.

"What can I do for you?" he yelled through the bolted door.

"Sir, we had a hunting accident. We need help," one stranger bellowed.

Tom looked at the wall screen to see the video from the front door camera. He let the two men in, and they lumbered into their home. The injured man fell onto the floor. A skinning knife was in his side, sticking up in the air. Blood, snow, and dirt soon drenched the spotless hardwood floor.

"I can't stop the bleeding!" the other man said, and paused, looking up at the family. "I'm Trevor Pumphrey. This is my younger brother, Willard."

"What happened?"

Mattie wet several kitchen towels and ran to the man's aid. The men took off Willard's hunting jacket. Ethan brought scissors, and they cut off his shirt and thermal T-shirt to reveal the intrusive knife. The entire twelve-centimeter blade had gone in and pinned the sheath to Willard's side, so they couldn't see the wound.

"We shot a deer. When we tried to load it onto the back of our truck, Willard slipped in the snow. He fell onto the knife he had in his jacket. It went right through the sheath."

"I'll call the hospital emergency room," Mattie said, activating her communicator.

When a nurse answered, she filled them in.

"Please focus your communicator's camera toward the wound, and I'll get the doctor. Please stand by."

Blood pulsed out of the laceration. Tom used water from a drenched dish towel to help clean the wound, and a four-centimeter-long cut was soon visible.

"Hello. I'm Dr. Burden," came a new voice on the line. "I see the knife and blood. Can you zoom in on the wound?"

"Okay," said Mattie, fiddling with the controls on the communicator.

"Can you work the sheath away from the lesion?" Dr. Burden asked. "Can you estimate how much blood he's lost?"

"I'd say one liter, maybe two," Trevor replied.

"The blade must have hit a vein or artery. He's bleeding inside too," the doctor said. "He needs to come to the hospital immediately. I'll call for an ambulance. Oh. Don't pull it out."

Tom and Trevor continued to apply pressure to the wound, but the bleeding did not stop. Willard moaned in pain.

"It's at least a thirty-minute trip from the hospital, one-way," Trevor said. "Even more in the snow."

"He's going to bleed to death right here on the floor."

"Should we pull the knife out?"

"The doctor said not to. It will hasten the bleeding."

A metallic iron smell filled the room. Willard's moaning worsened, and his eyes closed, and he passed out.

"He's going to die," Trevor said.

Jillian and Ethan stood next to the kitchen table, watching the escalating scene. Mattie ran to get more towels and a bottle of rubbing alcohol. She also rolled a towel and placed it under the man's head. She used another towel to wipe the blood from the floor. Once she completed cleaning the floor, she stood up and backed away, trying not to slip on the floor. Covered in blood and dirt, Tom and Trevor knelt beside Willard, who lay comatose. No one knew what to do.

They waited for the ambulance and looked at Willard with helpless gazes. Seconds, minutes, passed as they watched him bleed out.

A soft and familiar voice broke the quandary.

"Daddy, I can help."

Everyone looked at Jillian, who walked toward Willard.

"Briana, how can you help?" Mattie asked, bewildered.

"Mom, let me try."

She knelt down beside the man and said, "Dad, pull the knife out."

"What? You'll kill him."

"Daddy, he's dying. Pull the blade out."

Trevor and Tom stared at each other, and Trevor said, "Why not? He's going to bleed to death, anyway. I'll do it." He grabbed the menacing knife and with a tug, pulled it out of his brother's limp body. The knife made a slight, nauseating sucking sound as it came out. A steady flow of the man's blood followed.

Jillian moved closer to the man and held out her hand above his body. Her palm glowed brighter, illuminating the veins and bones in the back of her hand, and she placed it over the bloody wound. Her eyes closed, and her face relaxed, with a hint of a smile. Before long, a beam of intense blue light left her small, angelic hand and covered the wound. The blood bubbled and coagulated. As if directed by a hidden force, globules of blood moved away from the wound.

Trevor was speechless. Everyone watched in stunned silence. The cut was cleaned and healed before their eyes. After a moment, the brilliant bolt of blue light stopped. Only a modest scar remained.

Jillian withdrew her hand and sat down on the floor beside Willard. Her head hung low, and her arms fell into her lap.

Ethan ran over to his sister, and he hugged her, holding her upright. A wave of panic gripped Tom.

"Oh, my God! He's healed," Mattie screamed.

Trevor couldn't talk. What he saw baffled him.

Within one minute, Willard moved his arms and legs. After another minute, his eyes opened.

"Willard, this is Trevor, your brother."

Willard smiled at him, but did not speak.

Tom carried Jillian over to the sofa, and Ethan ran to the kitchen sink to wet a kitchen towel. Her clothes were messy, wet, and smeared with blood. He returned and wiped his sister's face and hands while his parents hovered above them.

Jillian awoke.

"What happened, Mom?"

"You saved this man's life."

The Hickorys knew what had happened. Jillian had used her elusive healing powers again. Would Trevor or Willard recognize who they were? Family courage turned to family fear.

In time, Jillian stood and walked around. She walked to the kitchen, opened the refrigerator, and poured herself a large glass of milk.

Meanwhile, Trevor attended to his brother, helping him into the kitchen to sit down on a chair.

"Did your daughter heal my brother's wound?"

"Uh, I don't know," Mattie said. "The wound may not have been as severe as we thought."

"Ma'am, my brother lost a lot of blood. Yet he sits here, healed and alive. It is a miracle!"

"Yes, we're glad you brought him here. It all worked out," Tom said, trying to downplay what had happened. The entire family understood they needed to protect their identity.

Mattie fixed some soup for everyone to eat, and they sat at the kitchen table and ate. Trevor fed his exhausted brother a few spoonfuls, then he helped him put his shirt and sweater back on.

"His wound is healed," he said with a perplexed look. Willard took another spoonful of soup and said, "Thank you. I don't know how it happened, but it did."

The Hickorys remained silent. Could this be the event that unraveled their masquerade?

As they were finishing their soup, they heard the shrieking sound of an ambulance, its disquieting sound getting closer. Within minutes, two emergency team members, carrying portable equipment and a big red bag, knocked on the front door.

"Who's hurt?" one said as Tom let them in.

Pointing to the skinning knife on the bloody floor, Trevor answered, "My brother fell on that knife. We came here for help. But he's fine now."

"Can we look?" one medic asked.

Willard was sitting at the kitchen table, his arms and chest leaning on the surface, his head down.

"Uh, I guess so," Trevor said.

The medic examined Willard's wound. Afterward, he said, "That looks like an old scar. Are you sure that's the correct wound?"

"Yes, sir, I am."

"Is anyone else hurt?" the puzzled emergency responder asked.

"No, sir. We're fine," Tom said.

After a moment of silence, the angry medic said, "The roads are treacherous, and the wound is healed. Your actions were frivolous. We could charge you with a misdemeanor."

"Sir, we got scared. We thought we had an emergency, but we didn't. We are sorry."

"We should have called back and canceled the ambulance," Mattie said.

The emergency responders stood in the kitchen, looking frustrated. "We need to get back to our station. Other calls are coming in. Please do not call us unless it's a genuine emergency."

After they left, no one wanted to discuss things further. Trevor helped his feeble brother stand and they walked to the front door while putting on their coats. Tom escorted them to their truck.

"Chris, thank you," Trevor said. "Amazing. You know, I've seen your family before. But I can't remember where."

Tom nodded but did not reply.

The two brothers drove off into the snow-covered countryside, and Tom reentered the home where he sat down at the kitchen table with his family. He picked up a soup spoon and tried to eat, but the tremors in his hands continued. He dropped the spoon onto the table, blushing. A panic attack was incoming, and the family knew it.

"Someone ought to call Agent Sutherland."

"I'll do it," Mattie said.

After providing a badge number and one other code, Mattie talked with Sutherland about how to handle what had happened. Sutherland told her she would research the two brothers. She would try to obtain a court order to monitor their communications.

"Do we have to move? Change our identities again?" Mattie asked despondently.

"No, I don't think so. We'll watch things and let you know."

"They'd better not try to split us up," Ethan said after his mother ended the call, having listened in to the call.

"Look, tonight, Jillian saved a man's life. We should rejoice. Now it is confirmed: we now know Jillian can heal people. She's been given a gift, though I'm not sure whether we can ever use it," Mattie said. After a moment of reflection, she added, "We shouldn't speak of this event again. Briana, what do you remember?"

"I remember the hunter. The knife scared me."

"Yes, it scared us. Do you remember anything else?"

"No, Mom. But I remember Dex hugging me. That's it."

For the rest of the evening, they focused on cleaning up the mess in their home. Afterward, Mattie went to bed. Tom was already asleep, having taken sedatives.

* * *

For the next few days, the family tried to recover from what they had experienced. Fear dominated them. They did not leave the safety of their home. They didn't even leave the house to go grocery shopping, leaning once more on the protection agency's kindness, and asking for more meals to be delivered. What if the hunters recognized them?

By January 11, the winter snow had melted. Winter in Salina happened in January and February only with temperatures ranging from minus ten to plus ten degrees Celsius. For the other months, it was too hot to snow. Later that day, Agent Sutherland called them to report what the surveillance had found.

"We have discovered no unusual behavior or conversations from either Mr. Trevor Pumphrey or Mr. Willard Pumphrey. We know they told their spouses about the event. They blame themselves for the accident, and are mostly focused on how the knife should not have been inside the jacket's pocket. It should have been secured to his belt."

"That's good news. I'll tell my family," Tom said. "Thanks for the update, Agent Sutherland."

The Hickory family tried to put the hunting incident to the back of their minds, in the most hard-to-retrieve areas as possible. They followed Mattie's advice and did not discuss the incident again.

But for those who hide the truth, fear has its ways of reemerging. Later that day, a news report brought the family to the edge of their seats.

"We found a family of four living in Cape Town, South Africa, who fit the physical characteristics of the lost Hickory family," The *British Chronicle* news anchor began. "Two anthropologists specializing in biometrics are studying public films of this family. Facial-recognition software has found fourteen matches worldwide. The anthropologists plan to investigate each. The highest probability of a successful match is the Cape Town family."

"The Cape Town family refused an interview, but we know that they have hired a security firm to escort their two kids to school, and that the wife called local police when being hounded while out shopping. Police freed her and took her home after thirty people surrounded and trapped her in a corner of a grocery store. The family has filed a lawsuit, asking for a restraining order against all news organizations and reporters."

The video showed a camera crew at the front door of a home in Cape Town. The besieged family opened the door a few centimeters with a chain lock, and asked the news reporter to leave their property. A camera panned around to show three more television crews outside.

"Dad, do you think they'll find us?" Ethan asked.

"I hope not, son."

"We're being hunted," Mattie said. "I hate living a lie."

"Hey, we shouldn't talk about the Cape Town family. Why get upset? We are safe," Tom said.

The daily news reports were an assault on their lives and forced the family toward isolation. Only Tom ventured out with fellow farmers and Mattie with Morgan or Dean, shopping for clothes and furniture. But Ethan and Jillian were confined to the farm; no friends or school activities. They needed to protect their identities, avoiding the unpalatable consequences of making a mistake. Tom considered reestablishing the wall screen blackout mandate they had followed in the past.

* * *

A slight dusting of snow covered the fields and highways that Thursday evening; Mattie prepared a premixed pasta meatball stew for the family. She heated the ready-to-serve meal in the convection oven, ready for when Tom returned from a farmers' association meeting.

"How did your day go?" Tom asked Ethan, sitting at the kitchen table.

"Good, Dad. My teacher thinks I'm ready for the seventh or eighth grade."

"When is the qualifying exam?"

"This summer."

"Wow, that's good news," Mattie said.

"We'll talk with your teachers after the test. It might be a good idea to not phase too far ahead," Tom said. Ethan nodded, showing he understood that logic.

"Briana, how about your day?"

"Daddy, we had a good day. My teacher is funny. I practiced free throws today too. I'm getting better."

"It's good that you practice, sweetheart."

"Yes, it takes my mind off our troubles."

Once they'd finished dinner, the kids helped clean the kitchen. In a momentary reprieve from rinsing off the dishes, Ethan asked, "Mom, will the orb return one day?"

Mattie considered the question and replied, "Yes, one day. But maybe not in our lifetime."

The family, who'd been ineluctably bound to sacrifice part of their lives for the sake of humanity, stood in silence, looking at one another. They understood the colossal burden they carried because of the orb's visit. Everything had changed except the family tradition of a sit-down meal in their kitchen.

*　*　*

After dinner, they watched a television show on how sea life adapted to warmer oceans.

"Today, ocean acidification, measured by pH levels, is at the same level as twenty million years ago. The rate of change in Earth's ocean acidification is one hundred times faster than in the past twenty million years."

"Our oceans absorb about one-third of carbon dioxide in the atmosphere. Terrestrial plants and our atmosphere take up the remaining carbon dioxide."

"A solution's pH is the measure of its acidity or alkalinity. The pH of seawater ranges from seven to eight pH and is becoming more acidic. If you were a fish or sea creature, would you want to swim in an acidic ocean? I doubt it."

The news reporter had invited Dr. Rabab onto the documentary to comment. She was an expert on how ocean acidification and heat affected sea life reproduction, fertility rates, and DNA. Everyone recognized Dr. Rabab because she had been a member of the original expert team on-site with the orb.

"What are the effects of ocean acidification on squid?" the reporter asked.

"People think of squid as seafood, but squid are a linchpin of our oceans. Our research shows the inner bones of the squid's ear are less dense and get smaller as the pH level decreases. Their inner ear helps them determine directions in the ocean. It also helps them keep their balance, much like the human ear. And, in more acidic seawater, squid eggs take longer to hatch, so they're more vulnerable to predators. These results lead to lower squid populations, and when the squid population decreases, the entire food chain suffers."

In another segment of the documentary, the announcer said, "Lobster prices, adjusted for inflation, have increased tenfold. Lobsters have moved to deeper waters and closer to the poles. Higher ocean temperature and acidity have caused some of this migration."

"In the late 1970s, Maine's soft-shell clam harvest exceeded eight million pounds. Today it's less than four hundred thousand pounds. Ocean acidification is one of the primary causes of reduced clam harvests. The mud flats are barren of clams, so today we treat the ocean water with chemicals to maintain the correct acidity. As a result, clam prices have increased fourfold, adjusted for inflation."

"Humans depend on the oceans and marine ecosystems for food, jobs, entertainment, and oxygen, but an acidic and hot ocean makes even our survival doubtful."

The video accompanying the broadcast included images of healthy and not-so-healthy sea life.

"What a mess," Jillian said.

"Humans are stupid," Ethan added.

"Briana, humans make mistakes," Mattie said. "We ignored the signals for decades, and now we are trying to catch up."

"But, Mom, you said in bible classes in Kentucky that humankind has dominion over the earth."

"Yes, I know. But we didn't exactly do what God wanted," Mattie said. Tom, who was listening to the conversation, did not respond. Instead, he turned off the house lights and turned on the home security system. Now only a few lingering fireplace embers provided a faint light.

CHAPTER 15
Stampede

The next morning, January 12, before sunrise, Mattie and Tom woke up to groaning sounds outside their home. It sounded as if a stampede of vehicles had slammed on the brakes, and below that, they could hear the scratchy sounds of human voices.

"What's going on?" Tom yelled, jumping out of bed.

"It sounds like a slugfest."

They put on their bathrobes and hurried into the living room. Jillian and Ethan also came down the stairs, dressed in flannel pajamas.

The harsh glare of headlights pierced through their home's windows, curtains, and door edges, breaching their privacy.

"Dad, what's happening?" Ethan said.

"I don't know, but I'm going out."

With his stun gun in hand, Tom opened the front door. He stepped out onto the porch, with Mattie standing behind him. Jillian and her brother stood in the doorway. Cold, inhumane air rushed into their home, a harsh foretelling of their future.

"Oh my God! It's media trucks," Tom said.

"They found us!" Mattie's knees buckled, but she stayed upright.

Tom herded Mattie and the kids back into the house, and slammed the door shut, locked it, and leaned against the door. Before he could say a word, his communicator rang.

"Are they there yet?" Agent Sutherland asked.

"Yes, the media found us," Tom replied, shaking from a panic attack.

"I know. Lock your doors. I'll get the state police out there as soon as possible."

The family huddled on the sofa for protection, the callous rays of light, the frigid air, and the obnoxious sounds invading their home and their life. They would have to begin their arduous journey anew.

* * *

Four television camera operators crammed onto the front porch. They waited for the family to open the front door. An alarmed family heard the commotion, but no one came to their aid.

"Dad, what do we do?" Ethan said, holding his sister.

"Nothing. We wait until help arrives," Tom said, hugging a tearful Mattie.

A minute later, a news reporter banged on the door. The indignant banging was another blatant intrusion into their lives. Bang! Bang! The family was not about to answer. Every few minutes, a reporter would bang on the door or peek in a window. The outside temperature of minus five degrees Celsius was not a detriment to the reporters. For twenty minutes, the family huddled together on their sofa, waiting for help.

As the sun broke the horizon, a stout young state trooper knocked on the door.

"Mr. Hickory, I am Officer Baon of the Kansas State Highway Patrol. We have moved the news reporters off your front porch, sir. Please open the door."

Tom cracked the door open with the chain lock engaged and said, "Thank you for getting them away from our home."

"Yes, sir, Mr. Hickory. It is an honor. We will protect you. We have four officers here now and more on their way."

"What happens next?" Tom asked, with the door still cracked.

"Sir, our orders are to protect your family and the farm until an agent from the federal government gets here. We have moved the media thirty meters from your home."

Mattie now stood at the kitchen window, watching the media chaos. A wave of despair overwhelmed her. Her neck muscles tightened, and her headache returned. Ethan also watched the carnival outside their home.

Finally, Jillian asked, "Daddy, does this mean we have to move again?"

"Yes, I'm afraid so," a dejected Tom replied as he put a bottle of medicine in his pocket. He had taken two more pills to help avoid a panic attack.

The Giffords' wall screen was on, but muted. When Tom saw the big black-and-red "Breaking News," announcement, he unmuted it. The announcer began by showing a video of their home and six news media trucks. She said, "They have found the Hickory family! They live on a farm outside Salina, Kansas. The family helped communicate with the orb. To our knowledge, Jillian Hickory, the voice of the orb, is in this home too."

The beleaguered family watched the wall screen. They saw their lovely home and sanctuary televised for the world to see. A polite knock on the door interrupted them.

"Arianna, Chris, this is Agent Sutherland. Please let me in." Sutherland entered the Gifford home. The Giffords' surrounded her, hoping she had a solution to their plight.

"A helicopter lands here in less than an hour and takes you away. Get ready. Pack only one suitcase each," an upset Sutherland said.

"So, we have to leave?" Mattie asked.

"Yes. We'll handle everything here. Get ready."

For the fourth time, the Hickorys packed their belongings. Mattie and Jillian cried as they jerked their bedroom dresser drawers open. In his bedroom, Ethan cried too. He realized he could not take his science project and basketball. The kids lugged their suitcases down the steps. Jillian's suitcase tumbled down the stairs. Tom and Mattie were already downstairs.

Sutherland sat at the kitchen table, looking at the horrified family running from their own species. They'd waited only fifteen minutes before they heard the hum of a helicopter. Four soldiers armed with pistols jumped out and ran to the front porch. Sutherland opened the door to the house. The Gifford family filed out and hurried toward the helicopter, with Sutherland following them. Troops loaded the suitcases into the helicopter. Kansas state troopers held back the growing crowd of reporters. The media trucks recorded every detail of the daylight escape, and it was telecast live around the world.

The family stepped into the helicopter, took their seats, and didn't talk. Their posture was limp, and their faces were blank; their pain was deep. With one hour's notice, they'd had to abandon their new life in Salina. The family's only redemption was that they remained intact and were whole. The black helicopter flew off into a beautiful pink and orange sunrise. Now, for a time, they had regained their true names Jillian, Mattie, Ethan, and Tom Hickory.

"Where are we going?" Ethan asked Agent Sutherland.

"We go to Fort Riley Army Base," Sutherland replied. "Within an hour, we catch a plane to a safe house in Brazil. We'll hide and retrain you for life in Brazil."

"Brazil! You got to be kidding me," Tom yelled.

Agent Sutherland turned toward Tom and stared into his eyes and said, "Tom, I'm sorry. We should have never placed your family in America; our mistake."

"Do we stay in Brazil forever?" a weeping Mattie asked.

"No, we'll set you up as teachers in an English-speaking high school. After five to ten years, and once the kids are grown, we'll return you to the United States."

"What a terrible plan," Mattie yelled.

"Mrs. Hickory, we have done everything we can to keep your family together, so it could be worse."

A dazed Tom looked out the helicopter's window at the countryside and held Mattie's hand.

* * *

The family's adjustment to life in a Brazilian safe house seemed easier than in the past transitions. They knew what to expect from their caregivers as they used encrypted wall screens, communicators, and computers. Here, they had a chef who prepared two meals a day and quick access to US government-paid medical doctors and psychologist.

On the morning of January 23, Ethan and Jillian continued their home schooling with new teachers. The teachers used holograms and virtual wall screen pictures to explain science concepts, like the solid geometry of a cone or the conceptual components of a living cell. They also studied Greek and Roman history and watched avatars in a Greek ecclesia debate in Athens and Michelangelo sculpture one of his masterpieces, Pieta. They ended their studies by taking quizzes on the day's work with avatar feedback on incorrect answers.

After lunch, Ethan worked on a school project while Tom and Mattie watched a movie using well-known celebrity avatars as actors. Jillian lay down in her bedroom for a nap.

At 1304, the astounding blue orb appeared in Jillian's bedroom. It hovered at the end of Jillian's bed while she slept. It moved toward her and merged with her body. Her legs and one arm jerked, but she didn't awake. The room and Jillian were silent. As before, a thin, blue hallo surrounded her pristine body. The orb needed to use her body for one last plea to humanity.

CHAPTER 16
Decisions

"If the world builds two hundred sixteen of these megamachines, the global economy will move into an economic depression," the Prime Minister of India, Indira Neelesh, said, speaking at the United Nations Ninth Committee meeting. Twenty-six of the largest economies were in attendance at the meeting, hosted at Beijing's world headquarters on January 23, 2148.

The Ninth Committee had been established after the orb's intervention, and the UN had charged them with two duties. First, they were to verify the scientific knowledge transmitted by the orb. They had issued one interim report to date. Second, the committee would plan the building of the two hundred sixteen megamachines. To free up national resources to build them, each of the two hundred forty-three countries had to sacrifice, agreeing to stop production of current projects, such as building seawalls, spaceports, solar farms, and new cities away from the coast.

The Ninth Committee's proposed megamachine allocation plan called for completing the build-out of two hundred sixteen megamachines within fifty years. Four economic powers—China, the European Union, Russia, and the United States—were to build twenty-seven megamachines each for a total of one hundred eight megamachines. The rest of the world would build the remaining one hundred eight megamachines.

The location of each megamachine was important. Based on the orb's advice, they should be located as close as possible to major latitude and longitude intersection points. To optimize the effectiveness, they should be below sixty degrees latitude north (i.e., the Arctic Circle) and above sixty degrees latitude south (i.e., the Antarctic Circle).

Indira Neelesh, who was also the chair of the Ninth Committee, ended her speech by saying, "India can't afford to build its allocation of twenty-one megamachines. I must protect our people's standard of living."

Prime Minister Neelesh introduced the next speaker, before leaving the podium to the applause of over four hundred people attending the UN meeting. A UN television channel transmitted the speeches live throughout the world.

The US Secretary of State, the Honorable Sebastian Heras, stepped up next.

"The United States will build the planned twenty-seven megamachines. It will lower our gross domestic product, but it has decreased or stayed flat for the last thirty years. This is because of the high cost of coping with global warming. First, the cost of air conditioning and cooling vests is high. Second, the cost to abandon real estate, build seawalls, rebuild seaports, move cities, and subsidize mass migrations is exorbitant. Our food costs have also increased because we must grow food in climate-controlled structures. These actions increase prices and drag our economy down."

"We have done many positive things to mitigate higher temperatures and pollution. Our electricity production uses no carbon-based fuels. We planted trillions of trees. National laws required zero-energy buildings and recycling."

Heras paused for a drink of water and continued.

"The citizens of the United States have experienced the devastating effects of climate deterioration. I'll cite two examples, one in Florida and one in New York."

"One of our states, Florida, condemned over 1.8 million homes and commercial buildings since 2100. Contaminated drinking water infested many coastal towns. Abandoned water and sewer systems dot the map. Real estate prices have tumbled to historic lows. Total population growth and tourists traveling to Florida are in exponential decline. It is impossible to build a seawall around Florida because the porous rock will not support massive seawalls. Even if technically possible, it would cost more than the asset value of the entire state."

"New York City is building several dams and seawalls to protect it from sea-level rise. The projected cost is ð380 billion ecoins. When completed in 2220, it will keep the city above water for a few more centuries. And we have put new construction laws and regulations in place along the coast. They do not allow construction in high-risk areas. New skyscrapers must move to higher-ground locations in New York and New Jersey. Our subway system floods daily. We have added more pumping capacity, but it is expensive. Higher subway ticket prices won't pay for these mitigation initiatives."

"If all ice on Earth melts, sea levels will increase over seventy meters. If this happens, we must abandon New York City and over one-half of Florida will be underwater. Our amazing technological advances are no match for nature."

"The Earth's biosphere continues to get hotter while ice disappears. The oceans store over three-thousand times more heat than our atmosphere. It takes hundreds of years to dissipate the ocean's heat. We must do more."

"Climate change presents humanity with a unique and complex problem; cooperating on a global scale. The time framework of nature doesn't fit with human life spans or political, economic, and legal time cycles and time frames."

Heras paused and leaned forward toward the audience and said, "The United States will build its planned allocation of megamachines to terraform Earth, regardless of the costs or consequences. It is a matter of human survival."

Prime Minister Neelesh next introduced a speaker representing the continent of Africa. His speech elicited a chorus of boos from the audience.

"The rest of the industrial world polluted Earth, not Africa. Africa is not responsible."

"The UN allocation wants us to use our national resources to build seven megamachines. We want to build schools, hospitals, factories, seawalls, and other infrastructure projects. The African nations propose a zero allocation instead of seven megamachines. Thank you."

Neelesh introduced the Asian Union speaker, a native of the Philippines. The union comprised an economic trading bloc of countries such as Cambodia, Malaysia, the Philippines, and Vietnam. China was an ex officio member.

"We agreed to build our allocation of six megamachines. The ocean has overtaken many of our coastlines, cities, and low-lying islands. Thirty-six million people have lost their homes because of sea-level increases. Relocation is expensive."

"We have displaced over one million people in the Manila Bay area alone. Rising seas have overwhelmed our historic wetlands and river deltas. The hotter ocean destroyed coral reefs, mangroves, and fishponds. Flooding and storm surges are more frequent and powerful. It is too expensive for our nation to build a seawall to protect the Manila Bay area, and our legal systems do a poor job of enforcing environmental laws. Our population of one hundred eighty-two million is overwhelming us."

"There are other effects of climate change in the Asian Union. The cost of electricity continues to skyrocket, due to the necessity of running air conditioning and cooling vests to survive the torrid heat. In Vietnam, the rising seas submerged nineteen percent of the Red River Delta. They moved 2.1 million people along the Mekong River. The Republic of Maldives is one of the lowest-elevation countries on Earth. Sixty-two percent of our one thousand one hundred ninety islands are submerged."

"The governments of the Asian Union will try to finance and build six megamachines. We will reallocate national resources against our countrymen's will to accomplish this task. We have no choice."

A speaker from the United Economic Union (UEU) spoke next, a union which included the countries of Albania, Great Britain, Iceland, Switzerland, and Turkey.

"The Greenland ice sheet is liquefying at an exponential rate. If it melts, ocean levels will increase by eight meters. The Arctic is earth's canary in the cage. The UEU will build the expected eleven megamachines, but it will destroy our standard of living. But we have no choice."

"Even with expensive new dams and locks on the Thames River, the city of London continues to flood. We prove our grand stupidity by ignoring these warnings. Humans have fatal flaws—we are myopic and self-serving."

The Russian minister of foreign affairs, Dimitri Stanislav, PhD, was the last to speak. He walked to the podium to applause, and bowed to acknowledge the audience.

"Russia has been ahead of global sea-level increases. For example, over one hundred years ago, we built a costly system of dams and a thirty-kilometer seawall to protect the city of St. Petersburg. So far, it has worked. Even today, US officials seek advice from our engineers and study our designs. The seawall system to protect New York City is like ours in Neva Bay in many respects, so it's possible, but expensive. To-date, we have abandoned many coastal seaports and naval bases and rebuild on higher ground."

"The weather patterns in much of Russia, especially Siberia, have also changed. Siberia is more susceptible to floods, droughts, insect infestations, and dying forests. And we calculate climate change has reduced our nation's gross domestic product by 3.4 percent per year over the past decade."

"Russian experts find the orb's system of equations fascinating for many reasons. But one reason stands out to us. If you examine the orb's equations, you will understand the role methane plays in warming our atmosphere and oceans. It is about twenty times more potent than carbon dioxide at trapping heat, and humans triggered the release of billions of tons of both into Earth's biosphere. This release takes Earth's biosphere beyond the tipping point. The main and interaction effects are huge. Yet, we have ignored such knowledge for one hundred years."

"Our permafrost is melting. If you stand on the little permafrost remaining in Siberia, you can watch gas bubbles pop out of the ground. And we don't understand how much methane our oceans release into the atmosphere. We have underestimated the methane effects."

"However, none of these things matter because our intelligence knows the United States is hiding knowledge transmitted by the orb on anti-gravity technology. We have suspended our commitment to build twenty-seven megamachines until President Barlow shares this information with all nations."

The audience grumbles and boos Dr. Stanislav's last statements. Some delegates, including the US Secretary of State, Sebastian Heras, stood up and walked out of the UN auditorium. Many who attended by telepresence turned off their screens.

Thereafter, Prime Minister Neelesh went to the podium and said, "Please, please, let Dr. Stanislav finish his speech. Please sit down."

After a minute of shuffling, the audience became quiet enough for Dr. Stanislav to say, "Thank you for allowing me to finish. Global cooperation depends on trust. That is why we bring up this anti-gravity issue now. Such knowledge could lead to powerful new weapons that would give the United States a huge military advantage. We cannot allow this to happen. If the US shares the anti-gravity knowledge, we will reconsider our commitment to build the megamachines. Thank you."

In the instant after Dr. Stanislav's statements, a wave of shock and outright depression moved through the UN meeting and world participants. Soon, the world heard of the crisis, and felt helpless to stop it.

"We'll take a three-hour recess for lunch and continue our meeting at 1300," Neelesh said, with no one listening.

* * *

"Mr. President, did you see the UN speech by Dr. Stanislav?" White House Chief of Staff, Jerry Bragg, asked.

"Yes, dammit. I did. Should we call Igor?"

"No, not yet. We need a formal reply and evidence we did not withhold any information transmitted by the orb," Bragg replied.

A White House aide knocked on the Oval Office door, opened it, and said, "Mr. President, General Carr is on line three."

"Steve, we have a new challenge. The Russian military increased their military readiness level close to our DEFCON 2."

DEFON 2 means the US armed forces are ready to deploy and engage in less than six hours. DEFCON 1 means nuclear war is imminent or has started and requires an immediate response.

"Oh, my god! What is Premier Vsevolod thinking?"

"What should we do Mr. President?" Carr asked.

"Go to DEFCON 2. Put all of our armed forces on alert."

"Yes, sir. I'm putting in the codes now."

After ten seconds, General Carr said, "It's done, Mr. President. All ships will go to sea. Our bombers and nuclear armed fighters are in the air or ready to launch. Our land- and space-based nuclear missiles will be armed and ready to launch. We are ready."

"Good," Barlow said. "Al, what do General Tucson and Colonel Preston know about the orb's transmittals?"

"Sir, they know general things, but Lieutenant Colonel Kash Kilbourne, who was killed at the India-Bangladesh border, handled security around the expert team and orb transmittals."

"So, you're telling me the officer in charge is dead."

"Yes, sir."

"Who else might have detailed knowledge of handling the orb information?"

"Sir, Dr. Breslin, the chairperson of the expert team, would know most of the security procedures and details."

"I want to talk with him; get him on the line."

General Carr arrived at the Oval Office. He turned toward President Barlow, sweeping his hand across his forehead to remove a bead of sweat, and said, "Mr. President, China, Europe, India, and Japan have increased their military readiness too. Our intelligence also reports that thirty-one of the forty-six nations who have nuclear weapons have increased their military alerts."

Before Barlow could respond, a call came in from Dr. Breslin. They discussed the situation and the security procedures of the orb's transmittals, work tent security practices, and what he knew about team members' communications inside and outside the restricted areas. They concluded Breslin would write a public letter signed by all expert team members describing the content of the orb's transmittals and state that they contained no anti-gravity knowledge.

After talking with Breslin, Barlow said, "How do we prove to the Russians something that never happened?"

"I don't know," Bragg replied. "Let's ask Agee if she has any ideas." General Carr nodded in agreement.

Soon, Barlow was talking with Ginger Agee, the Director of Homeland Security. Her idea was to have each expert team member make public testimonials on-line about the content of the orb's transmittals.

"Okay, I'll call Premier Vsevolod. Stay here, I want you to hear the conversation."

For forty-two long seconds, President Barlow and his advisors waited for Premier Vsevolod.

"Good day, President Barlow," Vsevolod said.

"Igor, the expert team will soon make public a letter from them stating there was no anti-gravity knowledge in the orb's transmittals. And we have asked each individual team member to post on-line their personal statements on the anti-gravity issue. The United States, in no way, is influencing these expert statements."

"Okay, but our intelligence suggests you lifted the anti-gravity information before you gave it to the expert team."

"Igor, what evidence do you expect us to provide?"

"I don't know, but our Russian team of experts on-site say one equation the orb transmitted provides insights into how gravity affects the energy required to terraform a planet's biosphere."

"Ugh, even if true, the expert team says none of this information could create a weapon or propulsion system. I'll talk to the experts again and get back to you."

"Mr. President, you and I both know the anti-gravity knowledge creates a huge imbalance in military capability. We cannot let this happen."

"We will collect all the information we have on the security procedures and the content of the orb's transmittals and send it to you," Barlow said. After a deep breath, Barlow said, "Igor, you are creating a worldwide crisis. Once a war begins, our automated systems will escalate to a nuclear holocaust. You must deescalate the situation. You must!"

"Good day, President Barlow," the Russian premier replied as he hung up the line.

* * *

Ms. Indira Neelesh, the Prime Minister of India, reconvened the UN meeting at 1300. But to her surprise, only fifteen of the thirty-seven nations attending the meeting returned. Of the two hundred seven nations attending by telepresence, only fifty-one continued to take part. Because of worldwide military alerts, governments summoned their delegates home. She walked to the podium, glanced at the scant audience, and said, "Fear is in the air. I feel it and I know you do too. We will take up the issues of building the two hundred sixteen megamachines at a later time. Please go home and be with your families and friends. Thank you."

As she left the podium, a UN security guard handed her a note. She read the note and walked back to the podium. She said, "Are the cameras on? Are we broadcasting to the world?" Video crews acknowledged 'yes' to both questions.

"Jillian Hickory, the voice of the orb, has sent us a hologram. Please direct your attention to the stage beside me and we shall play the hologram."

A clear hologram appeared of the eight-year-old Jillian at 1304, Tuesday, January 23. A blue hallo circumvented her youthful body. The sparse crowd in the auditorium was stone quiet; some kneeled down in prayer. Television commentators announced that over four billion people had their electronic devices turned on for her speech. A broad smile engulfed her face.

* * *

In the safe house in Brazil, Mattie, Ethan, and Tom's movie watching was interrupted by a national emergency message that the orb and its voice, Jillian Hickory, appeared in a hologram at a United Nations meeting on building the megamachines.

"Where's Jilly?" Mattie screamed.

Tom and Mattie rushed to her bedroom to find Jillian asleep on her bed with a familiar thin blue hallo surrounding her body. They dare not touch their daughter as they turned on her bedroom wall screen to watch the United Nation's emergency message.

They watched in amazement as their daughter said to the world in a hologram, *"I have watched your UN meeting and news reports with deep disappointment. Your planet is dying, yet you find yourselves on the brink of war. Through neglect, greed, arrogance, and war, you fail to take global cooperative action to terraform Earth's biosphere."*

"Earth is a living system, much like you. You disrespect Earth and it will disrespect you. Ironically, if you continue to squabble, delay, or go to war, your species will die in an oven of your own making."

"I conclude our gifts to humanity, with its hopes and aspirations, are being ignored. I pray you do not squander these immaculate gifts."

"Your nuclear weapons, in space and on the ground, defy logic. We shall mitigate these evils. Good day."

The hologram fades out, and people are confused. What did she mean by "mitigate these evils?"

After listening to the speech, Mattie and Tom watched as the blue hallo around Jillian's body, and the orb, vanished. Slowly, Jillian awoke and Tom and Mattie hugged her in a long embrace.

"Jilly, Jilly, are you okay?" Mattie yelled. "We saw a hologram of you on the wall screen!"

Jillian rolled over to look at her terrified parents. Jillian said in a soft voice, "What did you say, Mom?"

"Honey, your body image was at a United Nations meeting on the other side of the planet!" Tom said.

"Mom, what are you talking about? I've been asleep."

Mattie and Tom realized Jillian knew nothing about her fourth encounter with the orb. Jillian washed her face and brushed her teeth and joined the family in the safe house living room. They watched on the wall screen, like billions of people, the orb's fulfillment of its prophecy to "mitigate these evils."

* * *

The US Nuclear Command and Control Center (USN3C) buried deep in the Rocky Mountains noticed on their radar screens a new object orbiting the Earth. It measured twenty centimeters in diameter as it raced around Earth. The USN3C directed radar and telescopes from around the world to zoom in on it. They linked the US telescope video to the command center, Pentagon, and the White House.

The United States and over twenty nations had orbiting platforms that could fire laser and nuclear payloads to thousands of targets on earth. Soon, China, Europe, India, Russia, and many other countries identified this strange object as the orb.

In an instant, the orb spun faster and faster; obscuring itself with rainbows of bright lights. The light from the orbiting and rotating orb was brighter than the sun. People worldwide tried to follow two suns in the sky—one moving slowly as expected and the other racing across the sky.

To their dismay, government leaders and warriors from around the world watched as the orbiting orb dismantled their space weapon platforms and communication networks. The President watched a US telescope feed that showed a US weapon's platform break apart in chunks and quickly disintegrate into strings of spaghetti-like material. The unknown predator feasted on any material in orbit around the Earth and shredded it.

President Barlow, accompanied by General Carr, Ginger Agee, and Jerry Bragg, sat in Air Force Eleven with fighter planes providing an escort. In wartime situations, the US President and key leaders would board Air Force Eleven and fly toward New Zealand with many places to land along the route. The President watched the live video feed with the other US leaders, including a few US cabinet and Congress members.

"Is this thing a threat?" Barlow asked, hurriedly.

"Yes, sir. We should shoot it down," General Carr replied.

"Do it."

Carr ordered US laser weapons on the ground and on orbiting weapons platforms to fire at the mysterious orbiting orb. By then, most of the world's space-based weapon platforms had been demolished. Ground-based laser shots entered the ball of light but never came out the other side.

"Mr. President, I just received notice that eight of our orbiting nuclear weapon platforms have disappeared from USN3C radar," an upset Carr said in an angry voice. "We have also lost over one-thousand satellites in the last five seconds."

"What's going on?" the president asked, leaning over the table in the plane's situation room.

The Director of USN3C said, "Mr. President, our radar telemetry shows the orb is circling earth fast and clearing all space around it of debris, satellites, and weapons."

"How can that happen?"

"Sir, we think the object has created a gravity well, a black hole, in orbit around our planet, and it's consuming everything in orbit."

"How will we communicate?" Barlow asked the Director of the USN3C.

No one answered the president's query because the communication lines went blank, as did all electronics on the airplane. The pilots took manual control of the plane to keep it flying. Now all US government functions were cut off from one another. Similar disconnects were happening worldwide.

The orb continued to spin and consume its orbiting prey. Once the orb completed twelve trips around the planet at two different altitudes, it disappeared into other dimensions of the universe.

"Al, can we fire our land-based weapons?"

"No, sir. We cannot communicate with anyone; even computer to computer or transmitter to receiver."

"Mr. President," White House Chief of Staff, Jerry Bragg said, "The orb fulfilled its promise. It stopped humanity's ability to wage war. It disarmed the world temporarily. Nothing is orbiting our planet now, nothing!"

"I confirm, Mr. President," a shocked General Carr said. "We're back to the pre-Sputnik days of 1956!"

The omnipotent orb gave humanity one more chance to fix its wrongs—avoid war and terraform Earth's biosphere. Now it was up to humanity to avoid extinction.

THE END

POSTSCRIPT

Mattie Hickory (Arianna Gifford) lived to be eighty-nine years old and died in 2196. Mattie begrudged her new life and blamed the orb, the media, Tom, and the US government for the family's woes. She never healed from the repercussions of the orb's visit.

Tom Hickory (Chris Gifford) lived to be ninety-seven years old and died in 2198. The family moved back to the United States after seven years in Brazil. Upon their return to the States, the children enrolled in college and went on with their lives.

Ethan Hickory (Dex Gifford) earned a PhD in astronomy from the University of Texas at Austin. He joined the faculty at Arizona State University and married another faculty member. He died in 2238 at one hundred one years old. His wife didn't know his true identity until the reading of his last will and testament.

Titan, the family goat, died happy in Fort Knox, Kentucky. They fed him broccoli the day he died.

Jillian Hickory (Briana Gifford) earned a master's degree in education. She married a medical doctor, and they had one daughter and one son. Jillian experienced no recurring symptoms of cerebral palsy. She worked in administration at the same hospital as her husband. Every year, the hospital gained notoriety with a miraculous patient recovery. She died in 2245 at one hundred six years old. In her will, she recorded a hologram interview about her experiences with the orb. She also revealed her identity as the "voice of the orb" and said the following at the end of her funeral hologram, "Like my mother and father, I expected the orb to return to Earth, but it did not. I concluded it presented its gift to humanity, with its hopes and aspirations, and now humanity must save itself from the effects of dramatic climate change or risk mass extinction. I pray we do not squander this immaculate gift."

Author's Note on Today's Climate Change Crisis

On October 18, 2147, an orb arrives on earth to help humanity save the planet from catastrophic climate change.

Humanity's on- and off-again response to climate change weakens our capability to survive on Earth. Global climate destruction is the predecessor to human extinction with a second adversary, artificial intelligence, closing out humanity's final chapter in the third novel in the series.

Changes in the earth's climate are an even more powerful foe than the debilitating pandemic beginning in 2020. The massacre of our home planet's biosphere is strangling humanity so gradually that we don't perceive it. Every few months, there is a one millimeter rise in sea level, a one part per million increase of carbon dioxide concentration, and a one-tenth of a degree gain in temperature, yet each generation hands the grueling, long-term problem off to future generations. We humans are committing "ecological suicide" by our inaction, debates, and delays.

Humanity is not so good at creating a coordinated response among all nations to solve this multiple millennia-long problem. The big hope is that our technology will rescue us, but what if it doesn't? Technology has always been a tricky solution to our problems—it can liberate and empower us; it can enslave and destroy us; it can bankrupt us; it can arrive too late, or it can simply lack the capability.

Far more is at risk than losing coastal cities and land. The effects of climate change will upset everyone's life. Will institutions survive? Will governments fail? Will democracy endure? What will it cost to mitigate climate destruction? Will your standard of living perish? Will humankind survive? Does humanity have the political will to solve the climate crisis?

Who are our adversaries— technology, the universal laws of thermodynamics, or humankind itself?

What will life be like if global average temperatures increase over four degrees Celsius (7.1 degrees Fahrenheit)? What will life be like if sea levels increase one, eight, or seventy meters? What if both happen? What is the cost to mitigate these obstacles to ensure human survival?

The *Earth's Ecocide* science fiction book series (www.theentity.us) shows the reader a fictional one-thousand-year story of humanity's struggle to save Earth as a habitable planet. The series consists of three novels in the years 2147, 2647, and 3147. It takes that long to see the devastating effects of climate destruction and our collective demise. Trillions of tons of greenhouse gases, pollutants, and heat remain in Earth's atmosphere, land, and oceans. There is no quick way to dissipate this toxic and cumulative mix. In the series, by 2147, Earth's fragile biosphere will have passed the tipping point.

Who might you ask is persecuting Earth? The answer is us—humanity. Yes, we continue to bicker and delay strong, meaningful and global climate abatement actions. We continue to dump chemicals and plastics into our oceans and waterways, pump harmful gases into our atmosphere to trap the planet's heat, and so on. We are harassing, targeting, and destroying our home planet's biosphere. We are desecrating our very home. It is wrong on all criteria.

We need to think about our fate as a species using a different level of thought and consciousness. The second novel, in the series, *Earth's Ecocide: Desperation 2647*, and the third novel, *Earth's Ecocide: Extinction 3147*, try to do this by using Plato's ideas, paradigms, and philosophy.

Each novel is told through the adventures and experiences of a family, each one always being the protagonist. Each family fights the relentless antagonist of global warming and the havoc it causes. Artificial intelligence emerges as a second powerful antagonist in the second novel, which completes its plan in the third novel.

Many climate experts and champions, much more knowledgeable than me, have written books, reports, and blogs, and given speeches on why humanity needs to take immediate action. Most of these champions present mounds of data, graphs, scientific arguments, and narrate well scripted movie documentaries on the dire situation of Earth's biosphere. But not enough people, companies, and especially governments, heed these ephemeral warnings and take prompt action.

What is missing? A massive and global outpouring of human emotion, generating outrage and fear for what we humans do to our home planet. We need to create an "emotional connection" between our home planet and all people of the world as soon as possible.

Science fiction novels, movies, and other visual and entertaining stories can help create such emotion and invigorate champions of our humanoid species. I call such champions—champoids. To be a champiod, you must also be a champion of our home—Planet Earth. Through their beliefs and actions, champoids support all forms of life, and what we would call non-life, including Earth's biosphere. That is, all things are connected at an infinitesimal tiny level. Being a champoid is much more than a political, legal, economic, national, or moral view or issue—it is an issue of consciousness and way of thinking, and human survival.

I hope you enjoy the stories in this series and that they inspire you to protect and nourish Earth, so future generations can enjoy its majesty. Follow us on Twitter at We Must Protect Our Home@AChampoid.

— David A. Collier, 2021

ABOUT THE AUTHOR

A native of Paris and Lexington, Kentucky, **David A. Collier** earned two degrees at the University of Kentucky before entering the corporate world. He later returned to academic life and earned his PhD from The Ohio State University. For forty-one years, he taught all levels of students as well as participants in executive programs within the business schools of Duke University, the University of Virginia, the Ohio State University, Florida Gulf Coast University, and the University of Warwick in the United Kingdom. As of 2021, his research has attracted over twenty-six thousand reads and four thousand citations according to *ResearchGate*.

After decades of authoring award winning research articles, business cases, and five college textbooks, he wanted a new challenge: writing novels that make a difference. I could have written a science fiction book series with no relevance to issues of the day, but I didn't choose the easier path. The following quote embodies the approach I followed in past academic and novel work. "Do not follow where the path may lead. Go instead where there is no path and leave a trail." I hope you enjoy the stories in the book series and they inspire you to protect our home planet, so future generations can enjoy its majesty.

David is the author of a science fiction series, *Earth's Ecocide*, as well as *Romance in My Rambler* using the pen name David A. Bourbon.

David found the challenge of writing novels compared to textbooks quite different. He made every mistake a rookie novelist could make. Why does he keep trying? Because of his sincere love for our species, all lifeforms, and their home planet. We must protect our home.

In his debut science fiction novel, *Earth's Ecocide: Hope 2147* (www.theentity.us), the mysterious orb arrives on Earth offering a solution to an Earth ravaged by heat and flood. But humanity must overcome its greatest obstacle: itself. The burden of salvation falls on the shoulders of the Hickory family as fractured nations, ignorant governments, and ravenous media grapple with the orb's arrival.

Earth's Ecocide: Desperation 2647 continues the one-thousand-year struggle of humanity to save Earth as a habitable planet. The story ends with a unique solution for the Paris family—one of hope and eternal love.

Earth's Ecocide: Extinction 3147 follows the story of the Torg family as it fights for survival against climate change and a second ominous antagonist, artificial intelligence.

David lives in Florida with his wife and their two Shih Tzu doggies. When not doing the tasks of everyday life, David reads astronomy, philosophy, sustainability, climate change, and science literature, and enjoys golf, boating, sports, and of course, everything about nature. He dedicates the *Earth's Ecocide* book series to those who love this tiny speck of wonder called Earth.